African/American Library

GENERAL EDITOR
Charles R. Larson

A continuing series of works of literary excellence by black writers in the United States, Africa and the Caribbean.

THE BEAUTYFUL ONES ARE NOT YET BORN
  by Ayi Kwei Armah
    Introduction by Ama Ata Aidoo
THE HOUSE BEHIND THE CEDARS
  by Charles W. Chesnutt
    Introduction by Darwin Turner
NOT WITHOUT LAUGHTER
  by Langston Hughes
    Introduction by Arna Bontemps
AMBIGUOUS ADVENTURE
  by Cheikh Hamidou Kane
    Introduction by Wilfred Cartey
dem
  by William Melvin Kelley
    Introduction by Willie Abrahams
WEEP NOT, CHILD
  by James Ngugi
    Introduction by Martin Tucker
HARLEM GALLERY
  by Melvin B. Tolson
    Introduction by Karl Shapiro
BLOOD ON THE FORGE
  by William Attaway
    Introduction by Edward Margolies
THE SPORT OF THE GODS
  by Paul Laurence Dunbar
    Introduction by Charles Nilon
IN THE CASTLE OF MY SKIN
  by George Lamming
    Introduction by Richard Wright
AFRICAN SHORT STORIES
  by Charles R. Larson, ed.
    Introduction by Charles R. Larson
BOY!
  by Ferdinand Oyono
    Introduction by Edri
EMERGENCY
  by Richard Rive
    Introduction by Ezel
THE INTERPRETERS
  by Wole Soyinka
    Introduction by Les
THE BLACKER THE B
  by Wallace Thurman
    Introduction by Therman B. O'Daniel

TELL FREEDOM
   by Peter Abrahams
      Introduction by Wilfred Cartey

MINE BOY
   by Peter Abrahams
      Introduction by Charles R. Larson

BLACK SLAVE NARRATIVES
   John Bayliss, ed.
      Introduction by John Bayliss

KING LAZARUS
   by Mongo Beti
      Introduction by O. R. Dathorne

THE LOOMING SHADOW
   by Legson Kayira
      Introduction by Harold R. Collins

THE RADIANCE OF THE KING
   by Camara Laye
      Introduction by Albert S. Girard

BLACK NO MORE
   by George Schuyler
      Introduction by Charles R. Larson

LIBRETTO FOR THE REPUBLIC OF LIBERIA
   by Melvin B. Tolson
      Preface by Allen Tate

TROPIC DEATH
   by Eric Walrond
      Introduction by Arna Bontemps

CLOTEL, OR THE PRESIDENT'S DAUGHTER
   by William W. Brown
      Introduction by Arthur Davis

THIS ISLAND, NOW
   by Peter Abrahams
      Introduction by Austin C. Clarke

QUICKSAND
   by Nella Larsen
      Introduction by Adelaide Hill

PASSING
   by Nella Larsen
      Introduction by Hoyt Fuller

MASTERS OF THE DEW
   by Jacques Roumain
      Introduction by Mercer Cook

This Island, Now

THIS ISLAND, NOW

by Peter Abrahams

With an Introduction by
Austin C. Clarke

COLLIER BOOKS
NEW YORK, NEW YORK

CONTENTS

Introduction 9

One ⊞ The Legacy 19

Two ⊞ The Inheritors 99

Three ⊞ The Executors 179

INTRODUCTION

Aₙₙ WORK OF FICTION written these days by a black
author is automatically inspected to see what the author's
social commitment is to the problem, the people, or the
country with which his work deals. There is a growing
concern about the author's accountability to his people
that is not strictly literary. This accountability is almost a
prerequisite to any writing being done in this country by
black authors, and it is certainly an essential dimension of
the prevailing black consciousness in art, literature, and
politics. This is the case, the mood in the United States.

The Caribbean writer in general, one of whom is Peter
Abrahams (in an adoptive sense), apparently does not
consider himself restricted in his literary expression by
this accountability. Abrahams, who nowhere in his novel
seems to be mindful of this racial accountability, suggests
that some judgment can be made against himself and
other Caribbean writers who do not gear their work to
any literary vindictiveness against the social oppression
of the mind and body that, as black people, they have
experienced in various forms of colonialism and imperial-
ism. Abrahams, however, is black, and he was born in
South Africa. These two facts say something specific
about the man's outlook. But one still cannot burden Abrahams's work with the extraliterary consideration of ac-

countability—the relevancy of his subject matter, as well as the attitudes of his characters (his black characters, that is)—to the black nationalism in art, literature, and politics. Yet one is worried that a more precise racial function, a more clearly defined black aesthetic, is not present in this novel because, after all, anything of importance that is written by a black novelist is important precisely because it is the experience, translated into artistic expression, of a black man.

This Island, Now, the most recent novel by Abrahams, who has adopted the Caribbean as his home, is set in one of the islands, presumably Jamaica, although the author deliberately does not say so. It deals with a political situation involving black people; in fact, involving a black takeover of a corrupt political system and the accompanying moral consciousness of the people. At another level, the novel can be termed a social novel: it deals with the social reorientation of a group of powerless people faced with the possibility of wresting power, influence, and racial dignity from a largely expatriate and light-complexioned class of neocolonialists. It is a social novel also because it has something to say about the predicament of these black people, who are undergoing what Frantz Fanon calls, in his book *Black Skin, White Masks*, 'the psychoexistential complex,' a complex brought about by their having lived in juxtaposition with nonblack people. Their experience, in Abrahams's novel, is weighed on a scale that says definitely that the cause of their social predicament of ignorance and powerlessness in their native society is also the consequence of that predicament.

This Island, Now deals, then, with a psychoexistential problem. The author tells us that since 'the imagination is nurtured by reality, the point of departure of this story is the reality of the Caribbean.' This precautionary note about the nature of his novel is less important than the word 'reality,' which is used to give some kind of universal application to the problems being discussed. Abrahams the novelist is agreeing with the black intellectual who would argue that the only reality there is has to be the reality of the black people who are the subject of the novel. He shows us these poor black people living in constant social and political opposition to the half-black, disoriented middle-class group, who pretend that they represent the driving force, the spirit of the revolution, the correct morals, and the money of the island. In contrast to this group, Abrahams shows us the millions of unemployed, poor blacks, in whose minds (to paraphrase Frantz Fanon in *The Wretched of the Earth*) any political revolution has only one meaning: a greater supply of food and the possibility of inheriting the land that has always been their assumed possession, as well as their right. Although, as is seen in this novel, they might never be able to put this knowledge of ownership into the sophisticated intellectual terms of the middle and expatriate classes, their representative, the newly-elected President Josiah, understands that his power and his blackness are now indivisible, and he can therefore act as their intellectual spokesman.

While the middle class and the expatriate class are trying to justify their presence and their role in the new regime, the black lower class confronts them with a derisive truth: the very problem they are having with the new order, which defines the oppressing groups, is the strength and perhaps the hope of black success on the island.

The main political point that Abrahams makes in his novel is this: there can be no revolution by the proletarian group in any Caribbean island unless that revolution has both the blessing and the cooperation of the rich upper and middle classes. And since the upper class in the Caribbean is closely related through marriage and through business obligations to a foreign power, the possibility of such a revolution, or even the chances of socialization on the island, is extremely remote. (It was tried in Guyana, in the 1960s, and it failed for the very reasons put forward by Abrahams. This makes Abrahams an important political novelist.)

But Abrahams is to be criticized for a one-sided treatment of the island's society. We do not hear enough about the hopes and feelings of the lower classes. We hear about them through their power image, President Josiah, and his political aspirations, which can be accepted as representing the aspirations of the lower classes. But we hear more about them, more that is derogatory, from the wealthy Isaacs family, from the half-Chinese woman reporter, Miss Lee, and from the British expatriate editor of the daily newspaper for which Miss Lee works. On another level, this one-sided treatment of the society is a manifestation of the colonial nature of that society as it is organized in the Caribbean, and it can be interpreted to mean that Abrahams has understood the psychoexistentialism that operates in a Caribbean island. For to have refused to mention that revolutionary spirit in the society (which is, to a native West Indian, no other society than Jamaica's), the Rasta Fari, and to have refused to come to grips with that kind of spiritual-liberationist feeling suggests the colonialist's arrogance or ignorance.

Abrahams's treatment of the middle and expatriate classes in such clear, unexclusive terms makes him (in this book, at least) a novelist like John Hearne of Jamaica. Hearne is the only writer of the Caribbean to see the importance, the national importance, which Abrahams pretends to see, in this middle class—a class which is, if one considers its power and influence, predominantly foreign, either through birth or disposition. In *This Island, Now*, this class is alienated. It is a class that seeks not nationalism, not progress for the island of their residence and power and wealth, not financial stability of any sort (for the middle class is itself too much a reflection of colonialism for that to happen); but rather, it seeks an identity through its personal crises. It struggles, as Abrahams clearly shows, for an identity that is not consistent with the cultural ingredients of the island.

Abrahams has shown the murderous intent of these men and women caught up in their crisis of identifying with a proletarian revolution, an intent that is close to political assassination, an intent that does not hesitate to be disloyal to anything that smacks of country or of nationalism. When nationalism is born on this island, the financial interests, the business interests, and the middle classes (euphemistically called in Jamaica, "the brown man") get ready to take a boat to leave. What was previously home

—because their presence in the island was cushioned through privilege based upon colour, connections, and wealth—now becomes, in the face of the rising nationalism, a place to flee from. It is an effective touch of political reality, for many African countries have witnessed this exodus of disillusioned "margin gatherers," as President Josiah derisively calls them.

This brings us to a second consideration of the novel: the social aspects of the work. The only persons, or group, who are not obsessed with the crisis of identity are the black islanders. Before the institution of any viable black-power movement on the island, and even before any awareness of a cultural nationalism that might have come from a reversal in the power structure, this black group always knew that it was Jamaican, or Trinidadian, or Barbadian, as the case may be. This group knew, as Abrahams implies, that the country belonged to it. And it knew that the moment it got 'its thing together,' then the insistence upon power and leadership, which the brown man and the expatriate class regard as their natural right (and which Abrahams stated without equivocation), and the officially recognized claim to country and land and bread would be attainable through the chosen process of nationalism. And to them, nationalism meant, simply, revolutionary violence.

President Josiah knows this. And so, too, does young Andrew Simpson, the inheritor of the position of Chief Secretary. It is a truth, a conclusion to the seizure of power from the old leaders that is comprehended by Joel Sterning, the expatriate Jew who has married into the Isaacs family; and by Miss Lee (for whom nationalism is death, since she belongs to two worlds, neither of which she can choose); and by the brown man on the island. It is this truth which Abrahams makes the crisis in the relationship of blacks to whites in the novel. *This Island, Now* shows us that it is the black islander's place in the society that is the cause of the economic exploitation. What his place is on the face of the island has to be defined for him, and has to be prescribed against all improvements. It is his sweat and his profitability which

Abrahams tells us is essential to maintaining such institutions of exploitation.

By focusing most of his attention upon the identity problems of nonblacks in the novel, Abrahams has shown that he understands the main characteristic of the West Indian novel, and indeed, of the West Indian society. For it is a problem of identity in the same way that one can say that the main characteristic of the black American is a problem of meaningful manhood—a manhood which must flourish, if it can, in the teeth of racism. But Abrahams is not a West Indian by birth, and for him to have seen this in the first novel he has set in the West Indies shows a most perceptive understanding of the problems of those who exist in a psychoexistential relationship.

The strength of this novel is the information that it gives about life in the Caribbean. It is informative in showing the manipulation of the business interests by the new black leader, President Josiah, who realizes that political independence is hollow without economic independence. But the manipulation is temporary and is based upon his ability to stem the tide of the moral and economic boycotting of the new regime by the collusion of the Isaacs family and foreign capital. This collusion is at the heart of any mass movement in the Caribbean.

Peter Abrahams also makes a strong point when he shows that a family like the Isaacs not only constitutes economic power but also tries to tell the native what is good for him. This kind of patronizing motivates even Max, the expatriate editor, whose obsession with being seen in the best respects by the black inhabitants ceases to be sincerity and becomes instead racial and intellectual condescension. And Martha Lee, cut off from two peoples, (the blacks and the Chinese) but striving in the heat of the present island nationalism to identify with the black people of the land, becomes, as Abrahams suggests, perhaps the most vicious enemy the people can have. She is the sexual go-between for the Isaacs family. She is the intellectual go-between for the new black leader. She is the best-known journalist on the island. She is a fifth columnist. It is her rationalizations about the possibility of violence, her arguments about what truth is for the people (an intellectualism which is more understandable to Max than it can ever be to either President Josiah or Andrew Simpson), and her disloyalty to the cause of black nationalism running through the inarticulate people that, on one level, make *This Island, Now,* a most perceptive and pentetrating novel.

AUSTIN C. CLARKE

New Haven, 14 February 1970

Time: The present.

Place: An Island in the Caribbean.

Nature: A novel, a work of fiction, in which all persons and places are figments of the imagination; but since the imagination is nurtured by reality the point of departure of this story is the reality of the Caribbean. Each reader is therefore at liberty to decide the particular island on which he or she wants this story played out.

Part One
THE LEGACY

ALL DAY LONG the sleek little planes and the clumsy-looking helicopters had criss-crossed the hills, flying low and yet out of reach of possible rifle shot. The man thought: Almost as though they are looking for me. But he knew they were not. This was routine, part of the show of strength that had become habit even when there was no need for it and no one to whom to show it. The peasants of these hills now had to be shown this strength all the time. That was something Josiah had learnt from the Old Man. But whereas the Old Man had used this show of strength only in times of need, Josiah used it all the time. Josiah had once told him that you can never overdo a good thing, especially if it were simple and straight-forward. Since a show of strength is a good thing, do it all the time. Fly the planes even when the peasants are not cultivating their hillsides for a little corn and other ground provision. Make the show of strength all the same: make it to the trees and the earth and the warm late Sunday afternoon breeze. Perhaps these will impart it to the men of the hills when they come to their cultivations tomorrow morning. The earth does communicate with men: she does pass on unease and fear in precisely the same way that she passes on assurance and confidence. Once this earth had communicated a high sense of freedom to its children, especially in the years immediately after the withdrawal of the occupying power. Now fear was a long shadow over the land and its children.

At sundown the planes stopped their lazy criss-crossing of the hills. He came out of his hiding place, which was a small cave high up near the top of the highest of the group of hills where he had hidden since Saturday night after the peasants had gone from their cultivations.

He scrambled up to the highest point and looked down at the long wide plain. And, as always, his heart was filled with the beauty of his land. The plain was a carpet of lush green, three thousand feet below, beginning with the un-believably placid Caribbean Sea and sweeping inward until it touched the foothills and ceased to be plain. The port buildings, the city and all the other man-made scars on the face of the plain seemed particularly unreal, ephemeral, embattled in the misty light of the dying sun: the slightest relaxation, the slightest letting up by man, and the lush green would overrun all his works and make nothing of them.

Nearer, the sloping land climbed fast; at a sharp grade that raised the land to over three thousand feet above the sea in less than twenty miles. Immediately below the man's perch, twisting and turning like a long sinuous snake, was the one smoothly macadamized highway into the hills. At this point, the road swung to within three hundred feet of where he stood. There was a sharp, uninterrupted view of it for about twenty yards. For at least a quarter of a minute anything moving at an easy pace would be fully in focus. Josiah's car, with a screeching motorcycle escort front and back, would move at an easy pace. The man thought: I will have a quarter of a minute: that is all I need, just a quarter of a minute.

He looked at the plain once more. And this time he gave way to the wave of heartache that swept over him. Now, at last, with less than an hour to go, it was all right to admit one's weakness, one's softness, one's heartache.

He turned and went back to the little cave. When he came out he carried an army-type knapsack with him. He went back to the point from which he would have his quarter minute. He had found and cleared the spot the night before, so now there was no need to prepare. He went down on the soft, hollowed-out earth and undid the knapsack. First he took out the small brown-paper parcel containing the highly seasoned escovitched fish, the small loaf of wholewheat bread, and the small thermos with the chilled soursop juice. This was his supper. Perhaps my last, he thought detachedly, without any real interest in the thought. He put the food and drink aside. Then he unpacked the series of dull metal tubes and other objects that filled the knapsack. He laid everything out on the ground with a delicate care, as a woman preparing a special dish for her family. He sat back, checking over each item, even though he knew every single piece was there. Then he proceeded to assemble the pieces.

When he had done he had a rifle; one of those powerful modern ones that Josiah had imported to strengthen his growing security force. You had only to touch the trigger of one of these new ones for a score or more bullets to go streaking towards their target. But unlike the ones Josiah supplied to the men of his security force, this one was mounted with telescopic sights.

The man lay down on his belly and fixed the rifle between the two boulders through which he commanded a view of the road. He looked through the telescopic sights and the road was brought up close so that he could pick out the individual small stones that had rolled on to it. It would bring Josiah close enough to show up the huge mole on his right cheek; perhaps even to show his odd mannerism of going wall-eyed in repose.

With the rifle ready and pointing at the road, the man turned to his food. He ate slowly, savouring every mouthful of the crisply fried fish and the delicately sharp taste of hot green pepper, raw onions and vinegar. Then he drank the soursop.

Then he waited . . .

CHAPTER ONE

J OEL STERNING switched off the radio and turned to his wife. Her expression told him that it was true. The Old Man was dead.

'What does it mean?' Clara asked.

He tried to think, but how could he explain time coming to an abrupt stop, or the light of the sun being suddenly extinguished? Such things are beyond the range of experience, and it is difficult to reason about the unknown. He shook his head and his wife, Clara, understood the mental and emotional helplessness behind the gesture. They had long ceased to care about each other but they had been married a very long time, and they had worked out an understanding that made possible living together at a reasonably civilized level.

The announcer's voice had been strained, unbelieving, frightened, when he said: 'Ladies and gentlemen, the President is dead. A bulletin from the Presidential Palace announced that President Moses Joshua collapsed and died five minutes ago. The President was in the act of proposing an after-dinner toast to his diplomatic guests when he died.' There had been a lot more: the National Anthem, his favourite hymn, the voice of his wife.

He was very old and the whole island knew that he might die any day. People had discussed the possibility openly. The Old Man himself had often referred to it, especially over the past two or three years. Yet his death was shocking and unexpected because all the people were afraid to think of life in this land without him. He had straddled the island as unquestioned leader for nearly half a century.

Joel Sterning went to the telephone and dialled the un-listed number that would put him in direct contact with the Presidential Secretary. He was one of less than a dozen people who had that number. It was engaged.

Clara fixed a drink and Joel noticed how her hands trembled. He knew that her need, at this moment, was for comfort. If he put his arms about her now it might bring back memories of the love that had once been between them, and that had died. And his wife was a striking woman. Without having an ounce of excess fat there was a tropical lushness about her that most men found intoxicat-ing. She had that flawless alabaster skin that white-skinned people with a small weak strain of Negro often showed. But he had long ago learned never to refer to the touch of Negro in the Isaacs family. They were proudly Jewish but don't dare mention the slight Negro trace in them!

Once, many years ago, a social rival of the Isaacs women—Clara, her mother, and her three younger sisters —had dismissed them as the five 'crepe sole brunettes'. The hurt had gone deep but they had to wait ten years— till the family had grown rich enough—for their revenge. When it came it was terrible and complete. Because of this piece of female cattiness the Isaacs men systematically stripped the unfortunate husband of his business, took every penny he had, sold his home and threw him out on the street. In the end, broken and on the verge of being made a bankrupt, the poor man and his family had to quit the island. That was the end of all mention, anywhere, of the touch of colour in Clara's family. Since that time the wealth and influence of the Isaacs has grown even greater.

His wife had always been the brightest of the Isaacs women, the most influential with their menfolk, and he knew she had a big part in that piece of social and eco-nomic assassination.

But, as with everybody in Mosesville, the lesson had gone home and he dealt carefully and warily with his wife and every member of the Isaacs family. Even the youngest of the children knew and used, both at school and at play, the influence and power of the family wealth and name.

Sometimes Joel Sterning woke in the middle of the night to wonder whether he would not have ended this unsatisfactory marriage a long time ago if Clara had not been an Isaacs. Such times usually ended with Joel prowling the town's nightclubs until he was helplessly drunk.

Clara brought the drink and stood very close to him, looking steadily into his eyes. She was an Isaacs even in this moment of fear and confusion and so there was a hint of command in her need for comfort.

He took the drink and turned from her, making it something casual, so that she should not see it as an insult.

'Have I become that repulsive, Joel?' she asked impersonally, as though it did not really matter; then she added: 'What do you think will happen now?'

'I don't know. So many things are possible.'

'The power struggle that you predicted?'

'Not immediately,' he said. 'They may put that off for months.'

'If Josiah permits.'

'He hasn't much choice. If he forced a showdown now he would risk losing everything. The others will gang up against him.'

'But the others were always fighting among themselves.'

'Only for the Old Man's approval, and because the Old Man kept Josiah in check: the only way they can contain him is by sinking their differences and sticking together. They know the alternative is hanging apart.'

'Surely they can get rid of him. No they can't. He can outpolitic and outmanipulate them any day. He's a clever little brute.'

Joel tried the Presidential Secretary's private number again. It was still engaged. Clara took a turn about the spacious room. Joel followed her with his eyes. He realized that the physical beauty of this woman who had been his wife for eighteen years could still stir his mind. Only his

heart could not be touched; and there is no love without
the touching of the heart. She came to a stop near him.

'Another drink?'

He knew that was not what she wanted to say, and it
pleased him a little that she had contained the Isaacs arrogance enough to not say what she wanted to. And now,
for a passing moment, remembrance of how it was before
love died was with him, and there was about it the faint
nostalgia we feel for long dead things that were once beautiful.

She went and poured the drinks and carried them to the
L-shaped glassed-in balcony. She put down the drinks and
moved one of the shatterproof sliding panels. A rush of
fresh air flowed, like a temperate stream, into the near-
chilled air-conditioned room.

Joel followed Clara across the room, appreciatively conscious, as always, of the taste and beauty of his home.
Clara's good taste and money had created this, and whatever friend or foe thought or felt about her, all agreed that
she had created beauty here. Carpet, walls and ceiling
were a delicate balance of complementing pastel shades of
blue and grey with occasional touches of rust. And the
furniture, all especially made of native woods and treated
so that natural grain and line and colours were preserved,
was given quiet emphasis by the perfect balance of the
colours. One wall was a panelled sample of the wide variety of beautiful wood on the island.

'It's beautiful,' Clara said, and there was a hint of awe
in her voice.

We've lived here a long time, Joel thought. She has
looked out of this window, from this spot, countless times
—ten, twenty thousand times perhaps—and still there is
the wonder. Clara, with that rare Keatsian gift of making
a thing of beauty a joy for ever by constantly seeing it
anew; and Clara, with the Isaacs arrogance and insensi-
tivity and the Isaacs ruthlessness in pursuit of wealth and
power: and both the same woman.

'Yes,' he said, seeing it freshly through her eyes, and
feeling a small sickness at heart because of it. 'Yes, it is
beautiful.'

Clara turned her head quickly and looked intently into

his face. 'What now, Joel? What have I done wrong this time?'

Oh God! he thought: Oh God! Oh God!

'I don't follow you,' he said quietly.

He sensed, rather than saw, her slight shrug.

Below them, a little to the left, the lights of Mosesville twinkled more brightly than the stars in the sky. They gave the city a fairy-tale quality that belied its day-time ugliness. The slums, the grotesque shacks of shanty-town, and the offensive zinc roofs, were shrouded by the night, and darkness and the shimmering lights and the lush tropical vegetation, all conspired to create an aura of romance.

The sudden tinkle of the telephone was explosive. Joel hurried to it.

'Joel?' The voice at the other end was that of an old man, but one in full command of all his powers. It was old Nathan Isaacs. 'Clara there?'

'Yes, Nathan.'

'Good. Be at my place in an hour. Full family council. Understand?'

'Yes. D'you want to speak to Clara?'

'Not now.'

'What's happening at the Palace?'

'The damn fools are wrangling as to who should have what title, bunch of silly shit-arses!'

'Josiah?'

'You were right about him, Joel. We should have spent our time and money on him instead of those fools.'

'Wouldn't have made any difference.'

'Don't be a fool, Joel. Every man has his price. The trick is to know what it is.'

'Is Josiah with them?' Joel asked quietly.

'No; he just looked in at the Palace, wept over the President's corpse for the benefit of Press and TV cameras and then he handed in his resignation.'

'What!' Joel exploded.

'Don't you be a shit-arse,' the old man said. 'Not in that way. He gave them a letter putting his Portfolio and his services at the disposal of whomever they choose to succeed President Joshua.'

'I don't follow,' Joel said.

'And you're supposed to be our political expert. Josiah is the only one with a clear plan and part of his plan is not to be involved in the power struggle. But we better stop this telephone talk. You never know.'

'Where is he now?'

'Somewhere on the streets. While those shit-arses wrangle over power, Josiah is out on the streets.' The old man let out a cold mirthless bark of a laugh. 'They say that he is comforting the people. Hear that! Comforting the people! The bloody fools! . . . In an hour, Joel. You and Clara. Things could get ugly and we must make plans.' With that old Nathan Isaacs hung up.

Joel went back to the balcony where Clara waited.

'Papa?'

'Yes. There's a full family council in an hour.'

'Did he tell you what's happening at the Palace?'

'Much as we expected. Josiah's taking no part in what goes on at the Palace. He's out on the streets comforting the people.'

'Comforting the people? That what Papa said?'

'Yes. That's the word.'

'Then things may really turn ugly.'

'That's exactly what your father said.'

'Surely they'll contain him, Joel?'

'Not if what your father said is true.'

'We should have paid more attention to Josiah.'

'Your father expressed much the same idea.'

After a long silence Clara said: 'You think things might really fall apart here, don't you?'

He said: 'Life is a process of falling apart and coming together and falling apart.'

'We all depended so much on him,' she said musingly.

'Depended on him or used him?'

'Doesn't it boil down to the same thing, ultimately? . . . Joel . . .'

What now, he wondered, trying to follow the new turn of her thoughts.

'Yes?'

'Do you still get those bouts of homesickness for Europe? Remember, you told me of them once. You sug-

gested we should spend time in Europe and perhaps visit
your sister in Israel . . .'

'That was a very long time ago,' he said.

He felt her withdraw.

'Don't you want to protect your children against what
might happen?'

'By taking them away?'

'Yes.'

'Clara, Jean is seventeen and young Emanuel is fifteen.
You can't just uproot children at those ages. They will
have something to say about it. And you mustn't forget
that they are Isaacs children, my name notwithstanding.
Besides, I want to stay and see this thing out now.'

'What if I decide to go?' she asked.

'Then you go.'

'And what if I decide to take them?'

'That's up to you.'

'But whatever I do, you are staying?'

'Yes.'

'You really don't want anything from me any more, do
you, Joel?'

'Please, Clara . . .'

'Sorry: I'll go and get ready.'

She left his side and Joel listened for her movements, all
his senses on the alert, making the following of her
progress by sound a matter of major import. The thick
carpet absorbed almost totally the shock of high-heeled
shoes against floor. Still, he picked up each footfall. Now
she was half-way across the room; that pause meant she
was putting down her glass; at the door, and out.

He looked down at the shimmering lights of the city
then slid the glass panel shut and turned on his heels. Half-
way to the door he changed his mind and veered towards
the telephone. Again he tried the Presidential Secretary's
number. This time it rang. But it kept on ringing until he
was on the point of giving up; then there was a click and
John Stanhope's voice, loaded with weariness, said, 'Presidential Secretary.'

'John. Joel.'

'Thank God it's you!'

'How's it?'

'Bloody awful. They all seem to have lost their heads. You should see them. God help the island. Listen, Joel, can you come round?'

'Old Nathan's just phoned to say there's a family council.'

'He was here a while ago. Come when it's over. There's no sleep for me tonight.'

'What of the Ministers?'

'They won't arrive at anything tonight. I'll let them talk themselves out then pack them off till tomorrow. The confusion is mounting and you-know-who is out on the streets adding to it. Anyway, I'll warn the guards to let you in any time you come. Be slow and deliberate. They're all a bit jumpy. See you . . .'

Joel turned from the telephone to find Clara leaning against the door.

'Was that John Stanhope?'

'Yes.'

'Anything new?'

'The confusion is spreading. Where are the children?'

'They're all right. They're not on the street.' She crossed to the phone, suddenly brisk and businesslike, and dialled a number. She asked after her children of someone at the other end: she listened, ended the conversation and turned to her husband: 'They're both all right and they'll be delivered here after the party.'

'I promised to go round to John Stanhope after the meeting.'

'I gathered that much,' she said.

She led the way out. She had changed to a simple black dress and Joel wondered whether it was in mourning for the dead President. The line of the dress made her neck seem longer, gave her shoulders a tapering slope, her back a youthful erectness, and made her waist as slender as when he had first put his arm about it in the long ago carefree days of young love. And her hips flared out and he remembered how he and she had once shared the dance of love almost nightly, and how it had been.

She stopped suddenly and he walked into her. They grabbed each other for balance. She regained balance and composure first, she stepped back and watched his face, her gaze compounded of speculation and slightly derisive amusement. He realized that she had done this deliberately. His anger was tempered by his awareness of the softness and the warmth of the feel of her.

'I'm still your wife,' she murmured.

'What are you talking about!'

'Mentally stripping me, dear Joel. You don't have to, you know. The law says you have certain conjugal rights.'

'Without love?' he asked, startled.

She pursed her lips and looked judicious. 'It is of course preferred with but——' She shrugged slightly, turned on her heels and continued on her way out.

When he reached the car she was in the driving-seat. He started to remind her that he would be going to John Stanhope after the meeting, then he changed his mind. You do not have to remind Clara of such details. Tell her once and she remembers and provides for it without any further reminder. This capacity for remembering detail was a special Isaacs family characteristic. Whenever it had upset him, Joel had excused it by conjuring up some long dead Isaacs ancestor who might have been trapped in one of the physical and spiritual ghettoes of Europe, and whose survival and the survival of whose descendants, depended on his capacity to remember details. Thus, perhaps, out of the need to survive, was fashioned, and handed down, this extra family talent, as distinctive and sharply defined as an extra limb. But behind his thoughts, like a shadow to these thoughts, was the awareness of the feel of her firm warm body. And he knew this was as she wanted it to be, this was as she had planned, a demonstration of how to make things happen. And still the shadow was there behind his thoughts, and with it her voice gently urging him to further self-destruction with 'I'm still your wife'.

The car swung out of the imposing driveway and the twinkling lights of the city were hidden on the other side of the house and the high wide hill on which it stood. The road down was a spiralling corkscrew. Because of his affection for Clara the President had himself ordered that the office of Public Works use the best men and material available, and so this public roadway that served only

Clara and Joel Sterning's home was one of the finest on the island. The people of the island, depending on which section it was, had been exasperated, amused, moved, irritated, angered by scores of such presidential gestures based on an old man's caprice. At the time when he gave the order about the making of the road to the Sterning home, a formal opposition party was still in existence since the 'one-party state' law had not yet been passed. The opposition had tried to make an issue of it, tabling a motion of no-confidence in parliament, and outside it charging the President with acting like a dictator.

At an enormous function in the banqueting hall of the city's largest hotel, a mainly black-tie affair, where chicken and wine were served, the spokesmen of the opposition had sent out a rallying call to the nation to rise up and man the barricades and hurl back and destroy the creeping dictatorship of the Joshua régime. But the mass of the people could not afford to go to the great hotel to hear the call to the barricades. Besides, they said to each other, the Old Man was not doing anything new. He had been doing this sort of thing for as long as they could remember. So why the fuss now? And when the no-confidence motion came up in parliament the Old Man had appeared at the door of the Chamber, wiggled the index finger of his right hand at the Members on the government benches, laughed out loud and poked out his tongue at the opposition benches. The government Ministers had risen and solemnly marched out of the Chamber followed by their backbenchers. The Chairman of the Chamber had been forced to adjourn the session for want of a quorum. And that was the end of the no-confidence motion, and it was also the end of the opposition. By making a joke of it the Old Man had destroyed the opposition utterly. So, when the one-party law was passed later, it merely legalized reality.

At the time, Joel remembered, the joke of the Old Man's appearance at the door of the Chamber had seemed hilariously funny, especially as it was told and retold on the veranda circuit where it acquired, with each telling, a fresh cutting point. And it had all begun with this road.

He turned his head and tried to look at Clara's face.

The dashboard gave enough light for him to see it in striking profile, but not enough for him to see it in detail. He wondered whether she still remembered the making of this road. It was not a crucial thing on which survival or progress may depend, and the Isaacs gift for remembering detail operates at a highly selective level.

'The road,' he said, loud enough for it to be heard above the hum of the engine.

She turned her head to him, a quick doll-like jerk, then she turned back to watching the road.

'What about the road?'

Not a detail to remember, he told himself; aloud he said, 'Nothing.'

She slowed the car, brought it to a stop. They had made one complete spiralling downward circle. Again the lights of Mosesville could be seen far below. But now the lights did not twinkle. They were four hundred feet lower than the house, four hundred feet nearer the plain, and so there was no twinkle to the lights. They were, now, ordinary man-made lights, without any touch of fairy-tale magic.

She turned so that she faced him fully.

'What is it now, Joel? I've done something wrong again; but what?'

'You've done nothing wrong.'

'Yet you sat in judgement on me. I felt it, Joel. Am I not even entitled to know what I'm being judged for?'

'I was not judging.'

'All right. Reacting then.'

'I was thinking about the road, about how it came to be made and the politics surrounding its making.'

'And so when you said "The road", I should have made the connection immediately. Oh, Joel! And you the just and reasonable man. I wonder how you would have re-acted if I had made the connection. Sometimes a situation arises between two people, and there is a need for one always to see fault in the other: I hope we have not arrived at that point.'

'What do you want, Clara?' Joel sounded a little weary, a little impatient.

'Is it so wrong to care about being judged harshly by one's husband?'

'You surprise me!' he said bitterly.

'Why, Joel?'

'Because you know, and you've known for all these years, that the only reason why I'm still with you is because leaving you would also mean leaving the island or else being destroyed by your family. You've known this and you have not cared, so why this sudden concern now for what I think?'

'Is that all there is to it, Joel?'

'Isn't it enough? Isn't the taking of my manhood enough? What else would you like? Would you now invade my last privacy and tell me which of my thoughts are good and which are bad?'

The woman was silent for a very long time, and because the man knew how her mind worked he waited, knowing she was examining what he had said with the care a jeweller gives to a precious stone. He knew, too, that this act of examination meant she was deeply disturbed. But his mind protested against the notion of the woman being really profoundly disturbed. They had led separate lives too long for either one to now be emotionally disturbed by the other. Their children, the habits that come of being married long, what Clara sometimes called 'the forces of circumstance', these were the bonds now.

At last the woman came out of her reverie.

'So I'm to blame for your weakness and your cowardice. Even that is held against me. Aren't you a man, Joel? Couldn't you have left me any time you wanted to?'

'And what would you and your people have done?'

'What do you expect, Joel? Would you expect my father and my brothers to keep you on in the business after you had discarded me? They do have feelings, you know.'

'Yes, I know. And they would have vented those feelings against anyone who helped me or gave me a job.'

'And so, because you were afraid, you stayed. And because you stayed you blame it on me and you take out your resentment on me.'

'Did I start this?'

'Didn't you?'

'Yes, I did,' he said quickly. 'I'm sorry. I'd forgotten

how simple and clear-cut things are for you and your family.'

'What would you have me do?' she asked.

Inwardly, silently, he screamed: Restore my manhood! But he said nothing to the woman. The woman nodded as though she had heard that soundless scream. She reached out and touched the back of his hand, then she turned, started the car, and continued the journey down to the plain and the bright lights of the city.

On the way down the mountain it was as all the other nights of their lives had been. The circular road was dark and deserted; the stars were in their places; the homes of the half-dozen families who had built at the foot of the mountain showed the usual subdued lighting.

Then they reached the outskirts of the town and it was as no other night they had ever known. There were people everywhere. They moved like a flowing stream down from the hills that made up the hinterland and backbone and heart of the island: a silent stream of black peasant humanity.

Clara looked at Joel for explanation.

'I think they're going to the Palace,' he said.

'They're so silent,' she said.

'Be careful. Don't blow your horn. Take the first side turning. It may be like this on the other main roads too, so we'd better make our way by the side roads.'

'They're not hostile,' she said.

'Just bewildered,' he said. 'Like a household of small children who have lost mother and father.'

'I know,' she said. 'They are frightened; and like all frightened creatures they are likely to panic and run amok at the slightest shock. We'll have to be careful.'

This, too, is part of the Isaacs character, he told himself.

'Let us hope all people who are in cars tonight understand.'

'Yes,' she said, 'let us hope.'

They reached a point where a side street branched off the main road. Clara tried to turn into the side street, but the stream of people was everywhere about the car, so

thick and steady that moving against it, even at a slight
tangent, was impossible without the consent of that
stream.

Joel sensed Clara's mounting agitation and wished he
were in the driving-seat.

'Better come to a stop,' he said. 'Trafficator showing?'

'Yes.'

She put her foot on the brake and felt the reverberation
of many people bumping and pushing against the car. She
felt people peering into the car as they flowed past. She
thought: We are helpless here; we are at these people's
mercy; what happens to us now depends on the mood of
this mass. Then she thought of the Old Man lying dead in
his Palace. And fear touched her.

Joel felt the wave of fear sweep over his wife. He
thought: It comes hard to those who have never known it;
they don't know what to do, how to adjust to it. He
reached out and put his left hand over hers which rested
on the steering-wheel. Briefly, she gripped his hand.

A dark face peered into the window on Clara's side. Joel
leaned across her to see the face. He felt her breath like
warm steam in his left ear, and his left shoulder was
pressed against her right. This body contact had once been
a powerful bond between them, perhaps the strongest of
all the bonds. Joel lowered Clara's window a little more,
enough for the man outside to poke his head in.

The car was a piece of driftwood in the human stream
and the man outside held on to it to avoid being carried
along with the flow of the stream.

'What you blocking way for?' he demanded hoarsely.

'Help us, brother,' Joel said. 'We want to turn here.'

'Mek a light.'

Joel reached up and flicked on the small interior light.
The man outside had a long gaunt face with a lantern jaw.
The face shone a glossy black in the dim light. Other faces
tried to look in on Joel's side of the car. Momentarily,
there was confusion and indecision among the crowd
immediately about the car.

'Please help us, brother,' Joel said urgently.

'Me know you,' the man said and turned away.

Joel flicked off the interior light.

'Mek way for them turn!' the man said sharply, his voice slightly louder than normal conversation. He spread out his arms and those behind him came to a pause. A way opened to the left.

'Now!' Joel said. 'Carefully!'

Clara inched the car forward and turned left. A small group of people blocked the way into the side street.

'Mek way for them turn!' the long-faced man called again.

The small group stepped out of the way and Clara drove up the little street, freed, now, of the disturbing presence of the flowing stream of silent humanity.

Clara said: 'Thank you, Joel.'

He lit a cigarette for her and felt the trembling of her fingers as she took it from him. She was born here, she and generations of her forebears. She's as native to this island as any of those people back there, but because the Old Man is dead she has just discovered that she's afraid of them.

Twice they were held up by silent crowds at busy intersections. Each time they waited patiently, and each time someone from the crowd came to their rescue and helped them across a main road into another side street. Three times they saw other cars caught in the crowds. And they knew that whether the cars got out or not depended very much on what reaction the occupants provoked in some key articulate individual in the crowds.

At last, after spending nearly an hour on a journey they normally covered in twenty minutes, Clara turned the car through the enormous gates and into the vast grounds of old Nathan Isaacs's home. From the gateway to the house was a distance of a mile and a half. Only the Presidential Palace stood in larger grounds, and not even the Palace had such fine lawns and such a delightful and varied assortment of exotic flowering trees from every sub-tropical corner of the earth. For old Nathan Isaacs, this house was the outward and visible symbol of his success. He had started his working life inheriting a small dry-goods store that was mortgaged to the hilt and that carried more debt than his stock warranted. This had been the Isaacs legacy after four generations in the island. Starting with that, he had laid the foundations on which his three sons, Nathan Junior, Emanuel and Solomon, had later built the massive Isaacs economic empire that today touched every facet of the life of the land. He had spent a fortune to make this house the symbol of the Isaacs success.

Old Nathan's personal chauffeur opened the door for Clara and slipped into the driving-seat to park the car.

'Everybody arrived?'

'Yes, Miss Clara.'

Clara hesitated fractionally, looked at Joel, then led the way up the six steps to the large open door.

A radio was on full blast somewhere on the upper floor, and the voice of the announcer urged all people, especially motorists, to stay at home because of the mourning crowds from the hills. Not that there was any danger, the announcer hastened to add, everything was orderly and peaceful and under control. Then the Commissioner of Police came on to tell the people on the streets how they should behave and that they should try not to hold up traffic. He announced that buses would run all night so that people caught in the mourning crowds could get home.

Joel only half-listened to the voice of the Police Commissioner. Part of him fought against the loudness of the voice. He hated coming to this house because it was a house of noise. No one spoke softly here; everyone shouted. And there was always the conflict of noises from several radios, record changers, television sets, and human voices. While Clara lived in this house, when he courted her, she had tried to impose some control on its noises. Now there was none.

They hurried up the long flight of stairs to the upper floor, turned left, still pursued by the noise, opened a large oak door, slipped through, shut the door, and were miraculously free of the assault of sound. They had entered old Nathan's wing and he had insulated it against the noises from the rest of the house.

Voices came to them from old Nathan's study, which opened to their left. They went in and everybody was there except Clara's mother and sisters and the children. Her three brothers, Nathan, first son of old Nathan, Manny,

Solly, all flanked the old man. Nathan and Manny sat to the right of him, Solly to his left. Beside Solly were two chairs reserved for Clara and Joel. The three other men in the room, the husbands of old Nathan's three remaining daughters, sat a little apart, making it clear that Joel was the only non-Isaacs who was part of the family council. The family referred to Solly, Clara and Joel as the radical faction, while the old man, young Nathan (in his late fifties) and Manny were regarded as the conservative faction. When any situation demanded a conservative approach the conservative faction assumed authority and spoke for the Isaacs empire. When the need was for a radical line the radicals took over. Often in the past this had given the Isaacs empire a flexibility of approach that its rivals could not match.

'You're late,' old Nathan rasped. 'Crowds hold you up?' He was a tiny, dried-up little man with a large head and piercing eyes. He was darker than all his children but it was obvious that the slight Negro strain did not come from his side.

'It was terrible,' Clara said.

'Not really,' Joel said quickly. 'It was the surprise.'

'Yes; Joel is right.' Clara took her seat beside Solly.

'What do you think?' young Nathan said to Joel. He looked even more like a glum, very large and slightly overfed farmer than he usually did.

'Do you mean are they likely to run amok?' Joel asked.

'Yes,' young Nathan said. 'Revolution and all that sort of thing.'

'No,' Solly said. He was the youngest of the three sons; the long and lean temperamental one, Clara's favourite brother and the one Isaacs Joel Sterning liked without reservation.

'I asked Joel,' young Nathan drawled.

'Come now, to business,' the old man said. 'What do we do?'

'Solly's right,' Joel said. 'They won't run amok. At worst we'll have a few killings, a few demonstrations, a few cases of arson in field and factory . . .'

'Why are you so sure?'

'Because we know our people, brother,' Solly said. 'Traditionally they're on the side of the government, whichever it is; on the side of authority, of law and order, call it what you will. If you and I represent authority and law and order then they will obey us.'

'We're not here for a political discussion,' the old man cut in.

'We're coming to the point, Papa, to business,' Solly said. 'There is confusion because the death of the President means that there is now no authority for them to turn to. It is this that frightens them and so they all march to the Palace, the traditional home of the person in authority. It's a frightened, unreasoning action. But it's understandable and it gives us a pointer as to what could happen.'

'If I understand you, Solly,' young Nathan said, 'your point is that we have nothing to fear from the people.'

'That's right,' Solly said.

'D'you go along with him, Joel?'

'Yes.'

'Surely you make the reservation that we have nothing to fear for as long as they are not misled.'

'The point you are missing, Nathan,' Solly said, 'is the question: Misled by whom? By communists, socialists, racists? Which group do you fear?'

'Does it matter? Any of those you've named.'

'But that is just the point,' Solly said. 'They can only be misled by someone or some group in authority.'

'I get it!' young Nathan said quickly. 'If you're right then the real problem is who becomes the new father-figure in whom they vest all authority.'

'That's the real problem,' Solly said.

'Josiah,' the old man said, looking at each member of his inner council in turn. 'Joel, can't we do something to help those others stop him? Isn't there one of them we can back heavily who has a chance? You're our political man. Tell us.'

'There is,' Joel said slowly. 'But I think we'll lose.'

'I'm thinking of big money,' the old man rasped. 'One, maybe two hundred thousand. It's worth it to break him.'

'We don't think it can be done, Papa,' Solly said.

'Joel?' the old man said.

'If it fails,' Joel said slowly, 'we will all be finished.'

'So?'

'I think Josiah will win . . .'

'So?'

'I say don't get involved. Stay out. Do our business.'

Manny, the nondescript, pasty-faced brother, asked: 'Will *he* leave us alone? Will *he* let us do our business?'

'That is a chance we must take,' young Nathan said.

'Then you agree with Solly and Joel,' the old man said.

'I don't see we have any choice. It's not a question of agreeing. If they're right then our approach will have to become radical. I think they are. We'd better start by seeing that some of the darker workers are promoted to some of the special jobs.' Young Nathan's remarks, now, were addressed to the three men who were there by virtue of being married to Isaacs girls. 'Dark girls in all the front offices, and courtesy: you know the plan . . .'

'I thought that was already in effect!' Clara said sharply. 'We took that decision nearly ten years ago!'

'I know,' young Nathan said. 'This time it must be implemented.'

'No wonder they call us hypocrites!' Clara was possessed by a violent flash of uncontrollable anger. 'Why meet! Why make these decisions if they can be pigeonholed for ten years! The great progressive Isaacs empire dedicated to serving the nation!'

'Clara!' the old man said sharply.

'Come off it, Clara,' Manny, the silent one, said mildly. 'We could all see what was going on. You too. Let us not be hypocrites about it *now*.'

Solly put long thin nervous fingers on his favourite sister's arm. 'Easy, dear; Manny's right. We all allowed it to drift: all of us except Joel. He tried.'

'I didn't——' Clara began, then she looked at Joel and shook her head. 'Yes. Perhaps I didn't want to see . . .'

'This gets us nowhere,' young Nathan said. 'And when you've finished criticizing us, my dear Clara, just remember that our workers are still the best paid and looked after on the island. It's not our fault if standards are abysmally low. The thing is to adjust to the times. And this time it is up to all of us to see that the policy is carried out at every level. It is a matter of survival.'

'All right,' the old man rasped. 'Politically, we take no part in the struggle for power; organizationally, we project a more popular dark-skinned image. What else?' The old man turned to his eldest son.

'I formally resign the chairmanship of the board of Isaacs Enterprises,' young Nathan said. 'And I propose Mr. Solomon Isaacs as the new chairman and spokesman of Isaacs Enterprises.'

'I second,' Manny said.

'Objections?' the old man said, then in the same breath, 'None. Let it so be noted.'

Young Nathan smiled at his youngest brother. 'Anything special you want us to do?'

'You and Manny will of course continue to keep internal control.'

'Of course.'

'Keep up your political contacts. And you might both let it be known that you are not too happy about what looks to you like our support for Josiah.'

'Who are you? You and Joel?'

'And Papa and Clara.'

'Papa too?' Manny asked, startled.

'Yes. I want to speak with the authority of a very strong majority.'

'And just how unhappy are Manny and I?' young Nathan asked.

'Very. And you hope to win back control one day and reverse policy.' Solly looked at the three junior members, the three silent husbands of his three sisters. 'This will not be discussed again once we leave this room: not among yourselves; not even with your wives. Understand?'

The three nodded.

'Anything else?' the old man asked.

Young Nathan said: 'This is for your information, not discussion. I've just made a sizeable increase in our holdings outside the island. Senior members of the board can get details any time they wish.'

'Anything else?' the old man asked. After a pause he added: 'All right. Meeting's over.'

The old man rose and everybody followed suit. He led the way out of the study and into a large living-room with a wide balcony that commanded a sweeping view of the rear of the great house and the sprawling acres of floodlit garden. From the balcony they could see a small party in progress down by the swimming-pool. Manny's eldest son was home on holiday from his college in the States. He had brought half a dozen friends with him. And since grandpa Nathan's was the largest of the family houses, he and his friends had moved in and taken over a wing. Now they had collected a group of young ladies from nearby homes and were having a night-time swimming party, under strict chaperonage of course. Old Nathan always insisted that young people behave properly.

The sound of young laughter drifted up to the people on the wide balcony.

'The young people are happy,' the old man said, and slipped his arm through Clara's.

'It is easy for the young to be happy,' Clara said.

'Or sad,' the old man added. 'You very sad, my little Clara?'

'Not very.'

'But sad.'

'I don't know, Papa. It isn't so simple.'

'It never is, my child. Trouble between you and Joel?'

Two young black girls moved silently among them offering drinks and things to eat. Joel, Solly and young Nathan were in a corner by themselves exploring further the political and economic implications of the death of the President. Manny, the family organization and personnel expert, stood with the three junior directors, clearing up points they had been too nervous to raise at the full meeting.

'You understand I'm not trying to pry,' the old man said hastily when Clara said nothing.

'I know, Papa.' She patted his hand. 'There is no trouble. I wish there were. There is nothing. I didn't realize how proud he was.'

'I thought you were the one who was tired of him, my child.'

'I thought so too.'

'And I still don't approve of what you did. I would have blamed you if he had divorced you.'

'He did the same thing,' she protested. 'He did it first.'

'That makes no difference!' The old man was getting angry. 'He's a man!'

Clara choked back the angry retort that welled up in her. After a while she said very quietly: 'You would have blamed me, but you would have stood by me, against him. You and my brothers.'

'You are my child,' the old man said stiffly. 'You are their sister.'

'Yes,' she said heavily. 'Yes.'

'I—we—are very fond of Joel. He's one of us. He knows it.'

'He also knows you would have stood by me.'

The old man refused to follow where she was leading, so he led her to where Joel, Solly and young Nathan stood. He felt old and tired suddenly, and it showed on his face and in the stoop of his small figure.

'See me to my room, Nathan,' he rasped fretfully. 'Good night.' Young Nathan led the old man out.

'Don't see how I can get to the Palace tonight,' Joel said.

'Shouldn't try,' Solly said.

Joel looked at Clara and decided he could not let her make the journey home alone, or even with a chauffeur: not on a night like this. He would never forgive himself if anything happened to her, especially because things were bad between them.

Solly said: 'He's getting very old and we may not have him for long.' Joel and Clara knew his mind was on the old President lying dead in his Palace. There was no more than three or four years' difference, either way, between the dead old President and their living father.

Clara said: 'Papa's been rather more careful than old Moses.'

Joel walked across the room to where the telephone was

and dialled John Stanhope's number. Holding on, he turned and looked at Manny and the three junior directors who were there by right of marriage. There was an air of servility about them, an attitude of three untouchables in the presence of a Brahmin prince. It made Manny seem magnetic and powerful. Poor bloody brutes. The ringing of the telephone stopped and after a while a desperate male voice said 'Yes?'; but it was not John Stanhope.

'Joel Sterning here; Mr. Stanhope, please.'

'He cannot speak, sir; he's with the Ministers and not to be disturbed.'

'Will you take a message then?'

'I'm sorry, sir; the Presidential Secretary cannot speak!'

And you are on the verge of cracking, my friend, Joel thought as the man at the other end hung up on him. Again he looked at the three surrounding Manny. He wondered whether he, too, had once fawned on the Isaacs wealth and name as they now did. And it seemed to him that he remembered doing so, a little more subtly perhaps, with the sophistication of the European. These three were island-born. He went back to Solly and Clara.

'Get John?' Solly asked.

'No. Some fellow on the verge of breaking down who hung up on me. John's still with the Ministers.'

'Poor John,' Solly said. 'I'd tell that crowd to go to hell.'

'He can't,' Joel said, a little sharply. 'They're the government and John is a servant of the people!'

'Easy, Joel,' Solly was startled. 'I didn't mean anything: certainly not what you seem to think.' He looked from Joel to Clara.

'I'm going home,' Clara said quickly, and began to move to the door. 'You staying, Joel? If you are I'll leave the car.'

'I'll take you home,' Joel said.

They said good-bye to Manny and the three junior directors, and Solly went down the stairs with them. While they waited for the car they saw a special constable, a member of that branch of the police force that can be hired by private citizens, come round a corner of the house on his patrol. All through the night a 'special' will be on patrol duty around the house. Another will be at the gate, and a third will patrol the land at the back of the house.

Solly touched Joel's arm and said: 'Something's worrying you.'

'It's personal,' Clara said very quickly. 'Between Joel and me.'

'I see.'

'Do you?' There was a hint of bitterness about her now.

'Sorry,' Solly said, cold and withdrawn. He stepped back as the chauffeur brought up the car. The chauffeur opened the driver's door for Clara. She shook her head.

'Please drive, Joel.'

'Look you two!' Solly exploded. 'What the hell's the matter? I haven't done or said anything! I haven't tried to interfere! So why turn on me? When you've had trouble before I've kept the others off your backs to give you a chance to work out things by yourselves!' Then he calmed down as suddenly. 'All right. We are an oppressive bunch. Maybe things would have worked out better if you had gone away for a few years in the beginning.'

'Good night, Solly,' Clara said.

' 'Night, sis; 'night, Joel. I hope—' He swung on his heels and went back into the great house.

'You needn't take me home,' Clara said softly. She indicated her father's chauffeur. 'With him driving and a "special" beside him I'd be quite safe.'

For answer Joel started the car and moved off. The chauffeur touched his cap. As they passed him the 'special' threw an elaborate military salute.

The way back was easier than the way coming. Crowds were still converging on the Presidential Palace, but in smaller numbers now, and it was relatively easy to get the car through the crowds at the main roads. Joel switched on the radio at one stage and there was mournful, discordant hymn-singing as from a great and poorly guided multitude in the open under the stars. And when it was punctuated by the inevitable commercial, the announcer said that the broadcasting of this great and spontaneous expression of a nation's grief on the outskirts of the Palace where our fallen President lay had been made possible by the public spiritedness of Isaacs Enterprises. It later transpired that a young priest of one of the less socially respectable churches had joined his humble parishioners on their march down from the hills to the Presidential Palace. It was his efforts that had given the wave of sorrow its religious aspect. Other priests had soon followed his example. Now the approaches to the Palace gave the impression of a series of vast and mournful religious crusades. The organs of publicity had seized on this. When, five minutes later, the man with the commercial came on again, Clara switched him off violently. But the memory of the hymn-singing, sharp and clear, lingered with them all the way up the spiralling road to their mountain-top home.

Clara left Joel putting away the car and went into the house to see if the children were safely home.

When he came in she met him with a drink. She said: 'The children are all right. They're asleep. Something to eat? A snack? Cold chicken? Salami? Cheese?'

'No, thank you.' He wanted a snack, but alone, not with Clara.

He finished his drink quickly, checked to see that all doors and windows were securely shut, said good night to Clara, and went to his room. And because the President's death had come at the end of a long, hard day which was also the end of a hard week, he slipped into a very deep sleep almost as soon as he got into bed.

In the other room, Clara refilled her glass ensuring, as a matter of habit, that her drink was iced soda water with just a faint whisky flavouring. As the family hostess for all important occasions, which usually meant big political or economic or business dinners, she often had to appear to drink a great deal, so iced soda water flavoured with a few drops of whisky had become habit.

She carried the drink to the balcony. She opened one of the sliding glass panels. Below were the shimmering lights of the city, and the body of the dead President, and the mourning black crowds making discordant sounds out of their sorrow. She pulled a chaise close up to the glass and settled down, making her back comfortable by pressing it against the foam-rubber support of the chair.

The world was silent now, as silent and quiet as she had ever known it. When she was a child her room at her father's house had sometimes been as quiet as this, but never as silent. Always there had been the ticking of the clock that hung above her bedroom door. Here, in this all electrical house, the clocks were silent. And both the silence and the quiet were complete.

Her stomach felt sore and sick. Once, a long time ago, two big black girls had cornered her behind some bushes in the deserted part of the school yard. They had pushed her, playfully rather than aggressively. But she had become angry and slapped the bigger one on the face, hard. Without any change of expression the big black girl had closed her hand into a fist and hit Clara in the stomach. Then the two black girls had walked away. And Clara had leaned against the bushes, body doubled up, sore and sick in the stomach, unable to breathe properly for a long time. Now the sickness in her stomach brought back the memory of that dreadful day. She had known, instinctively, and as soon as the pain had eased up sufficiently for her to be able to think, that the big black girl would not have hurt her if she had not slapped the girl. The knowledge had been no help and no comfort. And now, more than twenty years later she felt the same sickness in her stomach and recognized it for what it was. She was afraid. And again the fact of knowing was no comfort. But she was an adult now, grown-up, the mother of big children, a woman of power and influence, so she did not allow herself to fall apart as she had done as a girl behind the bushes.

She thought of Joel in his room. He had comforted her once, long ago, when he had loved her. Now he loved that part-Chinese black woman. She felt the pounding of her heart, and she put her hand over it to try and still the violence of its beat. She felt the firm outward curve of her breast. He used to love cupping her breasts in his hands so, fondling them endlessly, even after loving, as though they gave him a pleasure beyond the realm of sex. That

woman would never be able to give the pleasure and satis-
faction of body that she, Clara, had given him. When sex
is as total and complete for as long as it had been between
them, then any after experience with anybody else is never
really important. That is why she could not feel jealous of
that other woman with her straight up-and-down boyish
body.

Where had it begun to go wrong? At what point had his
love started to wither? The way it came out from him now
it was as though the germ of its death was there at its
birth. But how then account for the good years and the
beautiful years and the happy times.

Then, sharp and clear, the thought was full grown in
her mind: We forced him to recognize the streak of fear
and cowardice in him; we challenged and proved wrong
his own estimate of himself. For that he will never forgive
me and mine.

She tried to deny the truth of the thought, but she knew
the attempt was futile.

She rose quickly and pushed her head through the opening in the glass panelling. Looking down at the twinkling
lights, she thought: Elsewhere it might have been different,
he would have been different and I would have been
different; not here, not on the island . . .

. . . It is a long time since I've crawled to anybody for
comfort. We are strong people, we Isaacs. We have to be.
Jews have always had to be to survive. But he's my husband and what is between us is wrong. How to right it? O
Lord how to right it? . . .

She shut the glass panel and secured it. She went to her
room, changed into her night-clothes, turned off all the
lights and groped her way to the door of her husband's
room.

He had opened all his windows and the night was clear
enough for her to see him as a shadowy figure in the bed.
She trembled violently now, as though chilled. She crawled
into the bed beside him, and the contact with his naked
body made the sickness in her stomach unbearable. He
stirred and pulled away. She put trembling fingers on him
and began to caress him rhythmically. He woke.

'What the——! Clara!'

Then he heard the soft sobbing of his wife. He reached out and switched on the bedside lamp. He sat up and turned to her. He choked back the angry words as he saw the tears flowing from her stark and frightened eyes. She was not given to tears.

'What's the matter?'

'I'm afraid, Joel; I'm afraid.'

'What of? What's wrong?'

When she said nothing, he thought: Another Isaacs stunt. Then, watching her, he felt ashamed of himself. Whatever the reason, Clara was really frightened. It was there in her eyes, and he knew this woman well. Then he became aware of her physical presence. He switched off the light quickly and settled back in bed, careful not to touch her.

'May I stay?'

'Yes.' She had not been in his bed or he in hers for nearly four years.

There was a long silence between them, punctuated now and then by a soft snuffle from Clara. Then she put her hand on him tentatively. Her touch was as fire to his skin.

'The conjugal rights business?' he asked coldly.

'Just comfort, Joel, please. Just comfort. I *am* your wife.'

He remembered how it had been. Afterwards, she had always made him feel as though he had bestowed a great and precious gift on her. But there had been total harmony only in this, and it was not enough. She pressed her thigh against his and passion rose in him. Then he pulled her to him with a mixture of bitter rage and high passion.

'So afraid,' she moaned as she received him, and he knew it was of the island because it was without its father now, without Moses Joshua.

CHAPTER TWO

THEY LAY side by side, naked, the tall handsome black boy and the statuesquely beautiful black girl. The song of the surf was the only sound in the moonlit world. And because they were on a private fenced-in beach they lay relaxed, unafraid of intruders or the night prowlers who preyed on lovers on lonely beaches. Besides, they were an hour's drive out of the city and the night prowlers operated at public beaches much nearer the city.

The boy was mute with wonder because of the unexpectedness of it all. It had not been what he had intended. They had been here, on this beach, many times in the past, and nothing happened. But unexpectedly, surprisingly and in a manner that he could not now recall, he had made love to her and discovered, with awed dismay, that it was the first time for her. She had taken him in quietly, as a mother suckling a baby at her breast and finding fulfilment in the very hurt of the act. He thought she had wept a little but he could not be sure of anything except that it had been the first time for her and the strange feelings of guilt and wonder this fact had evoked. You would not believe it, with the vast army of admirers always around her, with the whirl of parties and dances she attended, and especially after you'd experienced the competence with guardhouse and flopped down in the first empty chair she found.

All the way up the driveway, stretching to the very doors of the Palace, the place bristled with police and military. Even the guardhouse was unusually crowded, and there was a constant coming and going of policemen. The old sergeant in charge of the guardhouse seemed the only calm and composed person about. The old sergeant left his desk and went to the woman.

'Miss Lee . . . What a night, heh!'

'What a night!' she echoed him.

'Seen all the crowds?'

'Just been right round the Palace.'

'Never seen anything like it,' the sergeant said. 'Never!'

Miss Lee was tall and thin and her thinness and her tight slacks and longish face made her seem even taller. She was a deep dark-brown, nearly black, and her face was of a matte smoothness that glowed with a life all its own. But it was her eyes, wholly oriental and slanting and going round the corners of her face, and her straight thick blue-black hair, hanging down to the shoulders, that made for the striking appearance of the woman. She was almost completely flat-chested and the rest of her long lean body showed only the vaguest hints of feminine curves. There were laughter lines about the corners of the big mouth and a disturbing detachment in the gaze she turned on her world. Miss Martha Lee was the Political and Diplomatic Correspondent of *The Voice of the Island*.

'What's it like up there?' She moved her head slightly to indicate the Palace.

'Confusion, Miss Lee; confusion, Ma'am. All the Ministers except the Honourable Josiah have been there all the time since the news.'

'Yes,' she said drily. 'I saw *him* weep on television.'

'All that stop,' the sergeant said. 'No more television and radio people up there; they won't even let you in there now. Some of your friends are up there, but outside the doors. Anyway, a little warm coffee, ma'am? It not really hot again, but it strong and sweet.'

'No thank you, sergeant. It's kind of you. Can I try and reach Mr. Stanhope on your phone?'

'Not supposed to, Miss. Strict orders, and not from our Inspector either; a captain of the army is in charge up there now.'

Martha Lee tilted her head back and looked into the sergeant's eyes. For a while the sergeant met the steady gaze of the slanting Chinese eyes, then he looked away, disturbed; then, as though compelled, he looked back into those eyes.

'I'll lose my job, Miss,' he protested.

'I'll see you don't, sergeant; I promise.'

The sergeant shrugged helplessly, looked at the two telephones on his desk and made a rapid inspection of the three little groups of policemen in the room. The group in the far corner was immersed in conversation; the smaller group near the door was playing dominoes; and near at hand, only some ten feet away, four young fellows sat silent and tense as though afraid to breathe. These latter were young country constables, part of the force from the rural areas that had been flown in to stand by in case of trouble.

Martha Lee rose and touched the sergeant's arm.

'Sergeant, all I'm asking is permission to use your phone, understand? You don't know what for because I didn't tell you. As far as you know it is to get in touch with my paper. You know I've phoned my paper from here many times in the past.'

'All right, Miss,' the sergeant said unhappily.

In two long strides Martha Lee was across the room and at the desk. She picked up the phone that was connected only to the Palace. She dialled the numerals 2, 3. Someone answered almost instantly, but it was not the Presidential Secretary. She pressed her finger down on the rest, breaking the connection. Quickly she dialled again, three numerals this time, 1, 2, 3. In one of his moments of grand expansiveness, the old man who now lay dead up there had himself ordered John Stanhope to give her these private numbers as well as a bottle of rare brandy; and a week later he had publicly threatened to lock her up because of some article he did not like. Now, as the phone rang on the Old Man's desk, she half expected to hear the bluff, bullying voice rumble 'Yes!'

The voice that did say 'Yes?' was that of John Stanhope, gentle and charged with a terrible weariness.

'Martha Lee,' she said. 'Sorry to bother you.' Once she had thought herself in love with this man; but that had been a long time ago.

'Not now,' he said.

'When? I'm at the guardhouse. I can wait.'

'It may be very long.'

'I can wait.'

'All right.'

The old sergeant came to her, relief written all over his face.

'All right, Miss?'

'Thank you, sergeant. May I just make one more call, to my paper?'

'Yes, Miss!'

But it required three tries before she finally got on to the night man at the news desk.

'Malcolm? Martha Lee. Hold the front page till the very last minute. All right? . . .'

She produced cigarettes and matches from the deep pockets of her high-necked Chinese-style blouse. She and the sergeant lit up.

'Mr. Stanhope asked me to wait here, sergeant.'

'Then that makes it official, Miss.'

'That's right, sergeant. He said it might be a long time.'

'Doesn't matter, Miss. If he said so then you can stay here till morning. What about the coffee now, Miss?'

'I like mine black and bitter, sergeant; a little like me.'

That was what the sergeant liked about this young lady: big job and all and pretty enough to claim to be Chinese; but no, she doesn't claim to be coloured or Chinese-coloured or any of those fancy ways of denying the blackness in her. She comes straight out with the blackness in her.

In his pleasure he dropped his careful English and said: 'Mek me see what dem have in de back, Miss.'

So easy, Martha Lee thought, both touched and irritated; so easy. Say the right words, make the right gestures and my people eat out of your hands.

The sergeant soon returned with a mug of steaming black coffee.

'I got a little somet'ing to go in, Miss.'

She nodded and he brought a quarter quart bottle from the bottom right-hand drawer of the desk and quickly laced the coffee with a generous dash of white rum. Then he slipped the little bottle back into its hiding-place.

Martha Lee wrapped the long fingers of both hands about the hot mug and realized how cold her hands were. The island sometimes turned very cold at night as Christmas approached, and Christmas was less than two months away. She drank some of the coffee, still warming both hands with the mug, and as she drank she thanked the old sergeant with her eyes. He beamed at her. So easy.

Afterwards she went back to the chair. The sergeant returned to his desk and his paper work. A squad of policemen came off duty. The sergeant detailed the group in the far corner to take its place. The strong hot coffee and the stronger rum warmed Martha Lee and she forgot her weariness. She left the guardhouse and went to the Palace gates. They let her out and she was among the mass of mourners. Here, near the gates, everybody was silent, partly because of the noise from elsewhere, but also as though waiting for something to happen. Farther away, to the left and the right of the great iron gates, the hymn-singing took place. And it was those who were at the gates who were directly in the path of the meeting of the sounds of the conflicting hymns. From the left came 'Rock of Ages'; from the right 'When the Roll is Called'. And from farther away, immediately outward between left and right 'Abide with Me' was locked in combat with 'Lead Kindly Light'.

A woman put a hand on Martha Lee's arm, leaned towards her ear and shouted: 'You see him? Them let you in?'

'No!' Martha shouted.

'Me wan' see him! We wan' see him! Him belong wid we!'

'You will!' Martha shouted. 'You will! In the morning!'

'What?'

'In the morning! You will see him!'

'We wait! You see him?'

'No!'

'Don' go 'way!' the woman patted her reassuringly. 'You will!'

Just then a convoy of lorries carrying soldiers and po-lice worked its way through to the gates. The crowd heaved and pressed this way and that to get out of the way of the lorries. To escape the pressure Martha Lee went back inside the gates. She had some trouble getting past a soldier who had come to share guard duty with the po-liceman who had let her out. She decided not to go outside the gates again. Farther back the Palace grounds were rapidly beginning to look like a military camp. Tents were sprouting everywhere and armed soldiers moved about with the quiet purposefulness of people who knew what they were about.

Inside the guardhouse, the sergeant looked up as she entered and said: 'See how it is, Miss.'

'Yes; someone's really taken over.'

'I know I can trust you, Miss. Inspector just telephoned to say I must take my orders from the military.'

'As in an emergency,' Martha Lee said.

'Yes, Miss.'

An emergency operation against Josiah, Martha Lee wondered; and if it were that, by whose decision? That of the Ministers? Or that of John Stanhope? She thought about it and prayed that the decision was that of the Ministers . . . But John knows what is involved, and John is not mad, she told herself . . . Somehow she did not feel comforted. The sanest of us, the most reasonable, the most balanced, sometimes reaches breaking point; and then any-thing is possible.

She pushed these thoughts firmly out of her mind, set-tled back in the chair and closed her eyes. Her wait may be long, may stretch for two or three or four hours, or even into the morning. She made her mind blank; relaxed all her body. The clock above the sergeant's desk showed the time a little before one o'clock. The President had now been dead for just about four hours.

The old sergeant touched her shoulder and she woke immediately. 'Miss: the Ministers are leaving. Mr. Stanhope called through for you to come up.'

Martha Lee rose instantly and made for the door but the sergeant called her back. 'No, Miss! You must wait till a soldier comes to escort you. The military have taken over all security duty around the Palace.'

It was then that Martha Lee realized a soldier with the rank of corporal now sat at the sergeant's desk. She looked at the clock on the wall high behind the soldier's head. It was a quarter after two. Just then a soldier marched briskly into the room, saluted his corporal and presented a chit.

The corporal said: 'Miss Lee.'

The soldier saluted again, then stood aside for Martha Lee to leave the room first. They marched side by side up to the Palace, Martha Lee having to stretch her long legs to keep up with the brisk military pace. All about her soldiers were on guard, at fifty-yard intervals, along the driveway to the Palace, and making a vast ring, three deep, inside the shrub and barbed-wire fence that encircled the grounds. From the brightly-lit Palace itself the Ministers now emerged in a body. About them, outnumbering them, soldiers with automatic weapons were on guard.

Too many guns, Martha Lee told herself, much too many guns.

'This way, ma'am,' the soldier murmured and led her off the driveway and across the lawns at a tangent that would bring them to a small side entrance. She had a brief glimpse of Press photographers' flashbulbs popping, then they were round the side of the massive building. The soldier came to an abrupt halt, jarred his head with the violence of his footwork, and threw a massive salute that forced Martha Lee to step back in alarm. They had come up to a guardpost with a junior officer in charge.

The soldier handed over his chit and the young officer took charge of Martha Lee and led her into the familiar Palace which now had the appearance of an armed camp. Two soldiers stood on guard at the foot of the wide stairway that led to the upper parts. At the top, to the right, a soldier was on guard outside the Presidential Office; and two more guarded the entrance to the Presidential private quarters. To the left, and unguarded, were the offices of the Presidential Secretary. And although it was the very early hours of the morning, people were hard at work, everyone in his or her place. For these people the death of the President meant more work to ensure that the machinery of government did not break down as a result of the terrible jolt it had received. So the Presidential Secretary's senior assistants were on the phone to faraway places, talking to the island's representatives in foreign countries, explaining, reassuring, giving guidance.

Martha Lee knew this office well, but now the young officer prevented her from entering. Instead he waited till young Andrew Simpson, the brilliant cadet whom Stanhope was personally grooming for big things in his country's service, saw them and approached. And even now, in the hour of national tragedy, the very tall, very suave, very handsome and very black young diplomat in the making, could not quite restrain the impulse to switch on his charm.

His eyes lit up and he came towards her, both arms outstretched as if to embrace her. Martha Lee noticed a small twitch of contempt on the brown-skinned young officer's face.

'Miss Lee!' young Simpson murmured and made a deep bow over her hand.

The young officer clicked his heels as he saluted; he handed Simpson the chit, swung about and marched away. For a second the foppish air fell from young Simpson, and he was a sharp, alert young man with a hint of ruthlessness about his eyes. His lips moved and Martha Lee thought she lip-read, rather than heard him murmur: 'Silly toy toldier'. In a flash it was all gone and he was once more the smooth and charming young diplomat.

'Mr. Stanhope's up in his quarters,' Simpson murmured. He tucked his right hand under Martha's left elbow and steered her towards the very narrow and almost hidden flight of stairs that led up to the private quarters of the Presidential Secretary.

'You sometimes frighten me, young Andrew,' Martha said softly.

'Me, Miss Lee?' He gestured gracefully with both hands and his shoulders. Then he laughed out loud, gaily.

'Watch yourself, Andy. The President lies dead.'

He stopped abruptly. Again the amiable mask was dropped for a few seconds.

'You are so right, Miss Lee. Our beloved President lies dead and we must show due respect. But you will forgive me if I refuse to make a hero out of a bully and an autocrat who has lived high off the hog on my people, who has misled them and sold them into the hands of the margin gatherers. You will forgive me, won't you, for being glad that the old brute has finally been removed from our necks.' He said all this casually, lightly, as one might talk about the weather.

'Is that all there was to him?' Martha asked.

'For me and those like me—yes! That was all. He held us back. And don't remind me I'm a peasant boy from the hills with a top job in the Palace. This is only small part payment of a heavy undischarged debt owing to generations of poor peasants named Simpson; but here we are, Miss Lee, and you won't give me away, will you? My chief might think such thoughts subversive, and then I might have to go back to being a hill-peasant Simpson—or worse.'

Martha Lee put a firm rein on her mounting anger. She restrained the young man from knocking on the door at the top of the narrow stairs.

'Have you been outside, Andy? Have you seen the poor people from the hills weeping out there at the Palace gates, and all about the grounds?'

'I've seen them, Miss Lee. I've seen them.'

'And still you say what you do?'

'They are his biggest crime: the slaves weeping for the slave master. He put blinkers of ignorance not on one but on two and three generations of islanders.'

'So you dismiss those crowds out there?'

'No, Miss Lee. We don't dismiss them. But we know they are sick in the way all brainwashed people are sick.

They don't know what they are doing out there. So much of their humanity, of their dignity has been destroyed that they are afraid of standing on their own. Is this one of his blessings, Miss Lee?'

'But is that all, Andy? Wasn't there something more?'

He shrugged elegantly.

'For you; not for me.'

Martha gestured for him to knock on the door. He did so and they went in. He stood just inside the door for a while, waiting till John Stanhope, the Presidential Secretary, came forward. Then he bowed slightly and withdrew.

As he came towards her Martha noticed that Stanhope's normally vibrant pale chestnut-brown skin had a lifeless ashenness about it; the normally shrewdly twinkling eyes were dull; even the assurance, perhaps the single most important source of strength of the island's old coloured aristocracy, was gone. And because of this he seemed more pitifully human than Martha thought it possible for John Stanhope to be.

His fingers were ice cold when he took her hand and turned to introduce the European military type with whom he had been in conference. Martha recognized the soldier as the recently appointed Colonel Jones who had been imported to head the island's armed forces.

'Tell me, Colonel,' Martha said, 'has a state of emergency been declared?'

The Colonel opened his mouth then clamped it shut and inclined his head towards the Presidential Secretary. 'I'm only a soldier, Miss.' Then he touched his peaked cap casually and left them.

'Has it, John?' She stared steadily at Stanhope.

'There's no emergency,' Stanhope said wearily. He led the way through to his sitting-room.

'Then who called out the soldiers? And why?'

The man slumped deep in his favourite armchair near the large open window. He gestured for her to help herself from the array of bottles on the liquor cabinet. The woman quickly poured herself a small brandy.

'I called out the soldiers,' Stanhope said. 'And you know why.'

And now, suddenly, Martha was afraid of asking the next question, afraid of the answer Stanhope would give, but she asked it all the same.

'On whose authority?'

'My own.'

'My God, John! How could you! . . . Did you speak to any of them about it?'

'No. They'd all lost their heads and something had to be done to stop the spread of confusion and panic.'

'But John,' she protested. 'You're a public servant, not an elected representative. You have no authority for making this kind of decision. You have no power to call in the military, no power in law, John!'

'Someone had to do something.'

'Not in this way.'

'Let me tell you something, Martha. I've had them here since the death. I've been unable to make them do a thing. They can't even agree on as simple a thing as signing a decree ordering a carry-on until the problem of the succession is resolved. Each is afraid that anything he does might be held against him later . . .'

'I don't doubt your motives, John.'

'But I was wrong?'

'You know it. You know that you have now delivered yourself into the hands of anybody who wants to get you.'

'Like Josiah. But something had to be done, Martha!'

'There were many things you could do without manipulating the military. You had no right to manipulate state power.'

'If only he hadn't concentrated all power in his own hands . . .'

'That's cheating, John. We can make up a long list of "if onlys": if only his Vice-President hadn't died last year; if only he had appointed a Minister of Defence; if only his Ministers were a bunch of patriots instead of a bunch of cowardly self-seekers; and to this, among others, we can add if only the Presidential Secretary had not lost his head and usurped the powers of the people's elected representatives . . .'

'So, I should have done like the others; taken care of my

own interests and allowed the confusion to spread. What kind of patriotism is that?'

'Oh John; John. You have no real faith in your people, do you? This is the real tragedy of our coloured aristocracy, they don't have any faith or trust in the rest of us.'

'I'm awfully tired, Martha, and the going will be tough when daylight comes.'

Martha straightened up quickly. 'Sorry, Mr. Presidential Secretary. I didn't mean to presume.'

'Come off it, Martha,' John said wearily.

'Please John.' She was deadly earnest now. 'The country is going to need what you have more desperately than ever before. If the public service falls apart or goes rotten we will have no hope of surviving this crisis. So please make peace with Josiah. Save yourself in order to keep the service going.'

'Make peace with Josiah! You're mad.'

'John! You're not a political idiot. If you don't he'll break you for this night's work. You know as well as I do that the Ministers who just left you can't stop him.'

'He's no good for the country, Martha!'

'He is one of those who presented themselves to the people, and he was elected. They put him there, John, and nothing we say can change that. Neither you nor I have submitted ourselves to the people so neither you nor I have the authority vested in the least and the meanest of these people. It is either that or the will of the people is turned into a mockery we do not believe in but pay lip-service to.'

'Please, Martha . . .'

'I know. This is no time for a discussion on the nature and meaning of democracy. But you owe it to the country to try and get yourself out of this mess.'

'By helping to bring another would-be dictator to power?'

'*You* have taken unto yourself powers which have been entrusted only to the elect of the people. Think about that, John. Because you are our most senior public servant you are invested with considerable power and authority. You have the power to protect public servants from political interference and to safeguard the integrity of that service. Unfortunately you have, whatever the motives, compromised yourself so badly that you may not be able to do any of these things unless you retrieve the situation. . . . Now, may I please telephone my paper?'

Stanhope nodded and Martha Lee telephoned the night-duty editor and dictated the main lead story while the night man listened and a stenographer took it down. She spoke smoothly, quickly, not fumbling for words and putting the story together with the professional skill of the old hand. She began with the inconclusive end to the meeting of Ministers, pointing out that the only absent Minister was Mr. Albert Josiah who had entrusted the decision-making to his colleagues while he went out to try and restore calm and confidence among the bereaved people. She gave it as her personal view, based on all she had seen, that Mr. Josiah and Mr. Stanhope, the Presidential Secretary, were both more concerned about the need to comfort and reassure the bereaved people than about the problems of state and power. And so, while Mr. Josiah was out among the people, Mr. Stanhope was keeping things under control at the Palace. Then she instructed that what followed was to be set in a box and dictated: 'I am with the Presidential Secretary at this moment and he is trying to reach Mr. Josiah to get at least one Ministerial authorization so that the Palace gates could be thrown open and the vast army of mourners now outside be let in to view the body of their fallen President. With this end in view soldiers have been called in to mount guard to keep the crowds in order when the great gates are thrown open.'

She looked at Stanhope and covered the mouthpiece: 'Let it go or cancel it? It's the only way out.'

'Let it go,' he said, a faint suggestion of bitterness in his voice.

She uncovered the mouthpiece. 'And Malcolm, get the switchboard to try and locate Josiah and get him to call Stanhope, heh?' Then she completed the dictating of her story.

As she finished Stanhope took the telephone out of her hand, began to dial, then changed his mind. He put it down and picked up the other, internal phone. 'Send Simpson here, please.'

The smooth young black diplomat appeared in a very short while.

Stanhope said: 'I've been trying to get hold of Mr. Josiah, Andy. I need his permission to open the gates and let the people view the Old Man's body. Didn't want to do it this way but must; so get on to the radio station and ask them to ask him to get in touch with the Palace.'

'So that's it,' the young man murmured. 'Right away, sir!'

They waited for about ten minutes with the radio turned on and then the call to the Minister came over the air. Seven minutes later the Minister himself phoned.

Stanhope picked up the phone and recognized the cold, flat, impersonal rasp of Josiah's voice.

'Mr. Secretary? Josiah here. What is this radio call about?'

Martha saw the tic-like jumping twitch at the side of Stanhope's left eye. God how he hates Josiah!

'Mr. Minister; I'm so glad to reach you at last!'

'You are?' The man at the other end was mocking him. 'Why?'

'It's about the crowds outside the Palace . . .'

'Yes?'

'We'll have to open the Palace gates and let them in . . .'

'Have to?'

'You know what I mean . . .'

'No, I don't, Mr. Secretary.'

Stanhope took a hold on himself and suppressed his detestation of the man. He spoke rapidly.

'Mr. Minister, I've been trying to reach you for the last hour or so. I needed some Ministerial authorization for my proposal that we throw open the Palace gates to the people outside. You know how the crowds are growing. If we don't do this there is no telling what might happen . . .'

'Are you afraid, Mr. Secretary?'

'No, sir. When I took my oath of office I promised at all times to protect and further the best interests of my country.'

'All right; but why can't you get your authorization from my colleagues who are now with you?'

'They have just left, and I have been trying to reach you for over an hour, sir.'

'What are you trying to say?'

'I'm a public servant.'

'Come on, speak, man!'

'It was apparent over an hour ago that nothing would be done, no decision taken. I knew decisions had to be taken that lay outside the range of my authority so I instructed one of my officers to try and locate you . . .'

'The name of that officer?'

'Andrew Simpson.'

'I see. Did you know young Simpson is one of my supporters?'

'No!' Stanhope was startled and off-guard.

'No, you didn't,' the voice at the other end rasped. 'And you still say you asked him to reach me?'

'I tell you I did!'

'All right, you're said to be an honest man. Now what's the point of all this? What do you want from me?'

John Stanhope hesitated for a long time, and Martha Lee felt the terrible unhappiness in the man.

'Well . . . ?'

'I think you should come to the Palace, sir. I think you should broadcast from here details of our period of national mourning. And I think you should announce that as soon as there is enough light the Palace gates will be opened to all mourners. If you authorize me to I can arrange things so that you can make your broadcast the moment you arrive here . . .'

'I see.' The cold voice sounded preoccupied. 'Are you offering me an alliance?'

'No, sir. I'm a public servant and it is my duty to do everything to further orderly and legal government for my country. I think of all the elected Ministers you are the most likely to bring about an orderly and peaceful transition from one leadership to another . . .'

'And this is the basis for this call to me?'

'Yes, sir.'

This time it was the man at the other end who was silent for a long time. Stanhope put his hand over the mouthpiece, looked up sombrely at Martha Lee and said: 'He is checking it over for flaws. And this is what I've tried to avoid all these hours! Oh God! To think of the island in his hands, and I must help put it there!'

'There is no other way,' Martha Lee snapped, suppressing the compassion she felt for this unhappy man.

At last Josiah spoke at the other end.

'And you, John Stanhope: you ask nothing of me? Not even the security of your job?'

'Nothing other than that you uphold the Constitution and the rule of law.'

'I understand soldiers have taken over at the Palace?'

'I called them in when I decided on the course of action which has led to this conversation.'

'On whose authority?'

'I gambled on yours.'

'For the sake of the country?'

'For the sake of the country.'

'What if I refused your plan? You'd be in real trouble.'

'I know.'

'But it was for the sake of the country?'

'As you say, sir.'

'All right, Stanhope! Make your arrangements. It'll take me about half an hour to get over to the Palace.'

'One last point, Mr. Minister. I have Miss Martha Lee of *The Voice of the Island* in the next room. May I tell her of this? And how much?'

'They don't like me. . . . But let that be. Give her as much as we are likely to give out on radio and television. Anyway, the Lee woman's about the most independent writer they have, not in the pockets of the margin-gatherers. Still, we shall see what we shall see.' He hung up abruptly.

Stanhope walked across the long L-shaped room like a man who had suddenly taken a very heavy burden on his back. At the little bar he poured himself a stiff whisky and dashed it with soda. He looked at Martha Lee over the rim of his glass and she knew he was saying a silent prayer.

'When is he coming?' she asked.

'He's on his way.'

'Then I'd better go. And I'd better stay away for a while. He's no fool, John, so watch yourself. And, John . . . It's just possible that he cares as much about the country as you do . . .'

John Stanhope looked steadily at Martha Lee but said nothing. Martha Lee went out, down his private stairs, past the Presidential Secretary's office, down the broad stairway where the soldiers stood on guard, and out of the front door. Waiting Press colleagues pounced on her, and she passed on the news that Josiah was on his way.

Upstairs, John Stanhope was on the phone setting in motion the new chain of events. Young Simpson stood at his elbow.

Martha Lee hovered on the outskirts of the vast crowds until Josiah appeared. Recognition came quickly because he was in a small open convertible. She thought he looked very small and very incongruous standing up in that flashy little sports car. But the milling mass saw nothing odd about him. Those who saw him first shouted his name, informing each other that he had come. Others took it up, making it louder and louder, giving it shape and order and rhythm. Soon over a hundred thousand voices were chanting it in unison: Jo-si-ah! . . . Jo-si-ah! . . . Jo-si-ah! steady and insistent as drumbeats.

And then the little car stopped and the neat slender little dark-brown man, looking black in the bright lights from the Palace gates, got out. He raised both arms high above his head, palms forward as one halting a flood. The people immediately in front of him parted, making a narrow human lane for him to pass through. Raising his head, and squaring his shoulders, he walked down the lane towards the Palace gates. As he went forward the lane closed behind him, and soon Martha could see no sign of the presence of Josiah. But the sound of him was all about, rumbling after him, as thunder follows the flash of lightning.

So it is done, Martha Lee told herself. And if you ask these people tomorrow or the next day or next week or next month or next year just how Josiah came to inherit the Old Man's mantle, and who gave it to him, they will not be able to tell you. If you ask them what made them roar out his name, they will look at you blankly and shake their heads. And yet they know what they are doing. And that is the pity of it, that they know what they are doing even though they will plead ignorance now and tomorrow and next year.

Abruptly, she turned her back on the roaring crowds and walked away fast, as one flees from some frightening scene. When the crowds and their noises were far behind, when she entered a quiet and not very well lit narrow street, she transferred a small gun from the bag slung across her shoulder to the right-hand pocket of her jacket. She kept her fingers curled about the gun as she walked briskly through one narrow street after another.

There were lights in all the houses she passed. It seemed that all the world had stayed awake through the long hours of this night, that no one had gone to sleep, that everyone was waiting anxiously, with fear and uncertainty for companion. At last she turned into the main road which was the shopping centre of this upper suburban section of Mosesville. Here everything was brightly lit. Dress shops, jewellry shops, showrooms with the latest car models from all the world, shops filled with imported furniture, imported foodstuffs, all consumed vast quantities of high-priced electric current to show off their wares to best advantage.

She crossed the broad, tree-lined highway to the gas-station where she had left her car. Because there had recently been a number of well-planned robberies at filling-stations the two night attendants had locked themselves in. It took her nearly five minutes to wake them. She phoned the paper and Malcolm, the night man, told her the editor had left word that she should contact him at the Press Union Centre.

When she left the gas-station the first dawn streaks were coming up in the east. And because for her this was al-ways the loneliest period to be awake in any twenty-four-hour cycle, she gave in, briefly, to a mood of depression and wished desperately that Joel Sterning were with her now.

Maxwell Johnson was a big man, well over six feet tall and massively large without being fat; it was a question of bones and his were big and heavy. He could cover a sheet of paper, eight and a half by eleven, by simply putting his open hand over it. As editor of *The Voice of the Island* he frequently had to spread his enormous hand over a sheet of copy to ensure that his managing director did not know its contents and so could not interfere.

He had come to the island as a hulking young man in his early twenties, more than thirty years ago. He had found a job as a very junior sub-editor on *The Voice of the Island*, aware always of the resentment of his black and brown colleagues who knew that the owners of the paper would give him preferment over them. This had forced him to walk with delicate care in the presence of his fellow workers and to keep the representatives of the owners at a distance. In time his fellow workers had come to accept him as a man unwilling to trade on his own whiteness or their blackness or the colour bias of the country and of the representatives of the owners. Then there had been that wonderful day when all the invisible barriers had come tumbling down. The working Press, men and women, had organized a country feed for him at a little seaside village fifty-odd miles from the capital, and there, while they ate and drank prodigiously, and while talk flowed with a freedom and intimacy peculiar to the island, he had surrendered his heart and mind and he had become as committed to the island as the most patriotic of its native sons and daughters. There too, on that same night, on that sandy beach, he had become aware of Myra, a towering amazon all of six feet and strappingly feminine withal. All the racial strains found on the island seemed to have met and mingled in Myra, and the result was not African, not European, not Asian; and though all these had gone into the making of her, the Myra that emerged was a woman totally freed of all race or colour identification. And when they had lain together on a quiet corner of the beach, and the only sound was the soft and lazy lap-lapping of the sea, it was as though he had lain with a woman a thousand years hence in time, as though in making love to this woman he had been translated out of the twentieth century with its race and colour obsessions to a century and a humanity freed of this particular madness. And then he had marvelled at the physical strength of this woman and at the sweeping intensity of her passion. In the past, with other women, he had had to be careful in case he hurt them: with this one he had met his match.

Six months later he and Myra had married and for five years they, and their friends, had been dazzled by the intensity of the passion that bound their minds and bodies. It was a spur and under it he founded and became the first president of the Press Union and was the moving spirit in raising the money that went into the building of the Press Union Centre. He masterminded a strike that ended the era of low wages and for the first time in the island's history members of the working Press earned enough to feed and clothe and house their families properly. By then the representatives of the owners in particular, and the business community in general, had decided that the presence of Maxwell Johnson on the island was not in the national interest. The paper had suspended him and there had been a great agitation for him to be deported. But in one of his unpredictable interventions President Moses Joshua had invited a deputation from the working Press to come and talk to him, and after he had heard the deputation he had gone on radio and television and delivered an emotional, semi-coherent broadcast threatening to personally lead a street battle in support of the working Press if its just demands for a living wage and better working conditions were not met; and he and his entire government would resign rather than be a party to expelling someone from the island who stood up for the rights of workers.

The day after the President's broadcast the employers recognized the Press Union as the bargaining agent for the working Press and after one brief meeting they agreed to all the Union's demands; and Max Johnson was reinstated by the owners of the *Voice*.

After that the members of the working Press saw President Joshua as the great champion of Press freedom and when he invited the Press Union to become affiliated to his party the majority overruled Max Johnson's half-hearted opposition and did so. Thus when, a year later, the President ordered the expulsion of the resident correspondent of an international news agency, the Press Union protested, but very mildly and with a hint of apology for doing so.

It was while Max Johnson was worrying and arguing about this matter with the Union's executive committee that he received the call from the hospital, and the cool clinical voice at the other end ordered him to come at once. When he arrived Myra had just died in childbirth. The child died fifteen hours later.

Nothing had really mattered very much since.

When Martha Lee arrived at the Centre Max Johnson had already worked his way through half a bottle of rum. The only effect was to slow him up a little, to make him more deliberate in word and movement, and also to make him a little less withdrawn than normally.

She walked through the large members' lounge and the smell of stale tobacco and unwashed liquor glasses was oppressive. She opened two windows to let in the clean early morning air.

'That you, Martha?' Max boomed from the office behind the bar.

'Yes! Coming!'

'Well hurry up! And bring a cup!'

She sensed misery behind the brusque words, so she went quickly into the little office. There was a pot of coffee beside the rum on the little table under the window; he used the coffee as chaser. The office smelled fresh because he had opened all its windows, and he was standing at the window that faced in the direction of the Palace, staring out as though to see what went on where the great crowds were. He did not turn as she entered. She went to the little table, poured coffee into her cup and added a generous dash of rum.

'Hello, black girl.'

'Hello, Max.'

'Stanhope find Josiah?'

'Yes.'

'So everything was as simple as that. Withdraw and wait for the call.'

'You said it would be like that, Max.'

'Not that Stanhope would deliver power into his hands.'

'What difference does it make?'

'That's what you people don't understand!' He was impatient now. 'He was willing to wait for a call. I think he was prepared to accept a clearly defined mandate with that call. You people are so full of fear and hatred of Josiah that you don't even try to understand him. And so you've given him a blank cheque. I warn you, black girl, he's going to use it!'

He refilled his glass and poured some more coffee.

'Nothing could have held him back,' Martha said.

'He would have listened to the will of the people, if such existed. But we've made a mockery of it. Only the Old Man understood Josiah, and so only the Old Man could use him. Why d'you think the Old Man kept him on? He was the only one who tried to buck the Old Man's orders . . .'

'Even he needed at least one *man* against whom to test his old cunning,' Martha cut in.

'Yes; and there was also the Old Man's compulsive need to destroy any spirit of independence in those immediately around him. How he enjoyed that! But that is only part of it. The Old Man recognized something in Josiah that he himself lacked; Josiah believes, has faith, in the people of the island. The Old Man envied Josiah this; he wanted to have the same kind of faith: but you cannot have faith in puppets and he manipulated his puppets for so long that no matter how much he wished and tried to, he could not regard them as adult and mature and responsible human beings. He knew them for what they were. He also knew that they could have been more than just puppets. And he stopped short at this point of knowledge. To go on would have meant acknowledging his own responsibility for their being turned into puppets.'

'Even if you are right, Max, who could have given him a mandate?'

Max tossed down the remains of his drink and poured yet another.

'His fellow members of the Cabinet could have: that's one; the parliament could have: that's two; a powerful lobby such as those merchant princes and other friends of yours whom he calls margin-gatherers could have: that's three; and the people could have: that's four. I think he would have accepted it even from the margin-gatherers, if their price was not too high. But they, and the Cabinet, and the coloured middle-class, which is where John Stanhope stands, were rendered unable to think by panic. Was it the calling in of the military that undid John?'

'Yes.'

'We ride with the tide now, black girl. That is a directive. I'm meeting the directors later and I'm going to lay it on the line. I know they'll by-pass me with some of their hacks but you and I will see that the paper does its duty. It is just possible that he might breathe life into the puppets.'

'You really think so?' She sounded eager.

'I promise nothing!' he snapped. 'I'm no bloody prophet! Why the hell do you people always look to others for comfort and assurance! Look inward, man!'

'It's you who needed to look inward, Max,' she said quietly.

He turned to her then, a crooked smile on his face. He raised his glass.

'The king is dead; long live the king; and God help the island.'

'And you don't give a damn, do you!' She was angry now.

'My name is not Joel Sterning,' he snapped.

'That is cheap,' she said, 'cheaper than I thought you capable of being.'

'Yes . . .' He did not care.

'Yes.' There was a racial tinge to her anger. 'So cheap Myra would have been ashamed.'

She had reached him and the measure of his rage frightened her. His sallow puffy face turned blotchy red. His mouth became a twisted snarl. His two neck muscles stood out like rope pulled taut. His eyes threatened to burst out of their sockets. A violent spasm shook his massive body.

. . . He's going to hit me . . .

He did not; instead, with herculean effort he brought body and mind under control; he reached for the bottle of rum, half filled his tumbler, and turned his back on her and stared out of the window, as he had done when she had first entered the office.

After a long while she said: 'I'm sorry, Max.' She reached up and lightly touched one of the broad shoulders.

'Go to hell,' he said, but softly now, almost gently.

She left him and walked out through the members' lounge, now cleared of its depressing stale smell, down the dark stairs, and out into the deserted street and the fresh morning air. The street was empty except for a policeman on duty turning the corner by the supermarket. The policeman saw her and walked briskly towards her, curious and suspicious as his duty required him to be. She got into her car and waited for him.

'Morning, Miss. May I ask what you're doing out so early?'

The Commissioner's latest courtesy campaign had borne fruit here. She decided to meet courtesy with courtesy.

'Morning, constable. I've been having a drink with my boss. He's in there.' She indicated the entrance to the Centre with her head while she brought her Press card out of her bag.

'Mr. Johnson in there now?' The policeman sounded doubtful.

'You can go up and check, but I warn you he's in a foul temper.'

A drink with her boss at nearly five in the morning was a little far-fetched but he knew Mr. Maxwell Johnson's car and the woman's was parked immediately in front of it. More likely she's been giving him a piece of tail! No law against that if they do it in private. Wouldn't mind a piece of it himself!

The woman read his thoughts and snapped: 'If I did it

would be none of your business but I didn't sleep with Mr. Johnson so wash the filth out of your mind!'

He looked at the Press card and recognized the woman's name. This one could make a world of trouble for him.

'I had no such thoughts, Miss Lee.'

'Fine, constable. May I go now?'

He returned the Press card, stepped back and touched his hat.

We all do it, she thought bitterly as she drove off. We all pull class and position on them. We all undermine the concept of the law as above class and position; then we blame the police for going along and protecting themselves, and we blame the mass of the people, the so-called 'little people', for recognizing that the law and its servants operate a double standard, one for us and one for them. And we blame and condemn them for having no faith in the rule of law and for seeing the police as their enemies. If I had in fact been an anonymous working girl, caught after having a fling with the boss, especially one without a car, I would have had to appease him in the way he wanted or else risk being arrested.

In the half-hour's drive between the Press Centre and her home Martha Lee watched and heard her world come awake. First, the massed clouds, black and churning with turbulent fury in the west, were assaulted by the light rays from the east and fled farther westward; and fleeing they changed their massed nature and colour, became gentle snowy mountains in the sky, changed again and were just white clouds set in a rapidly clearing blue sky. The rays of the still hidden sun brought colour into the sky and into the earth. Trees, hedges, bushes, ceased to be darker shadows of the dark, and nature's green, the green of tree and grass, emerged once more as the dominant colour in the land. The shapes of the mountains cleared, and there were mists in their hollows and clouds on their highest peaks. And people came out from the mansions and homes and hovels where they had taken shelter during the night. They walked now, in ones and twos and threes, to their places of work; subdued, not saying much, most of them bone weary because the shadow of the death of their

President had made sleep impossible during the night just gone.

Instead of going to work, many dressed in mourning and made for the Presidential Palace to swell the vast throng of people who had already begun the slow procession to look their last on the dead President. Among them the ladies of the voluntary services had set up emergency soup kitchens, as they did in times of trouble, such as when a hurricane strikes.

It was just before six when Martha Lee entered her small house which was tucked far back from the road on a piece of rising land. She checked through the pile of message slips beside the telephone; there was no word from Joel. She went into her bedroom, stripped, then took a hot shower and crawled naked into bed. She looked at the clock. It was exactly eleven minutes past six and the sun was just rising.

Clara Sterning looked and felt refreshed; the fears and uncertainties of the night before were still there, but muted, subdued by the new sense of invigoration that flowed through her body. Odd that she should have forgotten this aspect of love-making with Joel, this wonderful afterglow that had always coursed through her for several hours of the following day; there had been one glorious spell when it had persisted for a whole series of days and nights, and both she and Joel had been in a heady daze with it. But that was long ago, so long ago that she had, until now, forgotten all about that afterglow . . . And even this will die because at the moment of climax last night she had been aware of a spiritual withholding on his part. He could not withhold any part of the physical side. Once started they went all the way together; but he had not given in, nothing had changed, and for Joel sex always had to be a renewal of commitment or else it turned sordid: he was one of those men who made sex spiritual.

Her son, young Emanuel, said 'The cream please!' a little impatiently.

'Don't give it to him, Mama! Are you too lazy to

stretch?' This was seventeen-year-old Jean Sterning, very grown-up and very considerate. She had been made head girl of her school a few weeks earlier, at the beginning of the Christmas term, and power and responsibility were still an exciting game.

'Shut up you!' The boy's breaking voice rose to a high, girlish pitch. He checked himself and repeated 'Shut up you!' in a rumbling masculine undertone.

'That's enough,' Clara said.

'Pompous cow!' the boy rumbled.

'Manny!' Clara warned.

The girl made it plain she was treating the boy's childishness with the contempt it deserved.

The morning sun streamed in through the open windows giving the breakfast-room a bright and cheerful cosiness. 'Winter' was coming and temperatures up in the hills might drop to between sixty-five and seventy degrees. This did not often happen but when it did the islanders talked about a 'severe winter'. Now the temperature was just above seventy and it was only the profusion of glass letting in sunlight that made this particular room as warm as it was.

The radio had said all schools and government offices would be closed today. The merchants had followed the lead. Instead of their usual commercials there were a string of: the House of So-and-So, agents and distributors of ———— as a mark of respect and mourning for our lost leader announced that it would remain closed so that all its employees would also be able to pay their personal respects to our fallen leader.

The children finished breakfast and first the girl then the boy wandered away. Alone, Clara went back to thinking about Joel. She knew herself, knew that having her own way had become second nature; controlling this, subordinating her will to his, would be the hardest thing in the world. And even if she did it, it might not be worth the effort; he might still want no part of her; but she had to make the effort. It was the only thing that might bring him back . . . Oh God! I don't think I can do it. I've had others doing the adjusting for so long. But I must. I must. I must.

Why? How the devil do you know why you want only that man? Why only he makes you feel as you are now feeling? Oh God, why? . . . There were the children and before them what led up to their coming. This had made him that special man in the beginning. Now there was something else as well, there was the fear of time, of growing old alone.

Joel entered the breakfast-room a little after half past eight. He was dressed for going to the office; jacket, tie, everything; all of which, Clara knew, was to make her know that what had happened in the night had changed nothing. In their younger days, before the children were born, he had told her of his first experience and because the woman had been older, very experienced, and casual, the aftermath for him had been a lingering sense of shame at the sordidness of sex. It had taken him a long time to recover from this, and even longer to discover that it could be beautiful. Perhaps he had looked as tightly wound up on that morning after as he did now. No, nothing is ever like the first time; nothing.

'Good morning, Joel!' The radiance that glowed within her came through. 'I hope you slept as well as I did. And—thank you; thank you very much for last night.'

Joel said 'Good morning,' trying to make it social and impersonal, but failing. The way she looked at him, the way she thanked him made it impossible. But why only in this? Why cannot the harmony they achieve so easily with their bodies become part of their words and thoughts and dreams? Or is it that this is all that really matters to her? But even as he thought it he knew he was being unjust. There was more to her than just sex.

She thought: He's thinking of me in terms that are tender now.

'Joel——' I love you; I really do; how can I make you understand that without any doubt and without any confusion: the only way I know is through my body; that way everything is clear and there is no confusion; please try to understand that.

She's doing it again, he told himself; and it disturbed him because in spite of himself he could feel a physical warmth beginning inside him, and he knew it was an involuntary response to the force she radiated.

He said 'Yes?' and used his mind to put a rein on his feeling.

I must not force things, she told herself.

'Nothing,' she said quickly. 'It's just that feeling got the better of me. You may have forgotten that it has always been like this for me—afterwards. Will you have your coffee now? And what would you like to eat? . . .'

And he told her and she fed him. And all the while he was aware of her sitting across the table, keeping some sort of check on the physical thing that she seemed to radiate whether she wanted to or not. Odd that he should have forgotten this part of it.

Solly arrived a little after nine. He was flushed and excited and more restless than usual. He had several copies of *The Voice of the Island*. He spread a copy in front of Joel.

'Your precious John Stanhope has sold out to Josiah! It's all there! Have you listened to the radio? They haven't the same detail that *The Voice* has, but it's all there! Not even a stand by anybody! And our principal civil servant, the man you said represented integrity in public life, he is the one to hand the country over to Josiah on a platter! And thanks to your faith in him he knows more about our operations and our real attitude than anybody else! If he were to tell Josiah how we felt about him. Christ, Joel! How wrong you've been!'

'Please shut up, Solly!' Clara snapped.

He stopped talking and prowled about the room while Clara and Joel read Martha Lee's report of political developments following the death of the President.

At last Joel finished his reading and looked up at Solly.

'I don't think you're right about John. I don't think he's sold out.'

'You don't! In the light of what's there!'

'There's some reason for John doing this.'

'Sure there's a reason: survival, maintaining his position and advancing himself by jumping on the bandwagon!'

'Of course!' Joel said with sudden anger. 'Everybody's

for sale! That is the gospel according to the tribe of Isaacs! You make me sick! Now shut up and don't do anything until I find out why John did what he did.' He got up and went to the door, growing more angry with each stride. He paused at the door. '. . . And let me tell you something, Solly, the sooner you and all the rest of your family stop holding everybody else cheap and buyable, the greater your chances of survival! The old days are dead!' He jerked the door open, and now he was shaking with anger. 'They died with that old man! And so did the ugly power you held in this land!' Then he went out and slammed the door shut.

Clara called: 'Joel!' Then she shook her head and moaned: 'Oh my God . . .'

Solly poured himself a cup of coffee.

'No need for him to flare up like that,' he protested.

'He was right,' Clara said bitterly. 'We do think everybody's for sale, and it has made us ugly.'

'What will he do now?' Solly asked.

'What he said. He will find out why John did what he did. And it will not be because John is for sale. And this will be another wall between him and me.'

She got up and went to her brother's side. She looked searchingly into his face. 'Why is it that here on the island wealth turns people rotten? It doesn't everywhere else, you know.' Then she left him.

CHAPTER THREE

JOEL STERNING rang Martha Lee in the early afternoon. He had spent the morning at his office, trying to get hold of John Stanhope and working out possible new lines of thought and approach for the Isaacs empire in the new situation: he had failed to make contact with Stanhope, and his thinking had been unproductive. He had lunched alone at the club nearest his office, the Mosesville Athletic Club. Because all the public places were shut he had expected the club's dining-room to be jammed. Instead he had been the only person taking lunch, and it was only towards the end of his meal that Maxwell Johnson had swept in. And because they were the only two in the room Johnson had joined him and ordered a beef sandwich and a double shot of rum.

'Seen Martha?' Johnson had asked brusquely.

'No.' Joel knew Johnson disapproved of him, had done so ever since the start of the affair with Martha.

'Since the death, I mean.'

'I knew you meant that, and I haven't seen her.'

'I'm surprised!'

'Just what does that mean, Max?'

'You know bloody well what it means!'

I'm not going to be provoked, Joel had told himself. He had pushed a silver coin under the edge of his plate, risen and nodded stiffly and formally to Max Johnson. The waiter had hurried forward with his bill and Joel had signed it standing. The waiter had bowed ingratiatingly and shuffled away. Joel had moved to the door.

'Don't you need her inside information even more than you normally do? It isn't just a sleep that you get from her, is it? She's a cold fish and you've got a piece of hot stuff right at home!'

Before he had realized what he was doing, Joel had swung on Max and struck him a stinging blow to the side of the face. Max had risen from his chair and Joel had braced himself for uneven combat and a beating, knowing that the type of beating he would take would depend on how soon anybody intervened. Then Max had relaxed, slipped back into his seat, and rumbled: 'Get the hell out of here before I kill you.'

And Joel had left, shaking. It had taken him an hour to calm down. Now, holding the telephone, waiting for Martha to answer, he was calm; bleakly, depressingly calm.

The phone rang for a long time, and he wondered whether she too would, like John Stanhope, prove impossible to get today. Then someone answered, a stranger; and behind that voice were other voices and the tinkling of glass. Martha's house was full of people, Press people most likely. This sometimes happened on special occasions: on election day and other days when public drinking is forbidden, or when there is some urgent matter that needs to be argued out freely and in private. At such times Martha's house became the gathering place.

The voice at the other end, a woman's and vaguely familiar, slightly slurred, demanded to know what he wanted.

'Miss Lee, please. Miss Martha Lee.'

The voice yelled 'Mar-tha!' with a shrillness that hurt his eardrums. There were noises as the woman put down the phone and then, for a very long time, there were only the voices in the background, picked up by an open telephone receiver that everybody seemed to have forgotten.

That woman's forgotten me; and if I hang up now no one might notice that the receiver is off and I may not be able to reach Martha for the rest of the day. Only way then would be to go round to her place.

'Yes? Martha Lee here.' She had to repeat it before he realized she was at the other end. The background noises had grown unusually loud.

'Joel' he said, raising his voice.

'Please hold on,' she said.

Then, as the sound of a radio is switched off, the background noises were instantly gone. He knew she had unplugged the phone and would now be carrying it to the privacy and silence of her bedroom. He waited, not concerned now about time passing. There was a faint sliding noise then her voice was with him, cool and clear and in a very quiet room.

'Hello, Joel.'

'How are you?'

'A little drained. You?'

'So-so. I had a run-in with your boss.'

'So I heard.'

'How?' He was startled.

'He phoned and told me. Said he provoked you and you punched him in the face, right there in the dining-room of your club.'

'Don't suppose he told you we were the only two there?'

'No . . . But he swore he didn't lay hands on you.'

'He didn't. That's partly why I'm calling you now.'

'He said he expected you would, Joel; and he asked me to give you a message. He said to tell you he could have been wrong, and his not hitting you was because of that, not because he was afraid of anything the Isaacs clan could do. Is this important to you?'

'Very.'

'He said it might be and I'm glad it is.'

'He accused me of using you; implied I didn't really care.'

'Do you have to go over it with me?'

'No; but it set up self-doubt. I *have* received special information from you; my association with you *is* an advantage to the firm.'

'I missed you last night.' She said it as though she had not heard what he had just said.

'I would like to come over,' he said.

'You've heard the racket here,' she said. 'We won't be able to talk.'

'I need you,' he said reluctantly, trying to make it casual and unimportant.

'Have you time to take me to the village? I'd like to see my child.'

'When?'

'As soon as you can. I want to be back early so the sooner the better. I can go by myself—but——'

'I'll drive you,' he said. 'But I must get hold of John first to find out something. I've tried all morning without success.'

'If it's what I think it is,' she said quietly, 'then I can tell you; but I know you'd much rather not get it from me.'

'Not after what Max said.'

'He knows he was wrong. John Stanhope had no choice but to take this line of action. I was with him and I literally forced it on him because . . .' And she explained crisply and clearly why Stanhope had to call in Josiah.

When she finished he said: 'Thank you. Give me half an hour.' He waited for her to say something but she was silent for so long that he said: 'Martha! Are you there?'

'Yes, Joel. What is it?'

'What do you mean?'

'Why are you beside yourself with rage? What is it?'

It is as simple as that, he thought; you reach out and feel the things I do not say. Aloud, he asked: 'Wouldn't time dull even this, Martha?'

'It wouldn't have with Max and Myra.' He felt her remoteness now.

'And for us?'

'You know it would.'

The cool clinical analyst, he thought; and there was a tinge of wry admiration to the thought. She faces up to things as no one else I know.

He hasn't answered me, Martha thought at the other end of the line. Perhaps he doesn't want to: he has a tendency to mentally veer away from the painful or the unpleasant, and so he is always reaching after an impossible standard of beauty and purity and happiness. And although you know it is a form of self-deception, it is also a form of beauty, which is what makes you warm towards this man.

'You haven't answered me,' she said.

'Solly thought John had sold out to Josiah.'

'Of course,' she said, making him feel guilty for the Isaacs clan.

'In half an hour then,' he said, withdrawn and remote.

'Make it an hour,' she said.

'An hour then,' he said and waited for her to hang up.

The sun was behind them as the car began the climb into the hills; there was a certain wateriness to it that presaged the coming of chillier times. The promise was that Christmas this year would be unusually cold for the island. To the right of them, and farther up, the slopes of the higher mountains had a purplish sheen that made you think of tenderness. And, of course, as a backdrop to all this there was the sea, placid as always, beautiful and clear with its constantly changing colours—the deepest blue to green to a breath-taking aquamarine to a subtle combination of the entire spectrum as a rainbow shaft rises vertically and unexpectedly because there is no reason for it— and with a hint of latent menace, of tempestuous violence and massive turbulence held in check.

They had been silent for the best part of an hour, almost from the moment they had started the climb into the hills. Martha sat huddled up in the corner absorbing the sights and smells about her. From time to time Joel took his eyes off the twisting, winding road and looked quickly at her face. She was oblivious of his presence; for her, now, the only reality was the fact of the physical earth about her and her communion with it.

Once, in the early days, he had tried to share this with her, to become a part of this strong bond between the woman and the land. He had sensed a connection as real, as physical, as that between a mother and her new-born child before the umbilical cord is cut; he had reached out and touched her, hoping to share and understand, hoping she would let him in. She had turned unseeing eyes on him and shaken him off as one might wipe away a strand of hair from the eyes. After that he had never tried to follow her into this private world of her relationship with the land. It had hurt in the beginning; it hurt less now because he knew what a source of strength this communion was to her. This and the child were the two most private things in her life, the only things she refused to talk about or to share with anybody.

Joel thought: Perhaps, one day . . . But he knew the futility of the thought even as it passed through his mind.

At last the climb of the road grew less steep, levelled off to a stretch of flat land. To the left, now, they could see the town sprawling out on the plain, a thousand feet and more below. Overhead, five of the huge carrion birds of the island circled with grace and power. Their presence suggested the carcass of some dead creature nearby. Then the climb began again, more steeply.

Joel slowed down and brought the car to a halt as near the edge of the narrow road as possible; but still anything passing would have difficulty. The land below the road fell away steeply, a sheer drop of three hundred feet; the land above rose equally steeply.

Martha got out and walked away along the edge of the road, always within inches of the drop. Joel lit a cigarette and became aware of the silence. When he had finished the cigarette Martha was out of sight around the curve of the road. He started the car and drove slowly after her. He picked her up quarter of a mile farther on. She had walked very fast and was slightly winded. After that he drove as fast as the road allowed, slowing only when he had to pass through the three villages that were on the way to where they were going. And so, still without speech, they came at last to a broad, gently rolling hill. A cluster of low houses, classrooms, workshops, dormitories, all washed with white lime, nestled on the brow of the hill. They drove through a gate above which was a wooden sign that said: Welcome To Sweetwater Children's Village. The sun now sat, far to the west, just above the rim of the rolling hills.

An elderly woman—one for whom the physical things had been rendered unimportant by time—waited for them at the door of the small administrative building. She was tall and bony, with a wiry strength that came from the earth; and dressed in tough peasant's shirt and trousers she could easily be mistaken for a man: her arms, shoulders, neck, stance, the parched and weathered skin, had all been hardened and disciplined and trimmed down to serve a will for which time had reduced life to one simple and clearcut reality. Sweetwater Children's Village was all this woman's life.

If you were perceptive and you looked closely the bone structure of this woman might lead you to think that once there was great beauty here. And if you knew her name and her family history you would know that once, in the dark and distant days when man owned man, her family, her ancestors, owned a massive piece of the island and vast numbers of its dark inhabitants; and knowing that you would also know that this woman was the last of her line on the island, and that just as she had trimmed down mind and body to serve a single idea, so she had, with the same deliberation, shed all wealth and property. The land on which the Children's Village stood was the last of that property, and she had long ago vested even this in a trust to perpetuate the village.

She stepped forward as Martha Lee got out of the car. They shook hands. Joel came around the front of the car and greeted the woman. They had met many times in the past at this same spot, so they knew each other. And since the woman was not interested in what went on down in Mosesville, there was little to say.

'She's on her way,' the woman said. 'I expect you'll want to go and meet her.'

Martha nodded and abruptly walked away from them, swinging round the corner of the building and going along a footpath that climbed, slantingly, to the children's dormitories a half-mile away.

To Joel, the woman said: 'Miss Lee is disturbed today. But of course her business . . .'

'Yes.' Joel said and thought that perhaps the day will come when this woman would not even bother to use words. He had noticed that she rarely used all the words needed to complete any thought. She gave you a clue and you joined her in completing the thought in silence.

'Would you like to . . .'

Joel nodded and followed her into the cool office. She went to her desk and he went to the window that gave a view of the direction Martha had taken.

. . . Here the death of the Old Man wasn't earth-shattering. And from here on farther into the heart of the island it would be the same. Perhaps not quite as inconsequential as to this woman in this room, but certainly not an event charged with the personal intensity that it had for the people of the city and those who lived in the foothills immediately about the city. Big news of course because the President *is* the President. But for all too many of the people of the island's hinterland what went on in Moses-ville was foreign news. What happened there, who was born and who died, who was in power and who had lost, did not materially affect their lives because the fruit of the progress the city folk talked about all the time had passed them by. Independence had not brought running water or electric light or more food or more and better homes or schools; it had been around for a long time and it had changed nothing and so it was as it was before it had come: just one more word used by politicians who only visited the remote village in the hills when they wanted votes . . .

'I see you, too, are disturbed . . .'

'Yes,' Joel said.

He could see Martha now; she was near the cluster of trees where the slope of the land ceased about two-thirds of the way to the children's dormitories.

Martha Lee came to a halt as she saw the two children. They came slowly from behind the nearest of the dormi-tories, a boy and girl. The boy tossed his limbs this way and that, twisted his body with each step, as you would expect to see a puppet move under the control of a drunken puppet-master, or one who is amused by distortion. His arms and legs and all his body were terribly thin; his head enormous.

Martha braced herself for the encounter . . . What manner of God is this who makes man in his own image? A joker? . . . Then she rid her mind of all thought and went slowly forward.

The little girl, *her* little girl, was as perfect in shape and form as it is possible to be: a sturdily upright young body, nicely filled out, straight-backed, square-shouldered, and a pretty little black doll face come alive, and gentle eys that caressed; a perfect little ten-year-old girl, led by the hand by a distorted little brown boy of the same age.

The two children stopped a few paces from Martha and waited for her to come closer. She noticed how firmly her little girl held the hand of the little boy. She noticed how lovingly the little girl looked into the distorted face of the boy. She knew they were saying things to each other without words; but you have to have words, or, at least, the memory of words, something you once knew and used, to be able to communicate. And this child of hers had been born without words and without sound, and all she knew she knew through her eyes only.

The little boy turned his head from the little girl and looked at Martha. He used his mind and all his will to instruct his lips to assume shape, and then he slurred out three words as a single, connected, animal growl: 'Heresheis'. Then he raised the little girl's hand and placed it firmly into Martha's; and then he turned and left them, tossing his limbs as he went.

Martha waited until the little boy had disappeared, tossing and twisting, behind the nearest of the dormitory buildings, then she turned and led the girl towards the cluster of cedar trees. The trees were fully grown and it was time for them to be cut down, sliced into board, and stored away till they were properly dried and cured before being sold to the lumber yards. At current prices the trees would earn enough to pay for at least a year's food and drink and clothing for the one hundred and fifty-odd

maimed and twisted, deaf and dumb, helpless and broken
children of this special village.

Inside the cool office the woman looked up from her
paperwork and stared with curious detachment at Joel
Sterning's back.

'Are they together now?'

'Yes,' Joel said without turning his head. 'They've just
gone among the trees and I've lost sight of them.'

'The boy?'

'He went back a while ago.'

The woman looked at the small clock on her desk and
noted down the exact time on a tiny desk pad; then she
returned to her paperwork. Sterning had once tried to find
out what had driven this last surviving daughter of what
had once been the island's most powerful and aristocratic
family to divest herself of her wealth and then found this
home for the most helpless of all the island's children.

She had laughed at him, the only time he had heard her
laugh. And she had said more than she had said either
before or since that time, and he had known her for all of
five years now, almost from the first day that he had
started the affair with Martha. The woman had said then:
'For none of the reasons you might imagine, Mr. Sterning.
I have no sense of guilt about the history of my family; I
do not feel I owe anybody anything; it has nothing to do
with my maternal instincts; I'm not sublimating anything; I
don't believe in a life after this world and so I'm not
working my passage anywhere. I do this quite simply because there is a need for it. Once one of my ancestors—
one of the slave-owning ones—was convinced that the
only way to stamp out an ugly and destructive atmosphere
of festering discontent was by breaking a father and son,
who were the ringleaders, on the rack. He did it and the
atmosphere changed overnight. The father had been his
playmate and the son as dear to him as his own son.
Because of this special relationship both had been taught
to read and write and both had access to the current
emancipationist literature. If you visit the archives down
in Mosesville you will find an account of this in my ancestor's own handwriting and you will read of the heartache it

gave him. But it needed to be done and he did it. In the same way there is a need for Sweetwater Children's Village.'

He turned now and looked at the woman: she was completely immersed in the paperwork that needed to be done. He thought: Whatever else they did, these people assumed responsibility for their actions. They paid the price of power. We, today's so-called merchant princes, want the power without paying for it. The question is: Will history allow it?

Martha and the child walked deeper in among the trees till they came to a log that had become smooth from constant use. The log was set against the base of one of the tallest cedars and the ground about it was bare of all other vegetation, so the long line of marching red ants, each large enough to give the impression of a distinct personality, stood out sharp. Martha and the child stepped carefully over the line of marching ants and sat on the log, still holding hands.

. . . When had it begun, this anchorage in holding hands? As far as she could remember it began when the child was three, on that terrible day when the maid didn't do anything in the house because the child clung to her and the maid had realized that she had suddenly become very powerful and had made demands . . . Now, holding a human hand was security . . .

Martha raised her free hand and touched the child's hair, feeling its wiry kinkiness. This child's father had been all black all the way and in her his blackness had completely swamped the Chinese streak Martha had brought to the creation of the little girl. He had had his fun and he had gone on, explaining to Martha, half defiantly, half appealingly, that he had to be free; telling her, and because of his fantastic charm convincing her for the moment, that all the repressed cravings after freedom of all the unfree Negroes had reached a point of culmination in his strikingly handsome black person. So he had to take what he wanted and go on. And Martha knew that somewhere in the world at this moment, in Europe or the Americas, he was taking what he wanted, and he would, after the taking, drift on to other takings. He was the kind who would get everything except the very last bit. Right at the end of the line he would be alone, probably sick and starving and with nowhere to shelter, deserted by his charm, and no woman to hold his hand. There would be a desperate loneliness to his dying. And it would be a long way from home.

The child looked up from the ants. Martha smiled and said out aloud: 'I was thinking of your father.'

It seemed to her that the child understood and, without words, asked: Where is he?

'I don't know where he is,' Martha murmured, running her hand over the child's hair, feeling its texture with her long fingers. 'But I know he's all right. He will always be all right until the very end. And then, right at the very end, in the moment of total defeat, his black pride will see him through. His only real fault, my dear, is that he turned his back on the island; he refused to have faith in its people and that makes him a party to all that has gone wrong here. That is the only thing I will not forgive him . . .

'But what of you, my little black one? I know they feed you well and I know you have love about you. But does a deaf-mute little girl laugh? And what causes laughter? Does she cry? And what causes tears? I want to wrap my arms about you, my little one; but that wise old woman says it would disturb you, and she knows . . .'

The long shadows were darkening the cool office so much the woman had to stop her paperwork. She peered at the desk clock, then leaned back in her chair and closed her eyes for three minutes. Joel Sterning seemed petrified at the window. Thought, for the moment, was suspended and a great tranquillity was inside and about him.

When the three minutes were up the woman rose from her desk.

'Time,' she said, and went towards the door.

Joel followed her out and waited while she locked up the office. The sun was nearly down and darkness was over the land. A sharp wind that came from the north made the evening air chilly.

The woman said 'Night,' and marched away round the side of the building, following the path Martha had taken earlier. Joel got into the car and waited, still enveloped in the tranquillity of the place.

The child was the first to see the woman coming and a little spasm in the little hand that was buried in Martha's communicated this new information. They rose from the log, stepped carefully over the line of still-marching ants, and walked towards the woman. Martha felt the tug of excitement in the child's hand. This woman had now become more pivotal to the world of her child than she herself was. You don't really need me any more, my little one. If I ceased coming tomorrow it would not really make any difference to you; you've crossed over into another world and so you are stronger. It is I who now need you.

She said it aloud: 'It is I who need you, my little black one.' And there was pain, physical in its sharpness, because the child could not hear the words.

They met the woman on the footpath and this time there was no need for the ritual of the transfer of the little hand. The child freed her hand from her mother's grip and herself placed it in the woman's hand. Doesn't need me, Martha thought.

' 'Night, Miss Lee,' the woman said, and the usually impersonal voice now betrayed an undercurrent of compassion.

Martha watched the woman and the girl till they disappeared behind the nearest building. Then she turned and walked briskly to where Joel waited.

All the way back to the city Joel was aware of the suppressed unhappiness that was like a cloud over Martha. Usually, and he had witnessed it often enough, this woman rode her miseries like a cruel horseman bent on showing a frisky horse who is master. Grief, she had once said—it was when Max Johnson's Myra had died—grief is a private thing: a private thing which is something you share with no one.

They were half-way through the last of the three villages when she suddenly ordered him to stop. He brought the car to a screeching halt.

'Back to that little rum-shop,' she said.

He reversed the short distance to the village square. The

shop, one-half of which was a general store selling everything from bread to salt fish to zinc sheets and nails and
cement, was the economic and social and political centre
of the village. The liquor-selling half was divided into two.
One part was called 'the beer joint', the other 'the drinking-
saloon'. The beer joint was crowded with young men and a
great deal of noise came from it. Four older men, all with
the stains of the earth on them and carrying cutlasses,
were quietly sharing a flash of white rum in the drinking-
saloon.

Martha led the way to where the older men were. There
was a brief lull in the conversation from the beer joint
while the young men examined the strangers speculatively,
then the noisy talk started up again, self-consciously
louder than before.

The old men moved closer together to make room at the
bar for the strangers.

A short round man with a little moustache and a very
greasy yellowish-brown skin came from the store part, a
gentle, friendly smile on his face. There was an odd mixture of speculation and ingratiation in the attitude of the
man behind the bar. The others, the four who had just
returned from a day's work on their small holdings,
waited, withdrawn, silent, emotionally non-committal.

Martha smiled at the man behind the bar and said:
'Gentlemen!'

The man behind the bar moved slightly and now his
back seemed straighter, the smile seemed, without any
visible change of expression, to be wholly friendly, without
any hint of fawning about it.

'Mum and sir,' the man rumbled in a deep gravelly
voice.

Martha named her favourite rum. The four relaxed,
returned to their quiet talk and drink, accepting the new-
comers as strangers but islanders and therefore not too
strange. The barman poured two measures.

'And yourself,' Joel said, so the barman poured a
third.

Martha made one long swallow out of her drink and
washed it down with water. A woman taking her rum like
this drew admiration from the barman as well as the four

others. It showed in their eyes. But Martha knew that if their own women had done this they would have disapproved. It was part of their ambivalence that things they approved of in middle-class women were terrible when done by their own women: like tossing down a drink or wearing slacks or showing too much of the female figure.

Joel stood back sipping his rum, consciously trying to efface his presence; acutely aware of Martha's emotional need to make contact with these people.

'The other half?' he asked Martha.

She nodded and the barman measured out two more drinks.

'You join us, gentlemen?' Joel invited the four casually.

They looked at one another, each unwilling to assume the responsibility for accepting a drink from the strangers. In the end the barman decided it for them by shoving a new flask of white rum towards them. The four made a ritual of serving themselves, then, having accepted the drink from the strangers, they abandoned their reserve, raised their glasses and each in his own way murmured 'mum' and 'sir' and 'health'. The barman helped himself from the flask of white rum.

'Sad t'ing,' the one who looked the oldest of the four said, delicately feeling out what seemed a safe line.

Another grunted and moved his head in a circular gesture that could be interpreted any way you wish: either a nod of agreement or a negative gesture of disagreement.

'Death is our sure reward,' the barman said solemnly.

'Some say he lived too long,' Martha murmured. 'So he held us up.'

'Some live longer than others,' the eldest one said.

The others nodded judiciously. Playing safe, Joel thought, just as we and the other merchants are doing: trying to feel the way of the wind in order to go with it.

'They say Josiah will take his place,' Martha said.

'So we hear too,' the barman said carefully.

'They say the merchants don't want him but the small people do.'

'We don't hear that one yet,' the oldest one said very quickly, very loudly.

'Tha's right!' the barman said.

'Yessir!' another one said.

'Not yet!' yet another said.

'You will hear,' Martha said. 'You will hear.' She put down her glass on the clean counter, looked first at the barman then at each of the others in turn. A broad smile cracked her face and tears showed in her eyes. 'Good-bye, gentlemen.' And she left them and went into the car and waited for Joel to pay the bill and come out to her.

When the village was behind them Joel said: 'You knew it would be like that; that they would not commit themselves, that they would bend with the wind.'

'I knew,' she said remotely.

'Then why let it cut you up as well?'

'As well?'

'You know what I mean: as well as everything else.'

'But it is everything for me, Joel. Do you still not understand that? Everything is part of what you call it.'

'This commitment to people who will not face reality? Who run away from everything? Who will only say what they know you want them to say? Who are always on the side of those in power? . . .'

'Yes!' she said, angry now, with the kind of blazing anger he had seen in her before. 'They're all that and more! I can make a longer list of their faults than you can! But you are not qualified to name that list because you are not committed to them! . . . Oh God! Oh God! I'm sorry, Joel . . .'

'But it's true,' he said sadly.

After that they were silent till they left the hills and were back on the plain. Then Martha touched his hand briefly.

'Those men up there, Joel, they are the measure of our failure; they are uncommitted because throughout their history every decent impulse in them has been used as a tool to exploit them. And we, the decent people, have failed to give them faith in themselves and in their own dreaming. That is our failure, Joel.'

Part Two
THE INHERITORS

⬛⬛ ⬛⬛ ⬛⬛

Against his will, he began to think. And because he was aware that he was unlikely to live beyond this night his thoughts were very sharp, very clear, very honest, but strangely without words. As a musician would think with sound, so he was thinking with feeling, thus giving the lie to the notion that man cannot think without words, even if those words are not shaped clearly in the mind. The use of words is only one vehicle of thought; the most important because the most universally used and understood, but still only one. Or is it? What a silly tangent to go off at at this time!

Josiah should come sweeping round the curve of the road any time now. Hope to God he doesn't choose this one day to be late. The light is fading fast. If he is late by as little as five minutes there might not be enough light to do what has to be done. What has to be done. How did we get to the point where this has to be done? Whose failure? His? Ours?

The man looked up at the sky, gauging what light still remained, and how long it would last. And then inconsequentially a picture jumped into his mind's eye and he was looking into a kitchen and at the straight back of a long thin woman who called to him 'The onions are brown'; and all his senses were filled with the strong smell of onions browning in coconut oil. The onions are brown. His eyes filmed over and a powerful nostalgia for life took hold of him. He used the back of his hand to rub the hint of wetness from his eyes. Then he leaned over the rifle and looked down at the road through its telescopic sights. Everything fell into place once more, and a man was a man because he was a creature with choice, a creature who could, unlike nature's other children, shape and mould the world in which he lived.

And looking down at the road along which Josiah had to come within the next five minutes, he could think calmly of that kitchen into which he had looked and from which had come the smell of onions browning in coconut oil, and of Martha Lee calling to him 'The onions are brown'. If only she had been younger or he had been older. That night he had forgotten the time gap between them and tried something. She had laughed cruelly at him and he had not been near her since. She had called 'The onions are brown' and he had gone into the kitchen and made the curry. It was after they had eaten that he had tried and she had laughed and he had left passing that fellow at the gate, coming in to her . . . The onions are brown . . . And the smell of brown is rich and warm.

Rich and warm and beautiful as the land is. Rich and warm and beautiful as its people. Rich and warm and beautiful as their dreams. Rich and warm and beautiful as the hope within them that has been betrayed and that must be restored.

It is getting dark now. Come on, Josiah.

Come on!

CHAPTER ONE

J OHN STANHOPE stood just inside the door of the long Cabinet Room watching the two senior clerks prepare the long table for the first meeting of the Cabinet since the death of the President. Outside, the day was clear and still. The soothing green of trees could be seen from the large open windows that took up most of three of the walls of the room. The great milling mass of people had gone, and so had the soldiers and the police, and all was quiet about the Palace and its environs. Old Moses Joshua had finally been put into the earth the day before. For three days nearly one-third of the three million people of the island had filed past the Old Man's coffin. Now he was deep in the ground and the land was turning once more to coping with the affairs of the living. And those who had worked closest with the dead old man, the senior Ministers of his government, were meeting without him for the first time this morning.

Stanhope crossed the room to the safe that housed all the key Cabinet papers. He was now the only one who had the combination of that safe. One of the things this morning's meeting would decide was which other person would also have the combination. But although Stanhope knew how, he could only open the safe when instructed to do so by the President, or, in the absence of the President, by the collective will of the Cabinet. He stared long at the small dial of the big steel box. Opening it would take him between fifteen seconds and half a minute. And inside this box were papers it would be best for none of these men to see; there were papers it would be especially dangerous for Albert Josiah to see. It was part of the Old Man's terrible capriciousness that these papers were not destroyed, were there to be used as weapons against others.

He turned away abruptly, stuffed his hands deep into his trouser pockets and went to one of the long open windows. The sun had not yet reached all of the sprawling lawns and on the ground immediately below the morning dew still gave the grass the appearance of a fresh, newborn dampness. A long time ago when he was a boy on the family farm deep in the heart of the island, he had always marvelled at the fresh dampness that seemed to be part of all new-born creatures. He had wondered whether it was so with new-born humans too, and so he had been very angry and upset when they would not allow him into his mother's room to see whether the baby brother they had promised him, and who took so long coming, would have that same look.

One of the clerks coughed artificially to attract attention.

'Finished?' He did not turn to look.

'Yessir.'

'All right. The windows then.'

He had switched on the air-conditioning as soon as he had entered the room so it would be fresh and cool when the windows were shut. The rule that the Cabinet always meet in a sound-proof sealed-off room was one of the few legacies going back to the colonial days that the Old Man had kept up. Behind him the clerks finished shutting all the other windows, then one of them came to the window where he stood. He left the spot and went to the door, waiting while the clerk shut the last window. Both clerks joined him at the door and all three men looked carefully about the room, checking to see that every detail was as it should be.

We've been doing this an awful long time, Stanhope thought: the three of us; the same three.

As though picking up his thought, the man on his left, the elder, who was in his early sixties, murmured: 'Won't be the same without him.'

The younger, who was in his fifties, turned speculative eyes on Stanhope: 'It will never be the same again. He made it seem the same for all of the twenty years I've been at the Palace. That's what's going to make it hard to meet the change.'

'All of life is change,' Stanhope said, feeling oddly paternal towards these men, the younger of whom was at least fifteen years his senior.

'He made us forget that,' the younger one insisted.

Stanhope shrugged so slightly there was hardly any physical movement; it was more a gesture of the mind pushing away a mood.

'Everything's ready,' he said briskly.

The two preceded him through the door, then he locked it, pushed the key into his pocket and walked down the passage to his office and the noise of the rest of the Presidential Office staff at work.

He found Andrew Simpson at his private telephone, the one that had no listed number and to which only a handful of people had access.

'Just a minute,' Simpson said, and placed the palm of a large black hand with beautifully tapering fingers over the mouthpiece. He looked sideways at Stanhope. 'Mr. Joel Sterning on the line, sir. Wants to know if you could dine with them tonight.'

Stanhope nodded and took the receiver from Simpson.

'Hello, Joel. Yes, I'd love to . . . Yes . . . Seven-thirty: fine . . . I'm expecting my Ministers any time now . . . All of them . . . No . . . Can't tell you anything now . . . All right . . . Tonight then.'

He hung up and was suddenly acutely, disturbingly aware of the presence of Andrew Simpson. He tried to shake off this new, oppressive sense of unease, but it persisted, would not leave him. Stupid, he told himself: I know this boy; I know him well and I trust him. I ought to. He's been with me five years and I've taught him everything he knows. Then, shadow-like, almost not there, he heard a small voice deep inside him: Do you really? You didn't know he was a supporter of Josiah till Josiah told you; so what else don't you know until you are told?

He looked quickly at young Simpson's face and felt ashamed of his foolish fancies.

'A suggestion, sir,' Simpson murmured.

'Yes, Andy?'

'Don't misunderstand me.'

'I won't.'

'Well, sir, Mr. Josiah has declared openly his view that the mercantile community of this island exercises a power and an influence out of all proportion to the contribution it makes.'

'Yes,' Stanhope murmured. 'The Minister of National Guidance has made no secret of the fact that that is what he thinks. So?'

'He has also made public his view that for the good of the society we need to bring into play a new pattern of power relations in which more value and importance and honour will be accorded those people who contribute more to the productive wealth of the nation.'

'All right, Andy. So what's the point?' Stanhope was becoming impatient and young Simpson sensed it.

'The point, sir, is that it might not be wise to be too closely identified with the most prominent mercantile family in the land.'

'I see.'

'Don't misunderstand me, sir. I'm looking at practical realities. If things go the way they look like going some sort of showdown with the mercantile community seems inevitable.'

'And the government's senior civil servant should not have any relations with any member of the mercantile community. Is that it, Andy?'

'That's not what I am saying, sir.'

'Then what are you saying?'

'That Mr. Josiah—and perhaps others—might misunderstand.'

'And think that I'm relaying government secrets to the mercantile community?'

Stanhope waited, knowing that his mounting anger was unreasonable, that the boy was only doing what he himself had taught the boy to do which was to examine realistically and dispassionately the political possibilities in any given new situation.

'I was thinking of your interests, sir.'

Young Simpson was stiffly formal now, remote and withdrawn. And I've hurt him, Stanhope thought. He does what I teach him to do, and he does it for me and I hurt him.

He spoke mildly, trying to undo the hurt: 'My relationship with Joel Sterning is personal, Andy. He's my friend; he's been my friend for many years. You know that, boy.'

Young Simpson went to the door, opened it, then hesitated and looked back at Stanhope.

'All right,' Stanhope urged gently, sinking into his chair, 'say it, boy.'

The thought was a flash of lightning across young Simpson's mind: God, I like this brown man!

'You told me, sir, that no area of the life of a good public servant, especially a very senior one, could ever be wholly private or personal.'

'Did I really say that?'

'Yes, sir.'

'Thank you, Andy.'

But now the young man would not accept his dismissal.

'You'll think about it, won't you, sir?'

'I'll think about it, Andy. And you, I suppose you agree with Josiah about this.'

'I do, sir. And about a lot of other things.' He hesitated then added: 'I think he'll be very good for the country, sir.'

And you know I have my doubts, Stanhope said to himself as the young man withdrew.

The first of the arrivals was the Minister of Youth and Community Affairs. He was a small man, sixty-five, and the colour of a piece of mahogany that had been left out in the open, to the mercies of sun, rain and wind, for as many years. He had a trim boyish little figure and a head and face too big for it. His dress was youthful in the extreme, what the young people of the island described as 'sharp': his trouser legs were stovepipe tight with razor-sharp creases: his high-heeled pointed shoes had large buckles and there was a conflict of shine between metal and leather; his jacket had no collar or lapels and followed every curve of the upper part of his body; he wore a creamy silk shirt and a spotted bow tie; enormous cufflinks displayed his monogram. His hair was cut in the style popular among the bright young men who were the island's fashion-makers.

In keeping with his dress, and the fact that he was the Minister responsible for youth, the Honourable Richard Young had carefully cultivated a boyish and bouncy manner and had sustained it for so long that it was now part of his personality. Any outsider coming into the island and meeting the Minister for the first time was usually shocked by the striking contrast between the youthful ways, figure and dress and the terrible old man's face of the Minister of Youth and Community Affairs. To the people of the island, however, this was how the Minister was: for him to have been anything else would have been shocking.

As Young got out of his car, two others drove up. Out of the first stepped the Honourable Ralph Smith, tall and thin and black and nondescript. He was the only member of the Cabinet who had been an ordinary working man before the late President had decided to make him a political figure and Minister of Labour Relations. He was modest, unassuming, and he was regarded as the best man in the land. The late President had once declared from a public platform that Ralph Smith and the word 'faithfulness' were one and the same thing. From that day on it had become customary to swear by Ralph Smith. And because he was completely without ambition even his Cabinet colleagues had helped build him up as the perfect party man.

From the car behind Smith's came K. E. Powers, Minister of Works, Posts and Telegraphs, a very big, heavily built light-brown man gone to fat on a large scale. Popular legend had it that the Minister of Works had a concubine in every large town on the island. Mr. Powers himself helped to promote the legend, of which he was inordinately proud. He also ate and drank heavily and he liked to be surrounded by big eaters and hard drinkers. In disgust Max Johnson had, a few years back, written an editorial denouncing Mr. Powers for making a public show of his gross eating and drinking habits and for boasting about the vast number of illegitimate offspring he had sired. Max Johnson had made it clear that he was not concerned with trying to change the Minister's ways but that he simply wanted the Minister to stop making a public show of what most of us did in private. 'Sexual license, massive drunkenness and gluttony are human weaknesses, and most of us are guilty of one or the other of these. Most of us, too, are ashamed of our particular weakness and try to hide it. Not so the Minister of Works! He parades his weaknesses as badges of virtue! And the values of our youth are distorted. Let us put an end to this stupidity.'

The late President had put an end to Johnson's campaign with a terse public statement: 'I see that our newspaper is trying to get rid of my Minister of Works. You should know Mr. Editor not all brains are in pens. I and I alone have the privilege of hiring and firing my Ministers. Don't you know your Constitution? Ha! Joke! Furthermore I like a man who is a normal and natural man and it is normal and natural to love woman and to love food and to love drink. So do not waste your ink and paper. Mr. Powers stays till I say he goes.'

There had been a brief, three-day national controversy. The churches had come out strongly on the side of Max and the paper; then word had filtered through that the mass of the little men had discussed the matter in their little rum-shops throughout the island. The majority had seen it the President's way. Mr. Powers, they agreed, was a natural man; and it was natural to love woman and to love food and to love drink. The churches had quietly dropped the matter. Max Johnson had accepted defeat. K. E. Powers had celebrated his victory with such vigour that he had, a month later, suffered a mild heart attack which had put an end to his orgies for nearly five years. And when he was restored to full health it was noticed that his deeds no longer matched up to his words: Mr. Powers was no longer the man he had once been.

Young and Smith waited for Powers; then the three of them entered the Palace. The two armed guards on either side of the great doorway saluted and young Andrew Simpson was just inside, waiting to shake each of the Ministers by the hand. He led them into the special reception room reserved for very important personages. A steward met them with cigars and cigarettes and a pretty waitress in black and white inquired whether they would take tea, coffee-tea, cocoa-tea or chocolate-tea. The Old Man had made a very firm rule about not drinking before or at Cabinet meetings. He had compensated by holding all such meetings early in the morning. Only in emergencies was the Cabinet called together at any other time; and then he overlooked any signs that one or more of his Ministers had had a few drinks. After all, going to cocktail parties and other social functions was part of a Minister's job. But he had been strict about the regular morning Cabinet sessions. So strict that he had once cancelled a meeting because he had detected the strong smell of white rum on the breath of one of his Ministers. The Minister had tried to explain that he had taken it medicinally, for a terrible cold, and only one small drink. But the Old Man had been firm and the Minister had been suspended from his duties for a month and from Cabinet meetings and the presence of the President for three months. After that all Cabinet Ministers, even the hard drinkers, retired early, and usually cold sober, on the night before a Cabinet meeting. This had been going on for well over twenty years and when a Minister was sacked, or died, the new one would automatically slip into the habit.

Richard Young looked pointedly at Andrew Simpson.

'Anything else, gentlemen?' Simpson asked.

'Stanhope ready for us?' Young puffed up his little chest.

Silly fool, Simpson thought, throwing his weight about: 'Of course, sir.'

'Hope none of the others are late.'

'They never are, sir.'

'All right, young man: that's all.' He waited till Simpson withdrew. Then, when the steward and waitress were out of earshot, he turned briskly to his companions and said: 'Well, gentlemen! Here we are without the Old Man. I know we can never replace him but we must choose a new head of state. If the three of us arrive at a mutually acceptable person it will be difficult for the others to resist us. I think Mabel Anderson will go along with us. I spoke to her last night. That makes four; not a majority but a strong group. What d'you say?'

'I spoke to the Prime Minister last night,' Powers rumbled.

'He's too old,' Young snapped. 'And he's not wearing as well as the Old Man. Choose him and we're in the same trouble in six months or a year. And he's not strong.'

Powers went on as though he had not been interrupted: 'He said Mathias and Donalds and Lowe are with him: and he also said Mabel will go along with them.'

'So he is making a bid!' Young was outraged.

'He didn't say so,' Powers snapped.

'But you said . . .'

'They'll act as a group: don't you understand that. I don't want to be personal, Dick, but you know as well as I do that as a group they won't back you. You've fought with all of them, especially with the Prime Minister.'

'I was doing my duty! I couldn't allow inefficiency to impede that. The Old Man saw with me.'

'Yes. But he's not here any more, Dick. Listen: Mathias said to me last night that he and Donalds would be satisfied to support me as a compromise candidate if the Prime Minister fails to win out.'

'You!' Young said bitterly.

'Yes; me!' Powers was suddenly blindingly angry: his face turned puce; his eyes popped; he struggled, arms pushing, legs kicking, to get out of the comfortable armchair but bulk and frenzy combined to defeat his efforts.

'Gentlemen!' Ralph Smith said; 'Boys!'

Powers gave up the struggle and slumped back in his chair.

'You and Smitty can decide between the Vice-Presidency and the Prime Ministership,' Young said grandly, taking a couple of jaunty turns about the room.

'You . . .! . . . You . . .!' Powers choked.

'We're getting nowhere,' Smith said. 'Let us think instead of arguing, like the Old Man always did.'

'He's dead, Smitty!' Powers snapped. 'No need to lie about him any more. He didn't think. Not in the way you mean. He bullied: he acted first and thought afterwards and we were the fawning claque trying to outdo each other flattering his so-called intuitive genius. If he had any genius it consisted in his lust to reduce men to ciphers.'

It was little Young's turn to lose control. He leaped across the room and lunged down at Powers, his manicured hands clawing at the massive neck. Powers heaved upright in his chair and swung his left arm in a large backhand sweep. It caught Young low on the chest and sent him staggering across the room and on to a settee. But for that piece of furniture he would have gone down.

'You my witness, Ralphy!' Young shouted. 'You heard him! Our great leader just in his grave and he's already smearing him! Disgraceful! You'll bear witness, Ralphy! He's not fit for leadership! Wait till I tell the little people what he said about the man they look up to as the father and founder of the nation! Its saviour and its salvation! Just wait till they hear! Just wait!'

Again there was a flurry of activity, of heaving arms and flailing legs as Powers fought to get out of his chair; again his bulk and the very violence of his efforts frustrated him. He gave up, puffing hard.

'Shut up! You little . . .' And he spat out the most violent obscenity he could think of. Then he slumped back, gasping.

'Ungrateful and unfit!' Young almost screamed.

'I'll kill him!' Powers rumbled: 'I'll kill the little . . .'

Andrew Simpson came quickly into the room. A 'fuss', he thought. In island parlance a 'fuss' was a row that fell short of actual violence. Pompous little Young sprawled trembling on the settee, as though Powers had picked him up and flung him there. And Powers himself looked as though he was on the verge of another heart attack. Only

Smith seemed unruffled. Fleetingly, Simpson wondered whether there was enough life in the man for anything to ruffle him. But his face showed no feeling as he said:

'Gentlemen, please!'

Smith began to say something but stopped as the waitress came in.

'Just a small political argument, young fellow,' Powers rumbled between gasps, 'nothing serious.'

The girl served them and withdrew hurriedly. A buzzer hummed in the great hallway and in the Protocol Officer's room upstairs to warn that more cars with more Ministers were passing through the great gates. The buzzer's hum became continuous.

Andrew Simpson forced a smile and said: 'Sounds as though they are all here, gentlemen; and there's still ten minutes to meeting time. Excuse me.'

He bounded up the stairs, taking them two at a time, swept down the passage, tapped on Stanhope's door and, without waiting for reply, entered.

'They're here, sir! I think it's all of them. Sounds like that.'

'Together?'

'Sounds like it. Signal from the gate was that it was being shut according to custom.'

'Then we'd better go down,' Stanhope murmured and rose from his desk. He thought: You're very excited, young man, like someone starting on a great new adventure; and like all the young you're unafraid because unaware of the dangers.

'Young and Powers had a fuss,' Simpson said.

'About the succession?'

'Most likely. Young was trying out different phases of the Presidential air on me when he first came in. They don't seem to realize their world has changed.'

'Do we ever, Andy?'

Simpson fell back into his official position one step behind the Presidential Secretary as they went down the wide stairs to receive the Cabinet Ministers. Young, Smith and Powers had come out of the reception room to meet their colleagues.

He's afraid, Simpson thought, noting the stiffness of Stanhope's carriage, the tautness of his neck muscles. Then he looked down at Stanhope's left hand: it was bunched into a hard, tight fist. A sense of startled wonder spread over him. He thought: God! He's not just afraid, he's scared stiff. And the questions and the doubt were born and flowered. Why is he so scared? Because he's a light-brown man? A shareholder in the old Establishment? Scared of the blacks in this changed world? And there was the devastating disappointment that comes when the pupil first discovers that the teacher is mortal and fallible, not all-knowing, not all-wise, not all-hero. The Ministers came through the great doorway and thought and feeling had to be suspended.

The first to enter was the Prime Minister and Minister of Financial Affairs, the Honourable Franklyn F. Freeways.

The Old Man's rubber-stamp, Andrew Simpson thought. And without the Old Man his rubber-stamp is without value.

Freeways was a tall, willowy white islander, distinguished in appearance, with a bluff open friendly face, twinkling blue eyes, and a deep and genuine love for the island and its people. When he talked about the island and its simple peasant people he often choked with emotion and his eyes filled with tears.

Shaking his hand, Stanhope recalled how Moses Joshua, many years ago, explained from a public platform why he had chosen a white man to be his Prime Minister and Minister of Financial Affairs: 'I know Mr. Freeways is a white man. I got eyes to see! And I chose him for that reason. When a white man speaks to other white men, there is respect and understanding between them, more so than if it is a black man speaking to white men. And it is easier too for a black man to speak to black men. I am not saying this is right or wrong or good or bad, or I agree with it or I don't agree with it. All I am telling you is that it is a fact. I did not make the world but I must act in it. The white people still have the money we need. It is better if we send a white man to ask other white men for money.

And all our big merchants here are white too and they like
to deal with their own kind. So I let them have one of their
own to speak to if it means we will get the benefit. It is like
using a good rubber-stamp!'

Next came the Minister of External Affairs, short and
round and ponderously judicious; very black and chosen
for that reason to speak for the island at the World As-
sembly where black and brown men outnumbered the fair
ones. The Honourable Z. K. Mathias loved the job of
being his country's spokesman in front of a world audience. He had quickly slipped into the habit of spending
more time at the headquarters of the world organization
than on the island. And since the Old Man, who in any
case made all the real decisions on external affairs, approved, everybody had been happy.

Then, in quick succession, Stanhope welcomes the Minister of Local Affairs, M. M. Donalds; the Minister of
Land Development, D. J. Lowe; of Industrial Development, Dr. W. R. Mathew, and Mrs. Mabel Anderson, the
Minister of Health, Housing, Education and Welfare, and
the only woman in the Cabinet. And finally, like a carefully stage-managed afterthought, Albert Josiah slipped
with dramatic unobtrusiveness into the room. Everybody
turned to him and for a few seconds the slender dark-
brown figure in the worn and nondescript old suit domi-
nated all else.

He seemed at once small and frail and long. He was
about five feet seven, slender and with long tapering fingers, long legs and a long body all scaled down. The
scaled-down impression ended at the neck and the long
thin face seemed made for a man at least six feet tall; and
so the very balance and symmetry of the rest of the body
made the face seem disproportionately large and slightly
ludicrous. But the sense of incongruity lasted only until you
looked into the eyes, rather close set, far back in their
sockets, reflecting no thought, no mood, no feeling. And
because man is a gregarious animal, made so by nature, he
is disturbed and apprehensive when he encounters one of
his fellows who seems outside the natural pattern. And this
man seemed not to need the comfort of others. This now

was the mood of his fellow-Ministers as they looked at Albert Josiah, Minister of National Guidance.

He said: 'Gentlemen . . .'

'Ah, Josiah!' Freeways boomed. 'You have an accounting to make to the Cabinet. It so happens that it turned out all right, but still . . . We can't just act unilaterally, you know . . .'

'I'm not aware that we're in the Cabinet Room,' Josiah said carelessly, as one brushes away a small irritation.

A mild shock rippled through the others. They had forgotten how this one was; that he alone had stood up to the Old Man.

'Then we'd better get up there,' Powers rumbled and turned to the stairs.

'Just a minute, K.E.!' Freeways swung about and strode forward until he was nearest the stairs. 'Our departed leader always insisted on the right form and order of seniority.'

'And on our shifting our tails!' Powers snapped, but *sotto voce*.

Freeways decided not to hear and started the procession up the stairs. The others fell into place behind him in accordance with the order of seniority the Old Man had decreed for them. Only Josiah did not take his usual place behind the Minister of External Affairs, but brought up the rear.

Stanhope unlocked the door of the Cabinet Room and the Ministers filed in. Normally they hung about in little groups of two and three until the Old Man strode into the room. Then they all stood to attention, waiting to see which of them he spoke to first. The one singled out for this mark of favour usually got most if not all of what he asked for from that Cabinet meeting; he was also the envy of his mates. Now, as they entered the long room the shadow of the Old Man hung heavy over them.

'Nothing to wait for this time.' Freeways was suddenly hoarse. 'Take your seats, gentlemen.' He looked at the seat at the head of the long table. Pad, pencils, the glass of iced water had been laid out. And now he sensed everybody waiting for him. He sighed inaudibly and sank into his customary seat. The chair at the head of the Cabinet table remained unoccupied.

'Well, gentlemen ... We have a lot of business to attend to . . .' Stanhope slipped his hand under the table and flicked the switch that started the recorder that taped every word spoken by every Minister at every Cabinet meeting. The Old Man had started this twelve years earlier after three Ministers he had sacked had gone about the country giving distorted information about what had gone on at Cabinet meetings. Since then he had twice released for public broadcast statements made at Cabinet meetings by Ministers he had fired and who had challenged his authority. In each case the Ministers had been so hopelessly compromised that all further agitation was pointless.

'If you're acting as chairman,' Powers said, 'the first thing we must decide . . .'

'No one's been elected to the chair!' Young snapped.

'I will remind you I'm the senior Minister, Dick!' Freeways said.

'Read your Constitution, man! It says nothing about the senior Minister automatically assuming chairmanship of Cabinet meetings in the absence of the President. Only the Vice-President can do that. And since there is no Vice-President we must select from among our numbers a chairman of Cabinet who will also act as head of state until there are new Presidential elections . . .'

Everybody started speaking at once; but the woman's voice finally prevailed: 'I'm under the impression that we haven't yet started our meeting and that Mr. Powers is concerned about a procedural point. Can't we just hear it?'

'The Constitution,' Young insisted, 'specifically says there can be no meeting without a chairman . . .'

'All I'm suggesting,' Powers bellowed, 'is that we start by discontinuing the practice of tape-recording what we say.'

'It was a decision taken legally within the framework of the Constitution,' Young insisted. 'It can only be discontinued in the same way. Instead of trying to shout me down, check your constitutional authority! I don't see how people can aspire to the Presidency of this Republic when they do not even know their own Constitution!'

'That is cheap and uncalled-for,' Freeways snapped, shaking with rage. 'The sort of thing only a petty person would say!'

'Gentlemen . . .' Ralph Smith appealed.

Again they all spoke at the same time.

'May I say something,' Josiah said. 'May I say something.' He repeated it, again and again, not raising his voice, until one by one, beginning with those nearest him, his colleagues fell silent and turned to look at him. When they were all silent, he said: 'Mr. Young is right in his insistence that we must do nothing to violate the letter of the Constitution . . .' Someone began to say something so he raised his voice slightly, insistently. 'Please! Hear me out! Mr. Young should know the Constitution provides specifically that in the event of any unusual emergency where neither the President nor the Vice-President are in a position to exercise constitutional authority, that authority devolves on the Cabinet whose members must collectively, until a new President is elected, exercise power. For the next three months, therefore, we as a group have the responsibility and the authority to run the country. During that period we can, among ourselves, make our own rules as to how we want to share out Cabinet authority. But the Constitution requires that at the end of that three-month period an elected head of state takes over from the Cabinet.' Josiah looked across the table to Stanhope. 'Am I right this far, Mr. Secretary?'

'You are, sir.'

'I wonder if Mr. Young agrees?'

He's taking over, Stanhope thought: quietly and easily; no fuss.

'Yes,' Young said reluctantly. 'I meant to mention that detail.'

Powers snorted. 'Then perhaps we can come to the point of the tape recordings.'

'Are you saying that we cannot elect an acting President?' Freeways was thoughtful and preoccupied.

Suddenly the blank eyes of Josiah had a message for Stanhope, and it was as clear as though the words were spoken. Stanhope felt chilled and all but shivered. He said:

'What Mr. Josiah means is that you do not have to elect an acting President in order to function; the Cabinet has the power to function without that.'

Powers asked: 'D'you mean we can rotate the chairmanship of Cabinet meetings?'

'Yes; if that is what you wish to do. On the other hand, you can, if you wish, elect one of your numbers to act as President for the next three months and to assume all the authority and responsibility of the Presidency.'

'This collective business never works satisfactorily,' Freeways grumbled.

'I don't like it!' Young snapped, and then he realized and was startled by the fact that he was agreeing with his rival.

'I would like the opinion of our Law Officers on this point,' Freeways said; but there was an air of hopelessness about him now, as though he had already lost the great prize.

'I think that's a good idea,' Josiah murmured, looking at one face after another around the table.

Freeways pulled himself together and tried to shed the air of hopelessness. 'I mean now; right now! I don't think it's good for the ship of state to drift, and this collective business would be drifting. I propose that we summon the Senior Law Officer immediately.'

'I second,' Josiah murmured.

Freeways blinked, like someone who had taken a solid punch. One by one the others nodded their approval. Stanhope got up and went to the telephone in the corner. He issued instructions quickly and returned to the table.

Powers examined Josiah's face with speculative intensity. He said: 'While we wait could we decide on this tape recorder business?'

Everybody was silent, each waiting for someone else to speak. At last Josiah said:

'What is your proposal?'

'That we end it!' Powers said violently. 'I've always hated it.'

'I've never minded it,' Young said. 'We all accepted it under the Old Man. Anyway, why didn't you object to it then, K.E.?'

'You know damn well why! He didn't give a damn about our opinions. We either knuckled under or he threw us out. That's why. Let's not pretend that we loved it!'

'I think some of us did,' Josiah murmured. 'No man could do the things our late President did without at least the tacit approval of a majority here in the Cabinet as well as a majority in the country. It is easy for his critics to talk about him as a bully and a dictator now that he is no longer here. I think he was what he was because we allowed him to be that, we here in the Cabinet and we in the country. He wasn't a fool. In fact I think in his way he was a great man, a realist who understood and used human nature. And if you say he loved power I will ask you what are we doing here? Isn't it love of power that has brought us here?'

'Then you are against the scrapping of the taping?'

'I did not say that.'

'Well, I'm against it!' Young snapped.

'And so am I,' Freeways said.

That's done it, Stanhope thought: you've given him his first win.

'I'm with Mr. Powers,' Josiah said softly.

Again Freeways reacted as though he had been hit. Then Freeways and Young watched their hopes fade as all the others, except the Minister of Land Development, supported the move to scrap the tapings. When it was over Stanhope switched off the recorder and dismantled the machine.

Powers looked down the long table and kept looking till he caught Josiah's eye; then he tried to send, silently and with the force of his mind, the message that was both question and promise. Stanhope intercepted Powers's look and thought he guessed its meaning. Josiah shrugged slightly, a faint smile flickered briefly on his lips, then he nodded and turned away carelessly. Powers slowly expelled all the air from his chest, as men sometimes do after pulling off something tricky.

He leaned towards Ralph Smith beside him and murmured:

'I'm going with Josiah. It makes sense and it's safe.'

'They say . . .' Smith began.

'I know what they say,' Powers cut in, 'but the people are with him and he can't lose.'

'You sure?'

'Sure.'

Freeways said: 'Well, gentlemen—and I'm certainly not forgetting our lady—I hope we don't live to regret this.'

'There will still be records of all Cabinet meetings but in the form of minutes,' Mabel Anderson said. 'You must admit, F.F., it was inhibiting to know that every cough and sneeze and linguistic mistake you made was there on record for the Old Man to mock at and use should the need arise. I'm frankly glad it's over!'

'You may be right,' Freeways murmured, using the expressive qualities of his voice to make plain his own doubt. 'Now, while we wait, perhaps we can look into the problem I raised with Mr. Josiah when we first arrived.' The Ministers grew alert and attentive. 'You will all recall the events immediately following the tragic death of our late President. First, we had the calling out of the military; next we had Mr. Josiah making a broadcast from the Presidential Palace to the nation in which he spoke with the authority of someone who had the powers of head of state. In that broadcast he authorized the opening of the Palace gates and announced the lying in state and the details of when and how the people could view the body. Now, all this Mr. Josiah did by himself and without reference to any of his fellow Cabinet colleagues. As it happens it all worked out for the best. But that is not the point. The point is that Mr. Josiah usurped those powers which he himself told us a while ago rested with us collectively. I have been advised that if these things were not done the national confusion might have led to the breakdown of civil order. I am not sure that I agree with this. Our people are not like that; they are not lawless or rebellious by inclination. But even if that were so, Mr. Josiah still had no right to assume the powers he did. Now, before I

propose that the Cabinet takes certain action against Mr.
Josiah, I think we ought to follow our usual procedure and
discuss the matter. In fairness to Mr. Josiah let me say
now that my proposal is that we strip him of his Portfolio,
expel him from the Cabinet and deprive him of all political
rights for the statutory period decreed by law on the
charges of gross violation of the Constitution. Whether or
not the law officers then institute action of any kind
against him is out of our hands. Perhaps this is a good
time for Mr. Josiah to indicate the lines of his defence or
excuse. I will conclude by making it quite plain that there
is nothing personal about my raising this matter: I don't
pretend I have ever liked Mr. Josiah's views but the country and the Constitution are more important than either he
or I, or our likes and dislikes.'

Freeways leaned back in his chair and waited, and all
the others waited with him. It seemed a long time before
Josiah spoke, and when he did it was with a casual mild-
ness that startled his Cabinet colleagues.

'I'm sure you will see with me if I prefer to wait till
you've all had your say. For one thing it would save a lot
of time if I got the complete picture of my alleged crimes
before answering; it might mean one answer instead of
three or six or perhaps even nine. For another it is customary for an accused to hear all the charges. Who knows,
there may be a number of additional charges. So I'll wait.'
With that he pulled pad and pencil towards him, and
waited.

Before anyone could speak the telephone rang and
Stanhope went to it. After a while he called out to the
room: 'The Senior Law Officer. Call him in?' Several Ministers nodded so he said into the mouthpiece: 'Bring him
in now.' He waited at the door and within half a minute
there was a tap and he let in the Law Officer.

'The question the Ministers wanted settled,' Stanhope
said, standing beside the man to give a little reassurance,
'is whether it is constitutionally correct to say that they
can either rule collectively for the three months before a
President is elected or else elect one of their numbers to
act till then; and that if they decide to rule collectively

then they can among themselves make internal rules such as rotating the chairmanship of the Cabinet.'

'That is the position exactly, Mr. Presidential Secretary,' the legal expert said. 'What they cannot do during this period is to either amend or propose amendments to the Constitution.'

Freeways said: 'Are you saying that it would be legal and constitutional for us, if we want to, to take turns playing at President for a week or so?'

'There is nothing in the Constitution and nothing in law to prevent it, if you make the decision properly in Cabinet, sir.'

'This is ridiculous!' Freeways exploded.

A flicker of feeling glowed in the expert's eyes: 'The law sometimes is, sir.'

'Thank you,' Stanhope said and ushered the man out.

'I'm sure that our late President never wanted the Presidency reduced to this kind of joke. President for a week, indeed!'

'I don't think anybody else wants to,' Mabel Anderson murmured.

'But it is legally possible,' Freeways protested.

'Many things are legally possible,' Powers said wearily, 'especially if we stick only to the letter of the law and forget its spirit. Which brings us back to the question you raised, Mr. Prime Minister. I for one am not happy about your punitive proposals against Mr. Josiah . . .'

'I protest . . .' Freeways began.

'You had your say uninterrupted,' Powers said savagely, 'now let me have mine. We all know there are people who are afraid of Josiah and what he represents, some of them right in this room, and that they would like to discredit him in the public eye. That is their right, provided they go about it in the right way, observing both the letter and the spirit of the Constitution and not twisting any part of it to serve private ends. I have no axe to grind. I don't owe Josiah or the merchants or the big farmers and estate owners anything. If I left politics tomorrow I won't starve. So my stand is based not on serving special interests but the public good, and I begin by questioning the motives of the honourable Prime Minister in trying to get rid of Mr. Josiah . . .'

'I really must protest at this misrepresentation . . .'

'Misrepresentation, my foot! I insist on having my say without any interruption. Now, let us go back to the night of the Old Man's death. We all know what happened in this room. For six hours Stanhope tried to get us to make a series of simple and urgent decisions. And for six hours we—let's call a spade a spade—we funked facing up to the fact that the prop had been kicked from under us and we were scared to function without him. The records are there on tape! They are there in Stanhope's memory! In mine! In yours! D'you want Stanhope to play back that tape so that we can all hear how each one fumbled? How we tried not to move lest we exposed our scary little tails?'

'Language, please, Mr. Powers,' Mabel Anderson protested.

'We decided not to . . .' Richard Young began.

'Of course we decided not to use the recorder in future. We did not decide not to play back past recordings. It might be salutary to hear ourselves again, to hear just what we sounded like, just how small we had shrunk, when we realized we were on our own, without our prop . . .'

'That's neither here nor there,' Freeways cut in decisively.

'But it is! It showed us up for the toy Ministers we were. That's why we panicked when faced with the need to decide. Is that why you want to destroy Josiah? Because he was the one who didn't panic? Or because of the other interests? If so, I'm not going with you. I've had my moment of shame!'

'Fine rhetoric,' Freeways said, 'but what about the facts?'

'That he acted unilaterally? He owed it to the state. With the rest of us he took an oath to preserve the peace, uphold the Constitution, promote orderly government and the welfare and stability of the people. When we failed that high oath, he did not. He too was elected by the people and when we failed to give them comfort and guidance, he did. Is that his crime?'

Stanhope said: 'In order for the Cabinet to get the record straight let me repeat here what I told each of you individually either by private telephone or in person the day after Mr. Josiah's broadcast. You will remember our six-hour meeting ended with no decision and that Mr. Josiah had left a letter saying he would abide by any decision arrived at by the majority of his Cabinet colleagues. You will also remember how hard I pressed you to make certain urgent decisions but we failed . . .' Quietly he went over all the details that led up to the Josiah broadcast, meanwhile noting down verbatim in shorthand his own words as he spoke them. When he had done there was a long silnece. Then Freeways said:

'Any other views?'

Richard Young cleared his throat then thought better of it.

'Mr. Josiah?' Freeways said quietly.

'I have nothing to say at this moment,' Josiah said.

'Nobody else?' Freeways looked from face to face. At last he nodded. 'It seems I'm alone.' He was old and drawn suddenly. He rose and held on to the table to steady himself. And now he was acutely aware, without quite knowing why, that he was the only white person in the Cabinet room. 'If you will excuse me I will retire elsewhere to write my resignation. Meanwhile you can decide whether you want to publicize the fact or not and as a loyal citizen I shall abide by the decision of the government of my country.' Then, with a slight bow, he walked out of the Cabinet room.

Young called out, frightened: 'F.F.! You can't, man!' Then when the door shut behind Freeways he looked from one to the other of his colleagues and said, wonderingly: 'I don't believe it! You're not going to let him.'

'He decided for himself,' Powers snapped impatiently.

Stanhope looked down the table at Josiah. He's as calm and casual as though this is a routine meeting; the Old Man would have dramatized this kind of victory, turning it into a piece of rollicking high-jinks: to this one it is a cold operation, carefully, even ponderously worked out. You were impressed by the exuberance of the Old Man even when he was being destructive or indulging in his favourite pastime of breaking men's spirits. He invested wickedness with a certain glamour and romance.

'You drove him to it by your cowardice!' Young snapped.

'Why don't you follow his example!' Powers said.

'Gentlemen!' Smith appealed.

'We have much to do,' Josiah said quietly. 'Many decisions to make. I suggest we select somebody to act as chairman just for this meeting and work out an agenda. The nation's business has been at a standstill far too long.'

Mathias, the Minister of External Affairs, broke his long silence:

'I propose Josiah as chairman for this meeting.'

'I second,' Mabel Anderson said quickly.

Young looked pointedly at Powers, who stared back with mockery. Then Young looked at Smith, who quickly lowered his eyes.

'I propose Mr. Powers,' Josiah said.

The operation, Stanhope thought: nothing left to chance.

'I stand down in favour of Mr. Josiah,' Powers said quickly, before anyone could second Josiah's proposal.

'I'm for Josiah,' Smith murmured.

One by one, in quick succession, the others cast their votes for Josiah. At last only Young remained.

'I would vote according to my conscience,' Josiah murmured.

Young pursed his lips, shrugged and said: 'Might as well make it unanimous. I like a good fight but when it's over the team must pull together.'

Stanhope just caught the passing flicker of disgust on Josiah's face, and he was startled by it because it was unexpected.

Then, very quickly, very briskly, Josiah rose, gathered his papers and strode to the head of the table. Casually, without hesitation, he sank into the chair in which no one except the Old Man had previously sat. An anticipatory hush fell over the room. Even Stanhope half expected something to happen. Nothing did and the tension slowly dispersed.

Josiah picked up the gavel and tapped the table lightly. 'I now call this meeting of the Cabinet to order . . .'

That, Stanhope told himself, is how easily and smoothly you climbed to power if your name is Albert Josiah and your will to power is as large as the world itself. Josiah was still speaking: '. . . I suggest we each cancel our other business and convert this into an extraordinary session to review policy and the work of all Ministries from top to bottom. The drift must come to an end. The country needs directing and expects it from us. The problems are immense and a start in tackling them is long overdue. If you agree . . .'

'An excellent proposal,' Powers said. 'Let us begin the long overdue work of shaping the future!'

CHAPTER TWO

'IT WAS the smoothest thing I've ever seen,' Stanhope said.

Clara Sterning sat on his left, sunk deep in her comfortable chair and very still in spirit. On his right Joel Sterning generated a mood of great restlessness. And immediately below, and seemingly surprisingly close, as the stars sometimes are on a black night, the lights of the city shimmered and twinkled, and the headlights of cars flashed on and off reminiscent of the love ritual of fireflies and glow-worms. They had eaten an exquisite meal with two very fine wines. And now he nursed, warming it with the heat of the palm of his right hand, a snifter of champagne cognac. On the little table between his chair and Joel's were coffee and a large box of Havanas.

Joel said tentatively: 'I don't understand about Freeways.' Then, quickly: 'Please, John: I'm not trying to pry Cabinet secrets out of you; you know that.'

'That was part of the smoothness,' Stanhope murmured. 'And yet he did nothing. He didn't fight back: didn't argue. Didn't defend himself; didn't even attack old F.F. He simply won over the strongest man and everything else fell into place. And he won his man over without a word or a promise: a passing of looks, that was all. It was like the night old Joshua died. He went out and waited and everything came to him.'

'It's frightening,' Clara whispered, more to herself than the others.

'But why the resignation?' Joel insisted.

'Old F.F. went out on a limb alone and when no one else backed him there was nothing else to do.'

'But . . .'

'I know, Joel. But before you judge them too harshly remember I was the one who called him in to make that broadcast.'

'Only because the others wouldn't do anything.'

'Are you sure it would have been different if they had acted?'

'What do you mean?'

'I'm not sure; but I have the oddest feeling that whatever we do now will change nothing.'

'Surely we can influence trends,' Joel protested. 'You in the service, we in business and the sane M.P.'s in politics. That's why it was such a mistake for old F.F. to resign.'

'But Joel, the resignation has meant nothing to the country! Look at your facts, man! A week after the death of the President the Cabinet meets for the first time and later issues a statement. It says it has gone into extraordinary session to make a comprehensive review of policy, suggests a radically new approach to the country's affairs is needed and that this is what it is working on under the chairmanship of Josiah. Then, almost as a casual afterthought, it says that the Prime Minister has resigned and that the Cabinet, acting collectively, has accepted his resignation because it could not agree with him that the Honourable Albert Josiah, Minister of National Guidance, should not have made the broadcast to the nation on the night of the President's death. And all the so-called "little people" applaud. And let me tell you one thing, Joel; making F.F.'s resignation public was not Josiah's idea. He was genuinely indifferent; F.F. was out of the way and he wanted to get on with the job; obviously something had to be done so he left it to the others and went along with their decision. And you know something, I know those men and for the first time today I've seen some of them behave like men instead of ciphers.'

'You sound as though he's got you too, John,' Clara said softly.

An abstract, worried smile flashed across Stanhope's face: 'I'm a public servant, my dear Clara, and he is effective head of state. I'm either his servant or I resign.'

'Then resign, John!' Clara laughed teasingly.

'It won't make any difference,' Stanhope said seriously. 'The country will accept it as enthusiastically as it accepted F.F.'s resignation.'

'I was only joking,' Clara said quickly, touching his hand.

'I had considered it seriously but it won't do any good. The idea of mass resignations by all the top civil servants is exciting. After all, we're supposed to be the backbone of the country, the guardians of its law and order. But just examine the notion seriously and you see how ludicrous it really is. You, the Isaacs empire, will make an opening for me at almost double my salary and everybody will say you are paying me off for favours I did you in the past. And the other chaps in the service will say "It's all very well for him to make this gesture; he gains by it because his moneyed friends are taking care of him. We have no moneyed friends and we're all of us in debt because we're all living way beyond our incomes". So . . .'

'It may yet come to that,' Joel said softly.

'I *was* only teasing,' Clara insisted.

'So where do we go now?' Joel asked.

'I don't know,' Stanhope replied. 'I do my job; I hold the service together as best I can and I do everything in my power to keep it free of political entanglements; beyond that I don't know.'

'You know, we may be wrong about him,' Joel said. 'He may do a lot of good.'

'I'm sure he will. I know he intends to. I'm worried about the price. But we'll have to pay it, whatever it is.'

'I don't mean that kind of good, John.'

'I know what you mean; but I do not share your sneaking sympathy for radicalism and radical solutions.'

A wave of rage swept over Joel. 'Of course not!' he

retorted savagely. 'If you had—and I mean you as a class —we might not be saddled with Josiah today! You, the brown-skinned *élite*, and the white mercantile and plantation crowd have literally brought Josiah about with your bloody ultraconservatism! Don't you see it yet, John!'

'Keep your shirt on,' Stanhope laughed. 'All right. So we are conservative. Show me any place on earth, your so-called radical states included, where people who have something to conserve are not conservative. You people have made money. Is it a crime for you to want to conserve it?'

'Yes! If we do it in such a way as to turn the mass of the people against us.'

'You know we're agreed there.'

'Then we ought also to agree that since the mass of the people are against us, the manner of our conserving, our conservatism, must be to blame.'

'If you are saying we are where we are because of the failure of the good people, I agree with you. But that doesn't make a sort of blanket radicalism right.'

'Perhaps not, John; but it does make your brand of conservatism wrong: Josiah is the proof of it. People like us will survive this. For the great Isaacs empire it is a question of using our wits, of adjusting ourselves to the new situation and so riding with the new tide. We might have to make liars of ourselves by being forced to say the opposite of what we said yesterday, by embracing those on whom we turned our backs yesterday, but that is a small price to pay. We will survive. And because he needs what we have we will use our wits, and go on making money.'

'You're awfully bitter for someone who'll do so well, Joel.'

'That's not the point, and you know it. How I feel about it is irrelevant to the fact that that is what will happen. The point is that we, the margin-gatherers as he calls us, will survive because he can use us and we can use him. You described what he did as an operation. Well, we are operators too. But what of the old families of the island? Of families like yours and what they symbolize here?'

'They have survived more than Josiah in the past.'

There was a new undercurrent of intensity to Stanhope's voice.

'The past is dead and you've never had a Josiah before!'

'That is where you've forgotten your European education, Joel.'

'The sole value of a European education——'

Stanhope cut in quickly: 'Is that it teaches us to survive.'

'I was going to use words like "flexibility" and "adaptability" but perhaps "survive" is the best word. All right, I'll buy your word; but survival today demands that you abandon the terrible conservatism which is the besetting sin of this land. If you don't he will destroy you, European education and all!'

Stanhope lit his cigar and savoured the first puff of it with deep sensual pleasure. He was aware that the stillness had deserted Clara and he knew that his exchange with Joel had brought to the surface of her mind the details of the conflict that had first eroded, and then destroyed, the great emotional and spiritual harmony on which their relationship had been founded in the beginning. He said, softly, reluctantly, knowing that it would upset Joel: 'But education, European or otherwise, is not an end in itself any more than survival is: it is either to a point or it becomes pointless itself.'

Clara made an audible noise deep in her throat and rose abruptly from her chair and walked away from them and the view.

I've touched a raw nerve, Stanhope told himself unhappily.

'But surely, John, the point is not this brand of conservatism that shuts its eyes to the monstrous extremes of this land.' Joel pointed to the little table with its coffee and brandy and cigars. 'This could keep two large families up there'—he waved at the hills—'for a month.'

'Then give it to them!' Stanhope snapped. 'But for Christ sake don't force your bad conscience on to me! I haven't a bad conscience, only concern for the land and its people.' And then he felt angry with himself for being angry.

They were silent after that for a long time; and because they were friends who cared for each other and who understood even each other's rages, the silence was without awkwardness, without embarrassment.

After ten minutes Clara returned from her bedroom, refreshed, and played one of Stanhope's favourite Beethoven pieces performed by Schnabel.

When Stanhope took his leave, a little over an hour later, Sterning said, with an off-handedness he did not feel: 'You're right about there having to be a point of survival, John. But even if there is not, life still goes on, pointlessly often, but it goes on.'

Stanhope hesitated, selecting the words carefully to ensure that what he said did not come out sounding arrogant or pompous: 'For more than three hundred years my family, families like mine, have tried to live usefully on this island; getting a living out of it and putting a great deal back into it. For us the notion of service is very real, and the people are very real, with all their faults and weaknesses. We are the people who've grown trees and made roads and built homes and created stability. I don't say we have not made mistakes, that we have not thrown up our share of idiots and knaves. But I cannot accept the new dispensation that would tear down the past as uniformly evil and that would build up hatred of class against class and against all the stabilizing forces in the society. I do not think it is a crime to belong to an old middle-class family. I do not think it is a virtue to teach the poor to be envious and jealous of what others have, and to promise that what others have would be taken from them and given to the poor.'

'But neither is the massive gap a virtue, John,' Joel cut in.

'You know I agree with you. But to promise people the moon for a plaything is to court disaster. There are no quick, easy solutions.'

'Isn't it your fault, the fault of your class, that the masses no longer believe in you and turn to him.'

'I've conceded you the failure of the good people.'

'But not that they have to pay a price for it.'

'And what of the good they've done? No credit for that?'

'That you must ask Josiah. I rather suspect he would

say you were paid and paid over-generous interest during the long rule of old Moses Joshua.'

'He hinted at something like that this morning,' Stanhope murmured. 'Anyway, there is a long day ahead even for this guilty, coloured, middle-class civil servant. If serving my country is a form of payment for a crime I do not recognize, I'm willing to pay all over again, starting very early tomorrow morning!' Thinking of the work ahead cheered him visibly. He kissed Clara on the cheek. 'Thank you, my dear, for a wonderful dinner as usual. I enjoyed it and I refuse to feel guilty about it. See you, Joel!'

They stood watching and waving till his car's lights slipped out of sight down the spiralling mountain road.

Clara turned back to the house and waited for Joel under the light over the doorway. She had gone out without a wrap and the chilly night air raised goose pimples on her arms. She rubbed them vigorously. She thought, clinically, of what might be the best line of action now in pursuit of the end of bringing Joel back to her emotionally. She knew that any hope of future happiness depended on that. She'd been wrong about one thing: She had bought the fiction that time heals. It did no such thing. Like God, it only helped those who helped themselves. She had thought that their being together in the same house—and time—would eventually tear down the invisible wall between them. So she had waited passively for four years, trying once to make him jealous by using other men. That had been disastrous in every way. He had withdrawn further, and she, though no puritan, had felt defiled and unclean. And then, the other night, after she had gone to him like a beggar, and after they had slept together, she had felt cleansed. He had withheld all of himself except the physical, which he could not control; and that by itself, she knew, would never be enough for him. But that, for the present, was all she had, the only key that might open the door back to what had once been.

He came to her slowly, hands stuffed deep into his pockets, head down; and she felt his unwillingness to be

alone with her. She turned with him and they entered the
house. The rest of the household had gone to bed, except
for old Jonston, the butler, who now waited to lock up.

She said: 'It's all right, Jonston; we'll see to the doors
and windows.'

The old man bowed slightly and murmured: ' 'Night,
Miss Clara, Mass' Joel,' and left them.

Clara waited for Joel to look at her, and when he did
she thought: He knows what's on my mind; not the details, perhaps, but the generality of it. The thing is if he
thinks I'm pushing he'll withdraw even more. Wanting
anyone is a very sad business.

'If you'll see to the doors,' she said briskly, 'I'll fix you a
nightcap.'

He thought: I thought the physical thing was really
over; and the thought was a mixture of excitement and
anger. And then he thought of Martha Lee and felt as
calm as only she made him feel.

He locked and bolted the doors and checked the windows. By the time he had done Clara was waiting for him
with the nightcap. She had, in the very short time,
changed into nightclothes that showed and concealed all
the things that had made her the most sexually exciting
woman Joel had ever known. He clung to the cool and
calming thought of Martha Lee but there was no stopping
the physical warmth that built up within him and spread
through his body.

It's all animal, he told himself savagely, but still the
passion grew within him. He felt guilty about Martha Lee
though he knew she would forgive him if he told her about
it.

'Excuse me,' he said, and went quickly to his room.

Clara waited. She thought she knew what he was about.
She was certain that the physical thing was only a beginning, but it was the right beginning, what she should have
done a long time ago; this was her only strong weapon
against that sexless half-Chinese woman who held his
mind.

Martha Lee's maid told Sterning her mistress was still at
the paper. The telephone operator at the paper said she

had left there more than an hour earlier. He gave up and put the telephone back on its cradle. He thought of undressing then changed his mind.

When he returned to the living-room Clara thought: He has not reached her. And then she was startled by the realization that she was prepared to accept the fact that Joel cared for that Lee woman, had slept with her and will sleep with her again, and that she, Clara, still wanted him and was willing to do battle with that other woman for him. Briefly, she was touched with a sense of great desolation. Joel saw her desolation and it stirred ancient racial and historic memories in him. She looked more Jewish than he had ever seen her.

She said, unexpectedly, humbly: 'Will you come to me tonight?'

He saw her humility and said: 'Yes.'

John Stanhope put his car in the garage and strolled slowly round the enormous Palace, making for the front. The moon was high and very bright, the sky a clear, cold, watery blue. The grass felt crisp and springy to his tread and the world was very quiet, very tranquil.

Suddenly, he was aware that Max, the great Labrador, was silently padding along at his heels. At one stage, about seven years back, the Old Man had briefly been interested in breeding Labradors. Max had been the first puppy of the first litter, and in a characteristic moment of impulsive generosity he had presented the puppy to Stanhope, making a great show of it. Now Max was all that was left of that great and costly, and very brief, show by the Old Man of his interest in 'dumb things'.

Stanhope reached down, patted the golden head and murmured: 'There, boy.' The dog made a low, deep-throated, emotional response, and man and dog walked up to the great doors now closed.

The two policemen on guard duty came smartly to attention.

'Easy,' Stanhope murmured and invited them to share a cigarette with him.

'Minister still here,' the corporal warned.

'Oh! Which one?' But even as he asked, he knew the answer.

'Mr. Josiah, sir.'

Then he saw Josiah's little car, sixty yards away, in the shadows under a tree. He opened the door and the dog slipped into the Palace hall. He said 'Good night' to the men and shut the door. He realized, and it came as a surprise, that he missed the presence of the Old Man. He climbed the stairs very quickly and looked in at the open door of the Presidential Office.

Josiah sat at the huge desk in shirtsleeves, his tie askew and a very loose band about his neck, the top three buttons of his shirt undone revealing his chest which was without a single hair and smooth as a baby's skin. About him the desk was piled high with official files and immediately in front of him was a large stack of sheets filled with neat close writing. He looked up at Stanhope and his eyes were bloodshot and his face drawn with fatigue.

They said he was a glutton for work, Stanhope thought: Plodding, persistent, patient. That was how he had earned a degree for himself, studying privately by himself. Perhaps our mistake was not admitting him to the Service when he applied six years ago.

'Ah, Mr. Stanhope,' Josiah said.

'I didn't know you were still here,' Stanhope said conversationally, and then regretted it as he saw the sudden flicker of anger in Josiah's eyes.

Josiah rose and stretched, working his shoulder muscles.

'Where have you been?' He was coldly impersonal.

'Out to dinner.'

'I know that; where?'

Stanhope hesitated, taken aback; then he made up his mind.

'Mr. Minister.'

'Yes, Mr. Secretary.'

'I've been dining with some friends of mine but I don't see . . .'

'Are you ashamed of your friends?' Josiah whispered. 'Afraid to name them?'

'I've been dining with the Sternings but with respect, sir, I don't see what business of yours it is.'

'Saying "with respect" doesn't change offensiveness.'

'No offence was intended, Mr. Minister.'

'I'll take your word for that, Mr. Secretary.'

'What is this?' Stanhope exploded, caught between anger and bewilderment.

'Don't you know?'

Then both men became aware of the dog's low angry growling; the hair on the back of its neck stood up straight; its eyes glared malevolently at Josiah; its fangs showed in a savage grimace.

'Home, boy!' Stanhope ordered. He had to repeat the order more insistently before Max obeyed and made his way to his master's private apartment.

'Your dog?'

You know, Stanhope said angrily to himself. 'President Joshua gave him to me,' he said aloud, stiffly. Then he said, knowing that this was the first of the encounters: 'My private associations and relationships are my business as much as your private relationships are yours. I think you know my public conduct is always guided by civil service regulations and I make sure that nothing in my private conduct does any injury to my public conduct and position.'

'That is how it was,' Josiah said carelessly, as if to dismiss the matter. 'From now on public and private conduct, public and private association, will be the same.'

'What does that mean?' Stanhope asked stiffly.

'In your case, that you will end all associations like that with the Sternings. You're an instrument of government policy. That policy will soon be in conflict with these people.'

'If you are suggesting the regulating of my personal and private associations——' Stanhope gave up the attempt at officialese. 'I'm sorry, Mr. Minister, but I cannot accept anybody's right to tell me who my friends should be.' He was shaking with anger now and he did not care whether Josiah saw it or not.

'I'm not interested in you or your friends, Mr. Stanhope.' Josiah sounded tired of the whole matter. 'I want to get back to my work. Your emotional problems don't interest me. As an instrument of government policy you will end all associations with all mercantile groups or, if you love them that much, you will resign your job.'

Damn you! Damn you! Stanhope fought to control his anger.

'You can't enforce either of your alternatives!'

'Can't I?'

'Not legally!'

'You seem to forget, Mr. Stanhope, that laws are made by the elected representatives of the people, not by the civil service, not by the head of the civil service. I suggest you retire and think carefully about it.' He abandoned his patient, explanatory air and said, briskly, sharply: 'And arrange for more coffee for me.' Then he swung about, went back behind the desk and settled down to his work with an absorption and concentration that banished the presence of Stanhope from his consciousness.

When his anger subsided a little Stanhope realized that his presence had ceased to register with Josiah. This made his anger flare up again. He stalked away shaking. But for all his anger he remembered, when he got to his quarters, to phone down to the kitchen and order more coffee for the man who sat working at the Presidential desk. Then he slumped deep into his favourite armchair, closed his eyes, relaxed all his body, and waited for the heat and passion to leave him. After a while he became aware of the warm breath of the dog on the back of his left hand. He opened his eyes. Max was sitting very close to his chair, mutely pleading for reassurance and some show of affection. Stanhope touched the cool damp nose and rubbed the soft velvety ears.

'All right, boy. We don't like him, do we? But stay away from him, heh. He's the kind that might even hate animals and show it. No. I'm not sure I'm being fair to him. Thing is, if I give in now. Come, let's find something for you to nibble.'

The man and his dog went into his little bachelor kitchen and both were equally pleased to see that the staff of the real and functional kitchen, where the food for the residents of the Palace was cooked, had remembered to send up the usual dish of bones for the dog. The man put down the bones but the dog waited till the man said: 'All right, boy.' Then he licked the man's hand before attacking the bones.

The low, happy growling of Max, at work on his bones, made Stanhope feel warm and comforted. He forgot his anger and he forgot the man who sat working in the Presidential Office. Instead he remembered the family farm on which he was born and where he had spent the earliest and happiest years of his life. The house on the highest crest of a series of green rolling hills would be in complete darkness now; even the caretaker's small cottage at the back would be in darkness: they still went to bed early in the country. And the land, too, would be silent and still and dark. Odd that he should remember the farm now; he had not done so in years. Before the house had become empty and silent and dark he had spent every moment of his free time there.

We're a dying breed, he thought. And in his mind's eye he saw not only the dark and empty and deserted farmhouse in which he was born, but all the dark and deserted and empty farmhouses on the island. It was the old families who were dying, and with them a whole world was dying: for a world is a way of living and thinking and working and playing and seeing. All this was changing, was being replaced by other ways and other values and the quiet drift into the new ways would now be accelerated and the number of the deserted farmhouses would be multiplied and more farmland would go into ruination. This was what the man down there at the Presidential desk represented; he represented a forcing of the change and the people were with him. He thought: Really, it isn't him I dislike or resent, or even the change, which is inevitable. It is the casual blotting out, without thought or feeling, of so much that was good and beautiful and that could still be used. There was no sadness to the thought; a heaviness perhaps, like the psychological heaviness and regret with which one recognizes the inevitability of death—but no sadness.

Only after he had left the dog, changed and got into bed did the sense of tranquillity leave him, and then for a brief moment only. Just before he fell asleep the thought flashed across his mind: Does he want to get rid of me? Then the counter-thought: But he can't; I'm the head of the civil service and my position is entrenched.

Josiah, meanwhile, worked steadily at the great desk.

At the other end of the town, Martha Lee parked her car in front of the great newspaper building. The long wide avenue was silent and deserted. She wondered how many of its citizens had ever seen the heart of their city like this, with the stillness of death over it. For the present, for the next half-hour perhaps, even the great presses were silent. She looked up and down the wide avenue, knowing what she would see and wanting to see it; and it was there, the unending black surface stretching in both directions, striking light from the overhanging street lamps and shining like mirrors, or like water, catching and throwing back the light. This, she told herself, is my city: this is my world, my beat. Then, abruptly, she swung about and entered the building. The lift carried her up to the top floor and the vast newsroom with its array of desks and typewriters and telephones. It was deserted, except for the night news editor, a couple of subs on late duty and one reporter working on a story. The cleaners had not yet come in and the wastepaper baskets were filled with discarded newsprint, and empty cigarette packets; and the floor, too, was littered with paper. Glass partitioning had been used to make half a dozen cubbyholes for the editor and his senior editorial staff. Martha entered the cubbyhole that said: M. Lee.

A sheet in her typewriter said: 'See the editor!' But first she went through the pile of telephone messages. One of them showed that Joel had called. She looked at the time.

It was a little after half past twelve and the slip showed that he had called less than an hour earlier. She picked up her telephone, hesitated, then dialled his home number quickly, as though driven. It rang once; twice; then she dropped it back on its cradle as though it were burning her hand. She leaned back and willed herself to be calm. The only other telephone message that interested her was from young Andrew Simpson. He had left a number for her to call when she got back. He had phoned two hours earlier. She called the number and when someone answered the background noise told her some sort of party was in progress. Then, through the din, she heard the gay voice of Simpson.

'Hello!'

'Martha Lee,' she said, raising her voice a little.

'Ah, Miss Lee! I'd given you up. I called earlier because I thought you might like to meet some of Josiah's key supporters. It's by way of a little celebration.'

'I would have liked to,' Martha said, 'but it's rather late now.'

'Not too late for us, Miss Lee. It is not far from where you live and I'll be glad to come pick you up and take you back afterwards. I really don't think you ought to miss this.'

'All right, Andy.'

'I'll be there in ten minutes.'

'No. I'm still at the paper.'

'I'll pick you up there then.'

'No; I'll be home in about three-quarters of an hour if your party is still going.'

'Fine, I'll be there,' young Simpson said gaily and hung up.

Martha Lee went to Max Johnson's slightly larger cubbyhole and sat down and waited till he finished tapping out a special front-page editorial for the coming edition of the paper. This was the last bit of matter before the paper was put to bed. When he had finished he passed what he had written to Martha. She read; then she suggested certain alterations and additions. They discussed and rewrote sections together. When they had done the finished product read:

'Special Page One Editorial

A WARNING

'Since the news of the resignation of the Honourable
F. F. Freeways as Prime Minister and Minister of
Financial Affairs, and coupled with the announcement
that the Cabinet has gone into continuous emergency
session to review all aspects of government policy, there
has been great ferment and agitation in financial and
business circles. This is understandable. It is right that
those who have a great stake in the country, either as
merchants, manufacturers, or the representatives of
overseas investors, should be concerned that the interests they represent are not damaged by any new
line of policy adopted by the government. And since
this island is as dependent as it is on foreign investment
we find ourselves in sympathy with those who insist
that nothing should be done to undermine the foreign
investor's confidence in the stability of this island and
in the good sense of its people and their rulers.

'It is precisely because we support this view that we
issue this warning to the representatives of some of our
mercantile, manufacturing and overseas investing interests. Wild and alarmist talk from them is as likely
to undermine the confidence of foreign investors as is
wild talk from any other section. Indeed, we venture to
suggests that wild alarmist talk is infinitely more dangerous coming from them than from other sections
because overseas investors put that much more weight
on what they say. Talk of dictatorship, of business
people packing up and pulling out, of a breakdown in
law and order, is dangerous, misleading and calculated
to spread alarm and despondency. To do this so shortly
after the death of our President is to do the country a
particularly grave disservice.

'The facts of Mr. Freeway's resignation are clear.
When we received the government statement we immediately approached Mr. Freeways, showed him the
statement and invited him to comment on it, add to it,
or subtract from it. We publish the statement and Mr.
Freeway's comments elsewhere in this issue. For anyone to suggest that Mr. Freeway's resignation was the

result of coercion or pressure of any kind is to fly in the face of the facts. We warn those who have started this whispering campaign to desist.

'The nine persons who now make up the Cabinet that governs this country are the elected representatives of the people. Their accountability is not to one group or section or one special interest. They are accountable to all the citizens of this island. They alone have the responsibility to govern, vested in them by the freely expressed choice of the people. These nine (since Mr. Freeways chose freely to resign) assumed responsibility fully for the first time, without the guidance and massive authority of the late President, just twenty-four hours ago. We urge everyone, especially our merchants, manufacturers, and overseas investors, to give them a chance to get on with the job. We do not say people should not lobby for their own interests. But we warn sternly that the type of wild talk and threatening postures indulged in by some of those we have mentioned are a greater danger to the island than the things these people profess to fear. Respect for a country and its people is expressed, in the first instance, by natives and outsiders alike showing respect for the elected government of that country.'

Max Johnson phoned down to the press room to say that the last piece of copy was ready, then he smiled humourlessly at Martha.

'Think they'll get the message?'

She shrugged slightly. 'Not if tonight's little do means anything. I think they've got old F.F. talked into campaigning as the businessmen's candidate.'

'Oh no!' Johnson groaned.

'Yes. Divine right to rule and so on. They didn't say it but I could feel it. Old F.F. sensed it and looked more miserable every time there was a hint of the latent white chauvinism coming to the surface.'

'What about the local people; the Isaacs crowd and so on?'

'Not represented. No Jews, Syrians, Arabs were there.'

'But surely old F.F. . . .'

'He didn't know how it would be, Max. He's being used; he's hurt and disappointed and it's always easy to use someone like that.'

'Hope to God someone gets him out of this mess,' Maxwell Johnson murmured as he got up. 'Come, I'll buy you a drink.'

'Sorry; young Simpson's going to introduce me to some of Josiah's supporters.'

'This time of night?'

'Didn't seem to bother him. So you may not see me at all tomorrow.'

'All right; but check in if you're away from your phone. I expect a run-in with some of our respected directors over our leader.'

'They'll be too scared and uncertain to be rough,' she said.

He nodded. 'Anything new on Josiah?'

'No. He's not been seen since the Cabinet went into emergency session. Saw Powers; smug as a sleek fat cat but uncommunicative. I hope to get something out of young Simpson.'

'Young man on the way up?'

'Yes; and he deserves to be. Very bright.'

'And very bitter,' he murmured drily, and added, as an afterthought: 'I hear.'

Trust you not to miss a trick, Martha Lee thought and said, a cool remoteness to her voice: 'With reason, bredda man; with reason.'

Johnson half turned away from her, grabbed the copy from his desk and handed it to the man who appeared at his door. He waited till the man was out of earshot, then he said, without looking at Martha: 'I think it's important to have a line on the Isaacs attitude at this stage.'

'Are you assigning me to the job?'

'Yes!' he snapped, suddenly irritable.

An odd little smile flickered across her face. Everything becomes personal here in our land; perhaps this is the last remnant of the African thing in us; and for all your being born somewhere else and of another culture, you are caught up in it too, Max Johnson. She said 'Right, sir!' and it was a gentle sneer. She walked away from him, down the large deserted newsroom to the door and the waiting lift. Just before she drove off the great presses started and a steady hum took over from the silence of the deserted avenue.

When Martha Lee reached home Andrew Simpson's car was parked outside her gate. She put her own car away, spent a few minutes in the house tidying herself up and changing her skirt and blouse for a pair of slacks and her favourite high-necked Chinese-style blouse with its wide deep pockets. The telephone message pad showed that Joel had phoned the house before trying to reach her at the paper. Must have been a matter of importance and for a passing moment she was tempted to try and reach him till she realized, looking at the clock, that it was a little after one in the morning. The thought began to form in her mind: He might not be alone. She killed it deliberately, as a person would step on a biting ant. She went out to Simpson's car.

'Hope I didn't keep you.'

'A little; but it's all right.' He got the car going then looked quickly at her. 'I'm glad you could make it. I—we—know you must be tired.'

Why this gratitude, she wondered.

'You said a celebration of Josiah's supporters. Why?'

'You'll see. You understand the invitation is personal, not to you as a newspaper person.'

'Just a minute, Andy. If you're saying I'm not to make use of anything I might hear or see at your party then you might as well take me home again . . . You should have known that.'

'I'm sorry I didn't make myself clear. We are not trying to impose any kind of restriction on you. It is just that we want you to know we didn't invite you for any publicity purposes and that for preference we would have no pub- licity at all right now. But that's up to you.'

'Who is "we"?' She wished she could see his face. She sensed a new seriousness in Simpson, and she wanted to look into his eyes and try to read its meaning.

'You'll see,' he said softly.

After that they drove in silence for ten minutes and then Simpson turned into the gate of the home of one of the key second-rank civil servants, a man whom Martha Lee knew. A large number of cars were parked on both sides of the street, the usual sign that a party was in progress.

Martha Lee recognized many of the people immediately she got out of the car. Most of them were senior public servants stationed at key administrative posts all over the island. The overwhelming majority were very dark: here and there, standing out in the uniformly dark setting, she saw a brown or white face, 'like spit on the face of the river' as one of her favourite Caribbean poets, the Haitian Jacques Roumain, once put it. But perhaps the most startling thing was the quiet, sober, orderliness of the party. It was going on for two in the morning, there was liquor to be had, but no one was tipsy, let alone drunk. The people sat or stood in groups, inside the house, on the veranda, on the front lawn, in the large garden at the side of the house, talking earnestly, arguing, exchanging ideas.

Martha thought: These are the people on the fringe, the people with the training and ability to become part of the *élite* but because they are black and have not gone to the right schools, and do not have the right social connections, they have remained just on the fringe of the *élite*; highly placed and highly paid, but knowing that were it not for their colour they would be higher than those above them because their abilities are greater.

Beside her, picking up her thought, young Simpson murmured: 'Not the wild and destructive and irresponsible lot that all Josiah's supporters are supposed to be.'

'No,' Martha said and looked quickly up at his face. 'But they are people who want to take over, not in order to improve things necessarily but to become the new *élite*, to replace the present pale-skinned political and social *élite* by a dark-skinned one. The question is: do they care any more about the people?'

The flashing smile lit up young Simpson's face. 'I think they care but that isn't the important thing. What is important is to shift the balance of power and responsibility.'

'And that will solve everything, Andy?'

'It is the indispensable beginning. Without it nothing is possible.'

'You sound as though we are on the verge of Year One, as though nothing has happened before and everything is about to begin with Josiah.'

'Basically that is how it is. This is *our* beginning.'

'Andy, let me ask you again. Who are the "we" you refer to?'

He led her towards an outside bar, past a group of strikingly dressed and beautiful young black women. The women suspended their animated conversation to turn and examine Martha Lee critically, frigidly, and for all her self-assurance their stares made her feel out of place. Andy Simpson took her arm, brought her to a halt, turned to the young women and said: 'This is Miss Martha Lee of *The Voice of the Island*.' The frigidity immediately disappeared. The women showed their teeth in flashing smiles; one by one they offered Martha Lee their hands. As soon as Martha and Andy left them the women dispersed, going from group to group to let it be known that the badly dressed woman with Andy Simpson was the famous Martha Lee, the political writer. And there was one woman who knew that she had an affair with that Jewish businessman, and this too was passed on among the women.

At the bar Martha received her rum and water from Andy and said: 'Thanks for the rescue operation. It was awfully cold.'

'About that "we",' Andy smiled thoughtfully. 'All of us here are representative.'

'Me too?'

'Of course—unless you feel you're not part of us.'

'What about your friend and mentor John Stanhope?'

'He's an islander, isn't he?'

'I see. I thought——'

'We're not racists, Miss Lee. You should know that. But we reject the notion that the only way we can prove that we are not racists is by perpetuating the present state of affairs where a tiny white minority is in control of all the key areas of real power in the land.'

'I thought real power was in the hands of the people.'

'Who have been misled and abused and confused and miseducated for three centuries and more. They've been made to see their vote in terms of dirty five-shilling notes, curry goat feeds and white rum binges at election times. They've learnt, in time, that the so-called real power of their vote was a face thing because their leaders, the people they elected, could be bought and sold by the money men.'

'Oh come now, Andy!' Martha protested. 'That's all right as platform stuff.'

'Yes, I know how crude it sounds; but you know as well as I do that this is what has happened—though not as crudely as I put it. And if you tell me not all of them have done this I will agree with you and then I will ask you why it is that in spite of all the decent people that you claim exist we still have such vast inequalities, such great gaps between those who have and those who do not and why the whites who represent less than five per cent of the nation still control something like ninety per cent of its wealth?'

'Haven't you got your villains a little confused, Andy?'

'There you go again, reading racism into what I say! I simply state the facts.'

'Laced with elements of blame which can be turned to bitterness and hate which will not make things better by one iota for your people and mine. I'm worried about your point of departure, Andy.'

Andy Simpson spread his feet a little and braced his body, balancing it as one who is about to make some physical effort. A shy, tentative smile made him look very boyish and young. Martha Lee thought: So young, so sensitive, so compassionate, I like you, young Simpson, and I'm afraid of what they might do to you: they seem to have a sick need to use clean and upright men like you, these shapers of the world.

Simpson was caught in Martha Lee's mood. He forgot the thought that had been slowly dressing itself in words. Instead he was enveloped in the disturbed and disturbing tenderness that radiated suddenly from this woman.

He said, and it was an involuntary exclamation: 'What is it?'

The woman smiled and the mood was gone, as though it were a thing of his imagining.

'Shadows,' Martha Lee said quietly, 'just shadows, Andy.'

And Andy knew that there had been something more than his imaginings. Briefly, without words, he and this woman had been close, intimate. And then the thought was there, sudden, unexpected: I wish this Martha Lee were twenty years younger. After that the realization came calmly to Andy Simpson that because of what had just passed between them he would always, from now onwards, be a little in love with this woman who was too old for him to do anything about it.

Martha rested her hand lightly on his arm for a few seconds and then removed it. He looked into her eyes and knew that she knew what had passed through his mind. Then, while he yet watched, she was transformed into the cool, detached, analytical Martha Lee of *The Voice of the Island.*

'You were going to say,' she said.

'I've forgotten,' he said, knowing he could remember very easily, but not wanting to. 'It'll come back.'

A tall, sallow, brown-skinned man moved purposefully to where they stood. His suit, of a light pastel shade, was cut in the latest style fashionable in London's Mayfair. He puffed a Blackfriar cheroot through an ivory holder. Each step he took was a study in the art of self-conscious loco-motion.

Andy Simpson turned on his diplomatic smile and shook the newcomer's hand vigorously. 'So nice to see you again. Have you met Miss Martha Lee of *The Voice of the Island*?'

'No-o-o,' the newcomer drawled, 'but I've been *wanting* to, you know . . .' He offered Martha a limp hand and cocked his head sideways. 'Professional *esprit de corps,* you know, though my main occupation is books, of course. These stints as foreign correspondent are good for discipline and keeping one's feet on the ground, you know . . . My editor gave me a letter to yours but I've not got around to seeing him yet. The people in the know on The

Street and at your Embassy said nice things about you. Everyone said to get to know the island you simply must meet Martha Lee. Of course, they tend to forget that I originally came from the island, probably because some of their best critics think I write better about their people than their own writers. I made it plain that I wanted none of this nonsense of being typed as a Caribbean writer concerned and restricted to the limited life of the islands and the limited lives of their people. Journalism's good enough for that: like this jaunt I'm on now. None of the islands are really worth more than a series of first-class articles, but they must be first-class, of course. If you must do a book, then make it funny; an exotic comic novel set in the sun and poking fun at the islands and their people. The English critics seem to love that. Look at the success of that fellow what's-his-name . . . Though I frankly didn't think the book was up to much, my dear. Didn't mind too much because it wasn't about *our* island, don't forget I still *feel* about *this* island though I'm now an Englishman with an English passport . . . Anyway, let's have lunch tomorrow and talk about all this, shall we, Martha dear? My room is three-three-three at the Imperial and I shall be free from twelve onwards unless those people at the Ministry keep me though I've told them I want *that* part of my programme cut to a minimum—seeing only really *key* people, you know. I want to do something good *for* the island and we have a circulation of . . .'

Martha Lee made a strangled noise deep in her throat. Andy Simpson saw she was on the verge of exploding. He grabbed the writer's arm and hustled him away, saying urgently: 'There's somebody important you really must meet, Mr. Mastering, one of the key people . . .'

Martha turned and looked appealingly at the young man behind the improvised bar. 'I need a strong one, please!'

The young barman laughed with his eyes as he served her. Then he asked:

'He really one of us?'

'He was born here,' Martha said, 'but one of us, I don't know.'

'One thing for sure,' the barman said, 'he didn't learn to chat so here.'

'That's for sure,' Martha agreed and felt much better. A new thought crossed her mind, making her feel worried. She offered her glass to the barman for a refill and said: 'Know something, until I went to England I had a false picture of Englishmen. I thought they were all masters and prejudiced and rude and rich, because that's how I found them here. It was only after I met them in their own country that I saw them as ordinary normal people like us.'

The barman nodded. 'And now you fear they think we all like this one.'

'Something like that.'

'It hard, heh, mum! And prejudice a hard thing . . .' He turned away to serve a group of bright young men.

Andy Simpson returned without the writer.

'That was the great Martin Mastering, our gift to English Letters. Trouble is his book—the one and only one— was good. Read it?'

Martha said: 'No.'

'You should. The story gives a new twist to the old one about the quaint habits of the "natives". The "natives" of his story are the English and a black anthropologist from an unnamed country goes and lives among them to study their customs, habits and beliefs in order to write a book. The result is the most hilarious kick in the pants for the English I've ever read. Trouble is, now that I've met him I'm not so sure that's what he intended.'

'And his visit here? Whose foreign correspondent is he?'

'London seems to see Josiah in much the same way as our merchants and Mastering's assignment is to come and see how close to dictatorship we are.'

'How's he doing?'

'Miserably. There's too much noise; there are too many dogs; too many babies; the streets are too dirty; people are unpunctual; the sun is too hot; service is poor . . .'

'Just keep him away from me!' Martha Lee warned.

'But he simply *must* see you and your editor,' Andy mimicked; '*esprit de corps*, you know.'

Martha let out an unladylike snort and spat out, softly but distinctly, the island's favourite four-letter cuss word. Simpson stepped back in mock horror. One of the young men who had come up to the bar for service murmured: 'Lady! Lady!'

There was sudden commotion among the different groups of people. They began to move towards the front of the house.

'I think this is what we've been waiting for!' Simpson took Martha's elbow and urged her in the direction everybody else was going.

'Josiah?' she asked.

'Yes!'

He was chauffeur-driven this time, in one of the Palace limousines. This particular house had a car-port that was part of its veranda, and the big black limousine drove right into it, and Josiah stepped out on to the veranda. Those on the veranda surrounded him, shaking him by the hand, but in orderly fashion, not crowding him, not pressing against him.

Simpson worked his way through the crowd, gently pushing Martha in front of him. People recognized him and made way, till they too were on the veranda. Close on, under the light, Martha saw how drawn and tired Josiah looked. His bloodshot eyes stood out in their sockets and every now and then he seemed to have difficulty keeping his drooping eyelids open.

Simpson said, 'Excuse me,' left Martha and went closer.

Josiah saw him and his face lit up. 'Ah, Andy!'

Simpson said softly: 'She's here, sir.'

'Good man!' Josiah reached up and put his hand on the shoulder of the tall young man. 'Bring her to me.'

Simpson saw the writer, Martin Mastering, some distance off fighting his way through the clusters of people. He whispered to one of the strapping young men who had formed an unobtrusive semicircle about Josiah. The young man went among the crowd, spoke to a person here and there, and then worked his way towards the writer. Now the writer suddenly found his way blocked and the people unco-operative, and even hostile, when he tried to bull his way through. At last the strapping young man reached the writer and spoke to him briefly. The writer gave up his attempt to get to Josiah.

Josiah raised both arms above his head. The waiting people fell silent. He said: 'My friends; brothers and sisters; there is no need for speech-making between us. You and I know what I mean when I say the great work is about to begin. The only ones who do not know what I mean are those who are not supposed to know.' He paused dramatically and a smile lit up his face. 'And they will know when they will know. I came so that we can be together for a small passage of time so that you should know our compact is still the main driving force in what is to come to pass. I expect all of you to go back to your posts and carry on, because the only reward for us is more work. You will hear many things that will test your faith and your strength: you will hear of dictatorship, of tyrrany, of collapse, and you will remember that we have waited a long time for this moment when we can begin our work, the hard work that none of us may live to see finished.' He lowered his head as though in prayer, then he looked up and smiled.

No one applauded. This is religious, Martha Lee told herself, feeling the mood of mystical commitment: the Rabbi, the religious, never needs, or receives, outward applause from his co-religionists; it is all inward and invisible, but palpable.

Then she was aware that Simpson had returned and was saying something to her.

'He wants to see you.'

'Me? Josiah?'

'Yes. Come.'

She was aware of many faces turned to her, of helping hands urging her forward, of friendly eyes caressing her because their leader showed regard for her. Then she was beside him. She knew him, had met him and spoken with him many times before; she had fended off many efforts on his part, as she had on the part of other politicians, to plant ideas and make use of her. But then he had been one of a number of politicians, one of the smartest, but still just one; now he was the man at the centre, and in spirit he seemed larger than he had been before, calmer, in control. Or was it because both he and she were aware of his new power. Is it the man who has changed and grown? Or is it my awareness of his new power that makes me invest him with these new qualities? Like how handsome and gallant an ordinary young fellow becomes when dressed in a dashing uniform?

His smile suggested that he had an idea of what was passing through her mind.

'It was good of you to come,' he murmured.

'My pleasure, Mr. Minister.' She knew this kind of small-talk was an effort for him.

'Come inside.' He signalled to Simpson and the three of them went into the house. No one else followed. Inside he stopped abruptly, turned to Martha and said: 'I've seen your editorial.'

For a few seconds she was nonplussed, then she connected and said: 'But you can't have!'

He smiled and looked at Simpson. 'It reached me just about the time Andy picked you up. Oh, I shouldn't bother to find out how.'

Martha felt cold suddenly, withdrawn and on guard.

'I'm not the only one, Miss Lee,' Josiah murmured. 'The Chairman of your Board also has a copy and so has a friend of yours in the Isaacs set-up. At least, I know copies went off to them. I have no way of knowing whether they've read them or not. The thing is: don't get angry with me or invest me with a new villainy because I do what my enemies do in order to know what's going on.'

'No one is supposed to . . .' Martha began.

'It's been going on a long time,' Simpson cut in.

'The thing is, I liked your editorial,' Josiah said. 'I would have emphasized one or two points a little more but it will do. I understand you yourself attended a meeting earlier this night and so I don't understand why your editorial does not mention the fact that the meeting represented a largely expatriate business group with strong anti-Semitic undertones. I should like you to follow this up. Forget the implied anti-Semitism if you like but give weight to the latent conflict between expatriate and local business interests.'

'Mr. Minister . . .' Martha began.

'In return,' Josiah said insistently, brushing her objection aside, 'in return, here is something special which you can use first. Presidential elections will be held as soon as possible. Instead of waiting out the three months we will call the election within four weeks of a resolution to this effect being passed in parliament. Parliament will meet in special session late tomorrow evening and the resolution should be passed a little after midnight.'

Martha Lee realized the timing had been especially arranged to ensure that she 'scooped' radio and television.

She said 'Thank you, sir!' warmly.

'You'll find that section twenty-three, sub-section sixteen of the Constitution gives us power to call such elections under certain conditions.'

'And who, sir, will be your party's candidate?'

Josiah pursed his lips and shook his head. 'I favour either Mr. Smith or Mr. Powers, but my colleagues seem determined that I myself stand.'

'May I say this?'

'Of course, but no direct quotes, you understand. And I suggest you talk to some of the other Ministers. In fact it might be an idea if you and your editor have lunch with me tomorrow. You will then be able to meet my colleagues for a little off-the-record chat. One thing, Miss Lee. I want none of this to get about until after it has gone through parliament. Tell your editor and prepare your story—and call on Andy for anything more you may want —but don't you or your editor discuss it with your friends: not with Stanhope and especially not with your friend Sterning.'

Martha began to raise a protest but before she could dress it in coherent words, Albert Josiah turned from her and walked quickly out of the room. She rushed out after him and was just in time to see his limousine drive off, and a small brown hand waving to his highly disciplined supporters.

Martha stood on the veranda and watched the car drive out of the gate and down the wide street. Then she became aware that she was trembling, aware that the beating of her heart was so violent that she felt it behind her ears, jarring her head. No one had ever told her what to write and what not to write, whom to see and whom not to see! And with that casual air which suggested that that was how it would be! And because she was an honest and intelligent woman she recognized and faced up to the primary reason for the violence of her anger: Josiah's quiet assurance had frightened her. And being afraid in this way, of some nameless, irrational feeling of impending disaster, was something new for Martha, creating a sub-area of shame-faced self-consciousness: and yet her awareness that her fear bordered on the superstitious did not in any way lessen the intensity of that fear.

Simpson touched her lightly on the shoulder. She shook her shoulder violently, making it plain she found his touch abhorrent. Then she walked away from him in long brisk strides. He followed and caught up with her before she got to the gate.

'You're a realist, Miss Lee. You understand the problem . . .' He took her arm and forced her to a halt, but gently, using only enough force.

'If this is your reality you can keep it and go to hell with it! I want no part of it!'

'And your people?' he said softly. 'Should they go to hell too?'

A great weariness swept over her. Of course, it had to be in the name of the people: always in the name of the people, for the people.

Andy Simpson said: 'Miss Lee, you know as well as I do—better in fact—that the so-called free organs of opinion, press, radio, television, have been used to serve certain special interests. You know this; I don't have to say it to you. You know—better than most—that for the hungry and the homeless and the illiterate and those in darkness in the bush your free press and free speech have not meant anything. Is he so wrong when he says let us for a change use the press in the service of the people, in the interest of making life better for them, instead of in the service of the margin-gatherers? So he inhibits you a little, but in the interest of the people. Is that so wrong?'

She thought: There is just enough truth in this to make

it hard to answer. Aloud, impersonally, she said: 'Tyranny
often has small beginnings, like inhibiting one journalist a
little.'

'So what do we do?' he asked, and added: 'In our context, to act in the interest of the people is to offend someone, some special interest. No matter what we do, someone will cry tyranny. He said it here not so long ago. So
what do we do, Miss Lee?'

'You make it sound very easy, Andy.'

'It is you who make it sound very easy; it is you who
talk about the small beginnings of tyranny. Tell me how
we can do a job, which I know you agree needs to be
done, without soiling our hands.'

'And when you've done the job, will we have any free
institution left? . . . Take me home now, please: I'm tired.'

He took her arm and they crossed the road to where he
had parked his car. 'It depends,' he said, 'on which are the
really key free institutions. When your belly is full and
you live in a nice house and your children are in good
schools and you have running water and electric light and
you can call in your doctor whenever there is sickness you
are likely to have a very different sense of values from the
man who is hungry and homeless and whose children are
not in school and who cannot get adequate medical attention. The values of free speech and free institutions are
relative. There are people—not only here but all over what
has become known as the third world—who will happily
trade free speech and free institutions for three square
meals a day, a roof over their heads and reasonable health
services. Are you prepared to say they would be making
such a bad trade?'

They got into the car and he drove off.

She said: 'So it's all worked out, like every other move
he has made.'

'He doesn't want to interfere with the Press unless there
is no other way.'

'And you and your friends back there are prepared to
do whatever he wants?'

'He wants what we want; without him we can't do it,
with him we can't fail. He is the spark our movement
needs.'

'And you have no doubts about him? I mean you personally, Andy?'

'None whatever, Miss Lee; not one.'

Martha looked at the houses flashing by like dark shadows. It would be a crime to try to undermine this young man's faith. All that mankind has achieved thus far on earth has been based on this kind of faith. Without it very little could have been done, very little achieved. But for the gifted and the perceptive and the genuinely compassionate ones the moment of recognition of the limitation of such a faith had often been devastating, sometimes fatal. She said, softly, tenderly: 'If things ever change, Andy, try to remember this night and our conversation, and that things are never as simple and clear-cut as the shakers and shapers and revolution-makers would have us believe. There are no interest-free short-cuts. If you skip a stage in one way, you pay for it in another. So if things ever change, don't let the change change what you are, and what you believe and hold dear. You are fine the way you are, and what you're after is right both for yourself and our people.'

'But you don't trust him; you don't like him. Why?'

'I don't know,' she said. She thought: How do you make someone who lives with both love and belief understand how it is to live without belief but with love. This Josiah of his is full of belief and without love and I am full of love without belief. Yet Andy's probably right. Josiah will bring much that is good: it is only the price that is frightening to contemplate. Aloud, she said: 'I'm not even sure you're right in saying that I don't like or trust him.'

'Then what is it? Why are you not with us?'

'I'm not against you.'

'It's not the same thing.'

'It's all I can offer.'

He said nothing but she felt his withdrawal. It was still there when he dropped her outside her gate.

CHAPTER THREE

MOST OF THOSE who worked in the great Isaacs building, which occupied a whole block in the very heart of the
city, had never seen old Nathan Isaacs. Those who started
the Isaacs empire with him—in the days when the extent
of its area was a single barn-like room thirty feet by forty
feet and its capital was one man's will and gluttony for
work—had either died or retired. So the coming of old
Nathan to the office was an event comparable to a visit
from British royalty or from the currently most popular
coloured singer from the United States. Between the time
when the sleek black limousine deposited the old man
outside the great building and when the lift carried him up
to the Board Room on the sixth floor, a matter of less than
five minutes, every one of the three hundred and sixty-two
workers knew that 'Old Mass Nathan' had come: and
everyone knew that this meant something very special; and
most of them guessed that there was a connection between
the old man's coming to the office and the sensational
midnight sitting of the house of parliament three days
earlier and the disturbing press and radio headlines an-
nouncing that Josiah would stand for President; that all
foreign companies on the island would be required to sell
half their shares to local investors; that the freehold ownership of property would be restricted to natives and that

foreigners would only be allowed to lease property up to a maximum time period of twenty-five years; that all natives must declare whatever stocks, shares, property and other holdings and money they may have deposited abroad; that all schools would come directly under the control of the government in an integrated education programme and that education would immediately become free and compulsory for all children between the ages of five and fifteen; that every young person, male and female, would give two years of national service to the country; that there would be direction of labour and of investment, control of wages and profits and a development tax levied on everybody. Josiah would fight the Presidential election on this programme. F.F. Freeways, former Prime Minister and Minister of Financial Affairs, had announced that he would stand against Josiah and against the programme. All the workers in the great Isaacs building knew, some vaguely and in a general sort of way, others sharply and clearly, that it was these developments that had brought old Nathan down to the office for the first time in well over twenty years. And the very few in the know, the private secretaries, the personal assistants, the key departmental heads, were aware that the old man, his two elder sons, Nathan Junior and Emanuel, and his daughter Clara, were all waiting for the youngest son and the chairman of the Board of Directors, Solomon, and the spokesman for the Isaacs empire, Joel Sterning, to return from a conference to which Josiah had summoned them.

'He's keeping them a long time,' the old man said, a little impatiently. He had gone carefully over the lead story and editorial in the latest issue of *The Voice of the Island*. Now he pushed the paper away from him. He almost knew the details by heart. He ignored the radio transcripts: the radio station (and its television subsidiary) operated under a license from the government, and since the terms of the license empowered the President to cancel the franchise at will, 'in the national interest', the radio station was always very careful—so careful indeed, that it sometimes ignored straight news, as it had now ommited from all its bulletins any mention of F.F. Freeway's candidacy in the forthcoming Presidential election.

The telephone rang. Young Nathan picked up the receiver, listened for a while, then snapped 'No!' and hung up. Even he seemed ruffled out of his normal ponderous phlegmatic solidity. There was little of the hearty overfed farmer about him now. Beside him at the long board table, on the right-hand side of their father, his brother Manny sat, more colourless and pasty-faced than ever, his eyelids red and swollen. But he seemed calmer than either his father or elder brother.

Clara, who stood at the window looking down at the road, turned her head and said: 'They're coming.'

Solly and Joel came up very quickly, aware of the tense anxiety with which they were awaited in the beautifully panelled and coolly comfortable Board Room. They entered the room and the old man rasped: 'Well!'

Solly said: 'Easy, father,' and went to sit on the left-hand side of the old man, close to him.

Joel paused at the door and looked at each Isaacs in turn, and they were all conscious of a new gulf between him and them and that it was a creation of his mind. Clara moved quickly towards him and in spite of the moment his mind registered the grace and beauty of her hips. She rested a hand on his sleeve, lightly, just above his wrist. He looked into her face and she saw and felt him grow less withdrawn, less remote. A sudden desire to put her arms about him, to press her body against his took hold of her. Instead, in a quick gesture, shyly self-conscious and wholly submissive, she raised the hand she had touched, kissed the back of it, then rubbed it lightly against her cheek.

'Christ! Not now!' Manny protested.

'Shut up!' Solly said sharply.

'It *is* an odd time and place for the love game,' young Nathan said, but mildly.

'All right!' the old man said; 'all right!'

Clara went back to the window, withdrawn.

'Just leave them alone,' Solly warned.

'It's all right,' Joel murmured, and joined the men at the table.

'I asked you . . . !' The old man raised his eyes to the ceiling.

'He asked for our co-operation,' Solly said abruptly.

'Josiah did?' Young Nathan sounded incredulous.

'Yes.'

'Begin at the beginning,' the old man ordered.

'That's the beginning.'

The old man turned his piercing eyes on Sterning: 'Joel . . . ?'

'It's as Solly said, sir. His first words were "Gentlemen, I called you here to ask for your co-operation, the co-operation of Isaacs Enterprises".'

'I don't believe it!' Manny exclaimed.

'All right!' the old man said. 'You tell it.'

'He was quite open about it,' Solly said evenly. 'He knows that all the business interests in the island are against him and he knows that he will have a very tough job if he is faced with united opposition from the business interests.'

'An impossible job,' Manny cut in.

'The way he put it,' Solly went on, 'the job is not impossible and I am inclined to agree with him; don't you, Joel?'

Joel nodded.

'It's impossible to buck the entire mercantile community,' Manny insisted.

'He said he knew that many merchants thought that. And he said they were wrong. He said he could buck the entire mercantile group and take over everything. He had no illusions about the result. The economy, here on the plain at least, was likely to grind to a halt; there would be dislocation, shortages, massive unemployment, political unrest and possible starvation.'

'And he's ready to risk this?' young Nathan asked.

'Yes. He said if it happened he would simply be forced to go further than he wants to. He would have to nationalize everything, beat the racist drums, drive all capitalists out of the country, and ask for help from the communist world.'

'This is blackmail!' Manny said angrily.

'He called it whitemail.' Solly smiled.

'Will he do it?' the old man asked quietly.

'Yes; he'll do it.'

The old man looked at Joel; and Joel nodded. The old man kept his eyes on Joel's face.

'Will he do it in any case?'

'I don't know,' Solly said.

'What d'you mean?' young Nathan asked.

'Whatever we do,' Manny said impatiently. 'Will he do all the things he threatens even if we co-operate?'

The old man said: 'What do you say, Joel?'

'Like Solly, I don't know,' Joel said.

Clara turned from looking out of the window and moved quickly into the room till she stood behind her father's chair. She put a hand on the old man's shoulder.

'What do you *think*, Joel?'

'I don't think he wants to nationalize or expropriate,' Joel said slowly, thoughtfully. 'At least I don't think he wants to do so now. He understands the problems involved, sees the difficulties too clearly.'

'Then call his bluff,' Manny said.

'But he isn't bluffing, is he, Joel?' the old man murmured.

'No, sir.'

'Go on, Solly,' the old man commanded.

'That's all, really,' Solly said. 'With us on his side the others would soon fall in line, or, at least, accept the new dispensation. He made it clear that he wouldn't then have to resort to extreme measures.'

'And our reward?' Manny asked softly.

'We become the government's principal adviser and agent on all trading and business matters; we get a basic commission of two per cent; you can be sure we'll make a lot out of it.'

'And we'll have power,' young Nathan murmured, 'a great deal of power.'

The old man had been studying Joel's face searchingly. Now, he half-turned and tilted his head upward till he could look into Clara's eyes. For the space of a quarter of

a minute father and daughter communed silently, then the
old man turned back and looked at his sons and son-in-law
sitting waiting on both sides of the long table. The old
man knew what he had to do; and the knowledge and the
mental effort needed for what had to be done made him
conscious of how tired he was, of how heavily the years
weighed on him these days. He tried to shrug off the
heaviness but it persisted. He sighed.

'All right, Joel. What is it? You predicted this thing; and
it has come to pass. We are safe and he asks for our help
because we followed your policies. Sure, most of us were
against your line. I myself was all for spending a lot of
money to try and stop him. So were the others. Perhaps
only Solly was with you, but only with half his heart
because he's a born compromiser. Clara couldn't come
into it because she's your wife . . .' He used his hands and
lips, miming out the rest of his thought on that aspect.
'The thing is, it came out as you said and you saved us.
But you are not satisfied. So what is it, Joel?'

Joel looked at the old man, then down at the table-top,
then back at the old man, and finally, up at Clara, standing behind the old man, her hand on his shoulder, her
index finger rubbing his sticking-out ear in a gesture of
absent-minded affection.

'I hope we're not in for a morality . . .' Manny began;
but the old man snapped 'Shut up!' and Manny swallowed
and was silent.

'Well, Joel?' The old man's voice was gentle to the point
of tenderness.

Joel kept looking at Clara. She thought: Like a drown-
ing man clutching at a piece of floating straw. He's a weak
man, really, and it isn't fair that one so weak should also
be so morally scrupulous. Then, with a tinge of bitterness
to it, the thought-pattern rounded itself off: And I'm the
victim of it all, of his weakness, his scrupulousness, his
hatred of this world of business and the ugliness of island
life; he blames me for all of them as a child gets angry
with its mother because it rains and the child cannot go
out to play.

'We're waiting, Joel,' she murmured, something of her
feeling coming through.

'He wants us to become his cannibals,' Joel said evenly. 'To do his dirty work and consume our own kind.'

'That's not what he wants!' Solly snapped hotly.

'Remember you sold him to us,' young Nathan said quietly.

'Stop it! All of you!' the old man ordered; then, to Joel: 'Is that what he really wants, Joel?'

'You know what I mean.' Joel made an effort to speak calmly. 'Whether he consciously wants it or not is unimportant. What is important is that doing what he wants will in fact mean our consuming our own kind. You know it, sir!' Emotion broke through. 'His proposal that half of all stocks and shares in all industries should be locally owned is a calculated blow at the foreign-owned businesses here. He told us himself there isn't enough money in the island to buy half of all the foreign-owned businesses here, which is why he thought up the device of the government taking up the shares and paying for them with low-interest bearing Bonds redeemable in twenty-five years. In practice the government will issue Bonds in exchange for half of a company's stocks or shares. These Bonds will begin to bear three and a half per cent interest from the date when they become negotiable, which is a quarter of a century hence. Meanwhile the government will, in addition to its taxes, collect dividends from its newly acquired and unpaid-for shares which will earn anything from seven per cent to fifteen per cent per annum.'

'So this is robbery,' the old man said softly. 'It was because I feared this that I wanted him stopped. You said he couldn't be stopped and you were right. So now he does what we feared he would do. You said if he did it, it would be for the good of the people. So?'

'Do we have to be involved in his destruction of the foreign businesses?'

'I see,' the old man said. 'You want us to refuse to co-operate with him. Solly, what would happen if we said to this Mister Josiah: "No sir; we do not like you; we do not like what you plan to do; we will not co-operate with you; we are business people, not politicians; leave us alone to do our business." Will he leave us alone, heh?'

'No sir,' Solly murmured, looking at Joel.

'Heh, Joel, will he?'

'No,' Joel said.

'All right then,' the old man said, forcing himself to a briskness he did not feel; 'let us face facts. It is a nice word you use, that cannibalism: man eat man, dog eat dog, cat eat cat. But don't we do it all the time in business? How do you think we made the money we have today? In business you must be a cannibal; you must eat your rivals or they will eat you. This is nothing new. And this Mister Josiah comes to us not because he likes us but because he wants to do something and he looks for the skills and know-how to get the job done. If we don't do it, he will find others to do it. And if we refuse him he will consider us his enemies and he would have to be a fool to want to leave his enemies alone at a time like this, especially if they are as strong as we are. So? I promise you that if we refuse to help him he will not leave us alone. It stands to reason. Unless he's a fool, of course. Is he a fool, Joel?'

'No.'

'So there we have it: cannibalism is part of business, it is how we got rich and powerful; if we don't do what Josiah wants others will and they will be the cannibals and we will be the eaten ones. And one more thing, Joel; when people get to where we are, when they have what we have, they cannot just resign or withdraw. When the politician loses an election he can withdraw till his turn comes around. We cannot.' Suddenly the old man seemed to run out of all stamina. His face and body seemed to shrink. 'I don't like it any more than you do but I'm too old to run away from where I was born. Besides, I don't want to.'

'So we go along with Josiah,' Manny said, breaking the long silence that followed the old man's last words.

'We have no choice,' young Nathan said. 'In any case, that's what both Solly and Joel advocated; and Clara and Papa went with them and so we went along. Come on, Joel, admit it; this was your line! I agree we thought you mad but you were right.'

'There is always choice,' Solly said.

The compromiser, the old man thought with weary

tenderness: half hard-headed businessman, half dreamer like Joel. And it is you two who must deal with the new ruler.

'Yes,' the old man said quietly. 'You can always choose to either live or die, and even when you're as near the grave as I am, you still find yourself choosing to live.'

Wash your hands of it now, Clara thought; and the thought became an act of will. Do it now! I'll go along; I'll be with you; look at me, Joel! Look!

And when he raised his eyes to her face she thought it was in response to the force of her mind, so she concentrated harder, mirroring the thought in her eyes so that he should see it.

. . . We'll go away, just you and I, to your beloved Europe; to Israel, if you like, and start again. It's not too late for that. They'll give me something as my share of the business; enough for us to live on. Tell them! And then we'll walk out together, free! . . .

Joel shifted his gaze from Clara's face back to the old man's.

The old man said: 'You yourself told us he will make things better for the poor.'

Yes, Joel agreed silently; yes.

'. . . And you know business, especially international business, can take care of itself. The home firms can put pressure on Whitehall and the State Department, and London and Washington in turn can, if they wish, make Josiah listen as all of us put together here cannot. Don't misunderstand me, boy, but I think you're *looking* for trouble. If he's going to do what you want, which is to better things for the poor, and if it suits our business too, then I would have thought you would be happy. Remember the people you're concerned about are not concerned about us: they would break and sell us tomorrow if they got a chance. And many of them make no secret of their anti-Semitism.'

'All right,' Joel said, trying to hide his unhappiness. And because of his own spiritual misery he did not see the unhappiness mirrored in the look that passed between Solly and Clara.

Old Nathan Isaacs closed his eyes and leaned back for a few minutes like one summoning his last remaining reserves of strength; then he straightened up, opened his eyes and announced briskly:

'Frankie Freeways came to see me at breakfast this morning. You know why. Told him I couldn't tell him anything till I'd met with the directors here but I warned him not to hope for anything. Don't suppose we can give him a little campaign money . . .' The briskness went out of the old man's voice and a wistful note crept in. 'Frankie and I went to the same school, you know; he was younger, of course, but he was in my House the year I was House Captain. Nice man, too; did some good work for the country.' The old man looked at Solly, not as his son but as Chairman of the Board of Isaacs Enterprises, and it made quite a difference. 'How you want me to tell him?'

'I'll do it for you,' Solly offered.

The old man shook his head. 'That would be cruel.'

Joel looked at his watch and said: 'Josiah wants to make the preliminary announcement in his midday news bulletin so that it can be raised in parliament tonight. He's expecting to hear from us about now.'

'I want to tell Frankie before it's on the radio,' the old man said. 'Clara, come with me to Solly's office.' He got up and Clara went to him.

'Are we agreed?' Solly asked.

'Yes,' the old man said harshly; 'we're agreed, aren't we, Joel?'

'We're agreed,' Joel said.

Solly picked up the telephone and dialled the number that would connect him with Josiah working at the great Presidential desk. After a while he said:

'Solomon Isaacs here, sir. My Board has just agreed to your request . . . We're at your service . . . Yes, sir. Unanimously . . . We want to make our contribution . . .'

Those watching saw Solly's jaw suddenly tighten as he clenched his teeth.

'. . . If making our margin also helps the country . . . Yes, sir, we're all satisfied with two per cent . . .'

At last Solly put down the telephone and stood still,

staring into space till some of the anger left him, then he shrugged slightly and lit a cigarette.

In Solly's office old Nathan Isaacs spoke on the telephone to his friend and former schoolmate, Franklyn F. Freeways, former Prime Minister and Minister of Financial Affairs, and now the man who would oppose Albert Josiah in the Presidential election due at the end of three weeks. He said: 'I'm sorry, Frankie, and take the advice of your friend and don't stand . . .' but before he could complete the sentence the line went dead at the other end. The old man looked at Clara and said, but without anger: 'He hung up. The bloody fool: this boy Josiah is going to mash him up.'

'Isn't that better sometimes?'

'Stop that, girl. I gave you a business head. Don't you go on like Joel.'

Solly came in and Clara asked: 'Where's Joel?'

'He's just left.'

She grabbed the phone but the downstairs receptionist told her Mr. Sterning had just driven away.

Josiah rose from the great desk and walked briskly out of the President's office past the Cabinet Room, down the passage, past the busy administrative offices and into the large conference room. Everybody in the room looked up as he entered and there was something of the air of a headmaster walking into a room of model pupils. All the Ministers were present, each sharing a desk with the Permanent Secretary from his Ministry. There was a pile of files on each desk. A large blackboard against the wall farthest from the door completed the impression of a postgraduate class at work.

The day after the Cabinet had gone into continuous emergency session Josiah had started these three-hour daily study classes that began at nine in the morning and ended at noon. He had told his colleagues that as representatives of the people they had to educate themselves into being fit for their jobs. And so days had been set aside when specialists from the university had come to instruct the Ministers in the history of their country, its economic and social and constitutional structure, its people and their

diverse racial and geographic origins and their social
habits and cultural history. Other days had been set aside
for each Minister, in turn, to explain in very great detail
the structure and function of his Ministry and its place in
the overall national picture. The first Minister who had
performed this particular task had been Mr. Richard
Young, the Minister of Youth and Community Affairs.
Mr. Young had been given the best part of a week in
which to prepare himself but it had soon become clear that
he had not done his homework and that he expected to get
away with 'fine language' and his: 'My Permanent Secretary will fill out the details for those of you who are not
familiar with them.' When he finished and sat down, obviously pleased with himself, Josiah had questioned him,
quietly, coldly, in devastating detail till it was plain to all
present that Mr. Young had only the haziest notion of the
structure and workings of his Ministry. Then Josiah had
said: 'A teacher must prove qualification before he or she
is permitted to teach our children, a doctor before he can
heal the sick; the people under you, Mr. Minister, your
Permanent Secretary and the lowliest established civil servant in your Ministry have had to prepare themselves for
their jobs, have proven fitness . . .'

'I protest!' little Young had begun angrily.

But Josiah had gone on. 'Fitness for the job is the least
we should expect of you, of all of us. If I were as ignorant
of my job I would resign!'

Little Richard Young had been stunned into silent
immobility.

The classes, after that, had been serious and hardwork-
ing affairs; and the next Minister who had held forth on
the work of his Ministry had come very well prepared.

Josiah looked across the room to where K. E. Powers,
Ralph Smith and Mabel Anderson worked as a little
group, their desks close to each other.

'I've just had a call from Solomon Isaacs,' he said, ad-
dressing Powers directly. 'They'll do what we want. I want
your people to become difficult with all foreign firms. You
know, permits, licenses, things like that.'

Powers nodded and whispered to his Permanent Secretary who left the room to phone the new directive down the line.

Josiah turned his head till he was looking at where the Minister of Industrial Development sat.

'You know what to do.'

The Minister nodded.

'Fine. Don't hesitate to consult; the matter is delicate and I'm available.'

Again the Minister of Industrial Development nodded.

Josiah beckoned to Mathias, the Minister of External Affairs, then walked down the centre of the big room, between the desks, till he stood by the blackboard. When Mathias joined him both the blackboard and the blackness of the Minister of External Affairs showed up Josiah's brownness, which was striking because he had projected so strongly the image of himself as a black man that everybody accepted him as a black man.

He said to Mathias: 'The howl will begin within the next hour so you'd better get down to your office. As long as we didn't have anybody to do the job for us they were prepared to wait and see. Now that we have the Isaacs crowd they will know we mean business. Refer anything from London or Washington to me. And you'd better not bother about these seminars till we are over this thing.'

'I'm worried,' Mathias said.

'Good!' Josiah said, 'so am I. Only fools don't worry. But this is only the beginning. The hard things are still to come, and from our own people.' Then he turned and walked back to the door, leaving Mathias deep in thought.

When Josiah was out of the room Smith and Powers signalled to Mathias. He went to them.

'What happens?' Smith asked.

'He's worried too,' Mathias said with a touch of wonder. 'Says only fools don't worry.'

'That's our boy,' Powers said, then: 'Because of this merchant thing?'

'He expects fireworks from London and Washington so I'm going to my office.' Mathias looked searchingly at Powers. 'Know something, he sounded soft just now, and kind and human and I thought it would be wonderful to have someone like that for a friend. And he said the hard things are still to come and from our own people.'

'Will he pull this off?' Smith asked. 'We'll be in a mess if he doesn't.'

You heard him say he's got the Isaacs crowd,' Mathias said.

'International big business is rough,' Smith insisted.

'I think he can do it,' Powers said, adding, almost reluctantly: 'I believe in him . . .'

'I'm beginning to, too,' Mathias said worriedly.

Smith made a slight gesture with his head. 'Don't laugh, fellows: he's a boy to me in years but I can't speak to him man to man; it's not exactly fear—you know how it is . . .'

And because they knew how it was the other two held their peace.

Josiah walked past the administrative office then changed his mind and turned back. There were flutters of excitement—men scrambling to their feet, women tugging at dresses and blouses and patting their hair—as he walked through the general office, tapped on Stanhope's door and went in.

Young Simpson, who was with Stanhope, rose to leave. Josiah waved him back.

'What I have to say concerns you too, indeed it concerns all public servants. I have been informed, Stanhope, that you have again told senior public servants to defy political instructions.'

'No, sir,' Stanhope murmured evenly, 'you were wrongly informed.'

'I think not, Mr. Presidential Secretary! Did you not veto three appointments?'

'Yes; because they were contrary to regulations governing appointments to the Public Service. If these appointments had been made by the Services Commission——'

'Of which you are the chairman!'

'Yes, sir. They would have been constitutional and valid.'

'Tell me, Stanhope. If I had personally recommended

these three appointments to your Commission, would you have confirmed them?'

He really wants me, Stanhope thought calmly, looking up at Josiah leaning against the door. 'I don't know, sir. The question did not arise.'

'You vetoed them on procedural grounds purely?'

'Yes, sir.'

'Without reference to the other members of your Commission?'

'I never act without reference to the Commission on such matters.'

'And they are with you?'

'Both the Constitution and Service Regulations are explicit on this point, sir.'

'All right! Now I ask you again: if I had personally recommended these three appointments what would you have done?'

'The question never arose, sir.'

'It has arisen now! Do you know anything about the three persons involved?'

'I do.'

'Enough to assess character and capabilities?'

'I think so.'

'I repeat then: if I had personally recommended them to your Commission what would you have done?'

'Only the Commission, as a whole, could do anything. With respect, sir, I think you should put that question to a sitting of the Commission.'

'You should have been a politician,' Josiah murmured sarcastically.

'You are the politician,' Stanhope said evenly.

Josiah shrugged slightly, a flash of irritation passing over his face. 'All right! Let us try once more. You know enough about these people, you have looked into their training, their capabilities, their backgrounds, their characters with sufficient care to have formed some sort of opinion. Can we agree on that?'

'Yes, sir.'

'The other members of your Commission would have expected you to brief them on these people. Right?'

'Yes, sir.'

'They would also have expected to be guided by your assessment and judgment. Is that right?'

'Yes, sir.'

'All right. We are back at the edge of the water: let us go in. Would you have recommended appointment or not?'

'I cannot answer that, sir.'

'You mean you won't, don't you?' Suddenly Josiah was angry. 'Come, man! Tell the truth! You won't! Isn't that it?'

'Yes, sir,' Stanhope said evenly. 'I will not tell you. In the interest of a non-political and independent public service those who framed our Constitution saw fit to put all civil service appointments in the hands of the Services Commission and provided freedom from pressure to that Commission. One of the guarantees of the freedom of the Commission is the provision that only in the event of a grave miscarriage of justice being proven can its decisions be voided; another is that no individual member of the Commission shall be called upon to reveal his stand on the question of any appointment.'

'I'm the head of state,' Josiah whispered with suppressed fury, 'chosen by the people who will confirm their choice very soon. As head of state I order you to answer me.'

'I'm sorry, sir. I cannot. I took an oath to uphold the Constitution.'

'Against the interest of the people?' Josiah thundered, wild with rage now. He turned blazing eyes to young Simpson: 'This gentleman! This Presidential Secretary! This head of the civil service! This gentleman who has been polished and made smooth by our former imperial masters! He tells me of his oath to uphold the Constitution. And I ask him: Against whom? Pray tell me, sir, Mr. Presidential Secretary! If I need to make certain appointments to serve the interests of the people and you block those and tell me you are upholding the Constitution, I ask you, is the Constitution against the people?'

Josiah swung about abruptly and stormed out of the room.

It was a long time before Stanhope was aware that

young Simpson was speaking to him, urgently, almost
pleadingly. 'It is only an instrument, sir, a document of
broad policies and principles and this one was written
under the influence of the occupying power. For all these
years old Moses Joshua has used it. We need something
else to go forward . . .'

'Then change it according to the rules!' Stanhope
snapped angrily. 'Now get out! I took an oath to uphold it,
faults and all! I don't expect you and your master to
understand that!'

'Mr. Stanhope, sir . . .'

'Get out!'

Young Simpson went out, trying to control the growing
resentment he felt against Stanhope.

After a while Stanhope rose from his desk and went to
the window. He was startled by the peaceful picture outside: the trees stood calm and majestic, hinting at un-
tapped oceans of tranquillity, and the grass suggested a
world made up of carefree Sunday morning picnics.

Back at the Presidential desk Josiah wondered briefly, as
a passing thought, whether John Stanhope was a political
idiot or a man who cared nothing about his people. Then
he pushed the thought aside and continued his work. He
worked steadily for two hours then he straightened up,
turned his neck from side to side loosening its tense muscles; then he relaxed all his body, slumping back in the
great chair, and allowed only his mind to work. But even
as he thought out the problem he knew that he had really
decided on its solution right there in Stanhope's office
while they were still jabbing words at each other: from
that moment till this the details had been working themselves out at one level of his mind, at what is now called
the subconscious level, while allowing the other areas of
his mind to grapple with the mass of important documents
on the desk. A man's most dangerous and tricky possession is his mind: the thought brought a quick, flickering
smile. He leaned forward, pressed his finger on a switch
and spoke into the tiny black box that connected him by
sound to the general office: 'Send Mr. Simpson here,
please.' He removed his finger and the circuit was broken.

Simpson knocked and came in. Josiah rose and walked round the desk to the young man.

'We'll have to do something about the Services Commission, Andy.'

'I know, sir. I tried to reason with Mr. Stanhope.'

'Don't misunderstand him, Andy. I have no doubt about his integrity. I don't think he's against me or us. It is just that for him the Constitution of this country is more important than are its people; in the name of legality he will hold up progress. The law and regulations governing the Services Commission will have to be changed, but we can't afford to wait till after the election to make these appointments that he's blocked. They are part of the pattern for winning the elections decisively: you know that.'

'Yes, sir.'

'D'you think anything could be done to win him over?'

'No, sir,' Simpson murmured reluctantly. 'I tried.'

'Then we have no choice, Andy. I want to see the two other members of the Commission as soon as possible. Arrange for me to have dinner with them tonight, and I don't want Stanhope to know anything about it or to contact them before I've seen them.' Josiah sensed Simpson's unhappiness. 'I dislike this as much as you do, but what are we to do? Abandon everything because one man, an honourable but misguided man, stands in our way?'

'How far do we go, sir?'

'You know the answer, Andy. You tell me: do we give up everything if he resists?'

'We can sidestep him.'

'You know the country and you know our people. Tell me, if we sidestep him how will the country interpret it?'

'I see your point.'

'All right! And if the country tells him that he's scored a victory it will strengthen his hand and comfort our enemies.'

'I'll arrange for the dinner, sir.'

'Just a minute, Andy. I'd like to hear you answer the question you asked me. How far *do* we go?'

'All the way,' young Simpson said firmly, 'if he does not give way.'

'And you know what that might mean?'

'Yes, sir.'

'There are no easy ways, Andy; no painless methods of breaking out of situations such as ours.'

'Doesn't he understand this, sir?'

'I don't think so; I don't think he wants to.'

'Does he understand what might be involved for him?'

'I'm sure he does, Andy. If you doubt me you try and explain it to him.'

'Then we have to break him,' Simpson said thoughtfully, unhappily.

'Yes, Andy: a decent and honest man who has served his country faithfully and who now stands stubbornly in the way of its progress. There is one consolation. Like old F.F. he will never do anything to subvert the legally constituted government so we don't have to do anything more drastic than force his retirement. See what I meant when I told you—all of you—that we'd sometimes have to pay a high price and that there would be times when we would hate the nature of the price.'

'He'll only be retired,' Simpson snapped, shaking free of his emotional mood and remembering how Stanhope had ordered him out.

'The thing is that's he's forcing our hand,' Josiah said, turning back to his desk.

Part Three

THE EXECUTORS

THE SUN was going down now, and darkness was racing on the land from the east, making black shadows of the higher mountains far behind the hills where the man with the rifle lay waiting.

The man listened and grew tense as a distant, steady, hum came faintly to him. He adjusted his body, making it as comfortable as possible. He had an urge, now, to test the rifle by firing a round . . . What if it would not fire? What if there were some flaw? This was something he should have done an hour ago when he had first assembled the thing. Too late now.

He concentrated on the approaching sound, determinedly, in order to get away from the wave of uncertainty. It worked: he grew calm, remembered the needs of the land and what had to be done.

The sound came nearer, grew louder, became identifiable.

Josiah's limousine, preceded by two motor-cycle police escorts, and followed by two more, was drawing near.

The man put his finger to the trigger and looked through the sights that brought the road close up.

The sound of the engines was close now.

The man prayed: Dear God, forgive me. It is not what I want to do; it is what has to be done for the sake of the land and its people. It is for this only that I break your sixth Commandment, for the sake of the land and its people, for he is destroying all that is beautiful in both. Amen.

Then the man braced himself.

The limousine came easily round the bend in the road and through the sights he could see how worried the preoccupied Josiah was . . .

CHAPTER ONE

THE PRESIDENTIAL ELECTION which took place six weeks after the death of old Moses Joshua was the briefest and most orderly in the history of the island. The two candidates were Albert Josiah and Franklyn F. Freeways. Josiah had the support of the Cabinet of Ministers, the trades unions, the farmers' organization, and the organization of civil servants (which for the first time in the island's history abandoned its stand of non-involvement in party politics). As the President of the civil servants' organization explained it: 'There is no sense in servants of the government trying to be politically neutral when the government pays their salaries and the needs of the country have dictated the setting up of one-party government.' All this had come about shortly after the Presidential Secretary had suddenly left the island on six months' pre-retirement leave. These developments had led Martha Lee to question, in her weekly political column, the legality of Mr. Freeways's candidacy. Her point was that if the law of the land permitted only one political party, and the official candidate of that party was Mr. Josiah, then it was as illegal for Mr. Freeways to stand as it would be for him to form a rival political party. She discussed the pros and cons of this point in great and funny detail and for a week the 'Letters To The Editor' page was crammed with interested and interesting responses from readers. Then Josiah summoned Max Johnson and all talk and writing on the point immediately ceased. Martha Lee was dispatched to one of the other islands to cover an important conference and her promised follow-up article on the Freeways candidacy never appeared.

Franklyn Freeways had the support of the mainly white and coloured upper and middle classes of the towns, the support of the majority of well-established professional people—the older doctors, dentists and lawyers—as well as that of those who ran small independent family businesses. Behind these groups, quietly and covertly, the handful of big foreign-owned companies worked hard for Freeways and put money into his campaign.

The local merchants bided their time, waiting to see which way the wind would blow, how the cat would jump, on the alert for any sign from the Isaacs empire. Unknown to the rest of the mercantile community Josiah had told Solly Isaacs and Joel Sterning that he expected the Isaacs empire to maintain an attitude of strict neutrality throughout the campaign. 'There is no political alliance between us,' he had said casually, 'only a business arrangement. You're doing business with me for a margin, not out of conviction or sentiment; let us keep it like that.' And so, in this election, the Isaacs empire remained strictly neutral.

Towards the last days of the campaign the rest of the mercantile community had grown suspicious. Perhaps the Isaacs neutrality was more apparent than real; perhaps there was some deep dark plot behind it. The quiet but open support the sugar interests were giving Josiah added to mercantile suspicion. Then, eight days before polling day, marching supporters of Josiah encountered marching supporters of Freeways and there was a brief, sharp eruption of violence. Because the Freeways supporters were mainly pale-skinned and well-dressed and the Josiah supporters mainly dark-skinned and ill-clad the violence assumed dimensions of race and colour. The police very quickly put a stop to the fighting. But many merchants were greatly alarmed for they saw it as the beginning of racial violence directed at all those who were fair-skinned.

One of the mercantile organizations petitioned the Cabinet to suspend the election. The Cabinet ignored the petition. First one, then another, then another of the local merchants sent out feelers to Josiah's campaign headquarters: if there was a shortage of transport, cars and trucks could be made available; printing bills could be met; free liquor for campaign functions.

At a great outdoor rally Josiah told a gathering of more than fifty thousand of his supporters of all the wonderful offers of help and money and transport and liquor he had suddenly received from the local mercantile community. He turned it into something that made his vast audience roar with great gusts of mocking laughter.

And when the votes were counted a few days later less than five per cent of the total had cast their ballots for Franklyn F. Freeways. And for twenty-four hours all life on the island was transformed into a jubilant fiesta celebrating the end of one age and the glorious and hopeful beginning of another. And Josiah, the new President, moved among his people, laughing with them, embracing them, and feeding the dream that made each man and woman, each boy and girl, self-consciously aware of a new sense of dignity and purpose in being alive and belonging to this land and this people . . .

Martha Lee returned three months after the inauguration of President Josiah. On the last day of the conference in the neighbouring island she had received a cable from Max Johnson ordering her to London and then the United Nations. She had tried to reach Max by phone that same night but the distant voice of the man at the night desk, guarded and withdrawn and suggesting more plainly than words the spirit of 'I'm not getting involved in this one' made it plain to Martha that Max did not want her to reach him. So she had followed instructions and spent three months in Europe and the States, sending occasional pieces about the doings of expatriate islanders and her weekly column which dealt now with the events of the great wide world instead of island affairs.

Now the great plane had landed and she was ready to disembark. The young man from immigration greeted her warmly, as one welcoming an old friend. Immediately, she felt better, more able to bear the mood of quiet depression that had been with her these past three months. This was home and it was good to be home.

The young man said: 'Want me to arrange about your baggage, Miss Lee?'

'Please,' she said. Nothing like coming home; nothing in the world. He took the luggage tickets from her, wrote a quick note and gave tickets and note to a porter to take to the customs house.

'Go along with this porter and they'll see you through quickly, Miss Lee.'

'Thanks very much.' Very good to be home. She looked quickly at the small cluster of people who stood waiting. There was no one she knew, no one to welcome her.

In the customs shed another friendly young man asked the usual questions then let her through without opening her luggage. There was still no one she knew outside the customs shed so she told the porter to find her a taxi. Then she saw, among the airport taxis and limousines from the hotels come especially to pick up tourists, a private car that seemed familiar and that was having difficulty getting by the hustling taxis. She went to the porter and told him, pantomime-wise, to defer trying to get a taxi.

At last the car got through and inched its way to the curb where Martha stood. Joel Sterning came quickly out of it and walked round the car to her.

An airport policeman sauntered up and said only taxis could stop there. Sterning ignored him. The porter explained, a little aggressively: 'He's only picking up the lady.'

Sterning took both Martha's hands.

'It's been a long time.'

'I thought I'd been forgotten.'

'Never!'

And the sudden tightening of his grip was part of the goodness of coming home. The porter, meanwhile, was trying, unsuccessfully, to open the trunk of the car so Sterning turned from Martha to show him how. The policeman sauntered away muttering about people not knowing where they were supposed to park. When he was out of earshot the porter snapped: 'Wait till Josiah fix him! Fat bloodsucker! Poleece, hah!' Then, the trunk finally opened, he packed in Martha's luggage, banged the trunk shut, collected his tip and went off, still inveighing against the 'fat bloodsucker poleece'.

When they were clear of the heavy airport traffic Joel slowed down, then, half a mile farther, he turned into a lay-by that faced out to sea. He stopped the car and switched on the interior light though it was still early evening and with much light in the sky. He studied her face closely for a long while then he switched off the light.

'How was it?' he asked.

'I should have enjoyed it. In other circumstances it would have been wonderful.'

'It could have been if you'd called me.'

'And precipitated an open scandal? In any case I wanted to be alone.'

He was tempted to argue the point, but changed his mind.

'See Stanhope?'

'Yes. He took me to dinner and the theatre, to dinner and the opera, to dinner and a concert; and it was marvelous each time and I was ashamed because I could not give him and the wonderful food and entertainment the appreciation they deserved.'

'How was he?'

A sudden wave of impatient irritation swept over Martha.

'How do you expect him to be? Full of beans at being forced out of his job?' Then her mood changed. She touched the back of Sterning's hand in a quick gesture of apology. 'Sorry. I don't know why I always turn on you. He tried not to show anything but it came through.'

'Tell you when he'd return?'

'Not till his leave's up.'

'Josiah indicated to Solly that he expects Isaacs Enterprises not to hire John when he comes back.'

'And they'll obey,' she said bitterly.

'As you say. They are now the official government agents at two per cent.'

She tried to look into his eyes in the fading light; she wondered what she would see there. But it was too dark to see anything but eyes.

'And you, his friend?' She made it as impersonal as possible.

'Nothing's changed,' he said, suppressing the violence he felt. 'He is my friend; he always will be.'

'Be careful, darling, they may need to make him a sacrificial offering to the new day. Anyone near him may get hurt.'

'Are you?' he asked. 'Another sacrificial offering?'

She laughed out loud, a sound made ugly by stridency. 'I'm not important enough, darling. I can be shunted off, as I've just been, into some siding like an unnecessary railway carriage. Besides, they know I can't be against them.'

'That may not be enough for our friend Josiah.'

'Perhaps not. It is not something I want to anticipate: I'm not as religious as you.'

'You will fight for press freedom, I know.'

'Then you know more than I do.'

'Of course you will.'

'There's no of course about it, Joel. It depends on what's involved. You know how important press freedom is to the vast majority of our people.'

'It is one of the basic freedoms, Martha.'

'For you and me, and those like us; not for those who cannot read and live without electricity and running water and scratch the earth like beasts of burden grubbing for a little sustenance. But you know this, so why waste time talking about what we know?'

'Because knowing settles nothing; one is still split—at least, this one is . . . It's good to be able to talk again, I've missed it—and you.'

She felt the stirrings of emotion in him. All he needed was a slight gesture of response and he would let it flow over her, because for this one, now, no matter how it was earlier when he married Clara Isaacs, loving that satisfied wholly had to be the child of calm cool creative thought, the aftermath or accompaniment to a meeting of minds. So it had always been between them; and this had often made their loving appear bereft of passion.

She said, very carefully so that he should not feel called on to commit himself: 'D'you want to take me home?'

'You don't want me to.'

'It may be a mess.'

'It isn't for that only. It is to be with you; to talk or to be silent.'

'I know.' She touched him and now he had his slight gesture.

He pulled her to him and kissed her tenderly, lingeringly.

'Even to make a mess of it would be better than not to be with you.'

'I've missed you too,' she said. 'Take me home if you want to.'

'Your friends are waiting for you,' he said. 'Fact is you're overdue at your welcome-home party.'

'To hell with that,' she said briskly. 'Take me home.'

'The party is at your home.'

She turned away from him and looked across the harbour. A ship, majestic and unusually white in the fading light, rode the vast ocean in lonely splendour. Like people, Martha thought irrelevantly, not quite sure of the meaning of the thought.

'This Max's idea?' she asked softly, not turning from the sea.

'Yes.'

'All right. Let's go home.'

He felt the woman withdraw and grow coldly frosty; guessed at the reason for it. He had feared that she might react in this way and had tried to warn Max Johnson, but Max had been in no mood to be warned; we rarely are when there is a need to atone.

'He meant well, Martha.'

Martha turned her face to him and it was a thing of shadows; and because he knew her there was no need to see her face to recognize the mood. He started the car,

reversed a little, then swung it on to the highway that led
to Mosesville.

The town seemed unchanged, unchanging, as it was
when old Moses Joshua straddled it, and the island, as the
bragging, blustering, bullying, wheedling manipulator. The
old bully was dead but the town remained, unchanged,
undisturbed by his going; almost as though he had never
been. And when the young man who has inherited the
Palace and its power reached the end of his reign the town
would still be here; grown a little and perhaps with a few
newer and taller buildings, more cars, a more efficient
public transport system, but basically the same, equally
undisturbed by his going. The town, like man in the mass,
will always outlast and therefore conquer the individual.

She lit a cigarette and in the brief flare of the light
Sterning saw, before he turned his gaze back to the road,
her face as a skeletal death-mask, drawn and bloodless.
This, he realized, absorbing the shock, was how she would
be immediately after death and before decay takes over.

He said: 'Martha!'

And the intensity of his disturbance reached her, forcing her to come alive with concern for him. 'What is it,
Joel?'

He shook his head as though she could see, then added:
'The light plays tricks.'

'Duppy tricks?'

'Duppy tricks,' he said, alarmed, as so often before, by
this woman's capacity for reaching at his unexpressed
thoughts and feeling.

It was dark when they reached Martha's house; all light
had fled from the sky and neither moon nor stars had yet
appeared, so the heavens were a deep black ceiling. They
heard the noise of the party before Sterning brought the
car to a stop.

'Want me to come in?'

'No; I'm feeling ugly and racial and you deserve better.'

'Shall I come back?'

'I'll be uglier when this is done; uglier and more hate-
ful.'

'I'll phone you later,' he said.

She touched his hand and walked towards the house and the strong savoury smell of roasting sucking-pig coming from the back of the house. Then, abruptly, she swung about and went back to where Joel was taking her luggage out of the car. She took two big bags, one in each hand.

'I think it was the racial thing that made me play the grand lady. That's why I wouldn't marry you, Joel, wouldn't take you from your Clara. I'd never be able to be bitchy or nasty to you without the fear that it might be the racial thing and that would be unbearable and you don't deserve that kind of mental block in a relationship.'

'It isn't a block now,' he said.

'Then why did I come back to help carry my bags? There is the consciousness of it; and for me that is a block. Sin only exists in our recognition of it.'

'We've been over this before!' His exasperation came through.

The door of Martha's house opened and a gust of human sound burst out. The stars, now, were beginning to show themselves, and in the west there was a hint of the moon about to rise.

A woman's voice yelled: 'She's come!'

'I know; but we each live with ourselves first of all, before we live with anybody else.'

'Your standards are impossible, unattainable,' he snapped.

'Isn't that your problem too? Would you want me to come to feel about you as you feel about Clara?' She turned her head and saw a group of tipsy people bearing down on them. She touched his hand and said, hurriedly: 'People like us shouldn't marry. Our standards are all wrong. That's why I feel sorry for your Clara.'

'I shouldn't have married her?'

How he yearns for me to be possessive, she thought and said: 'For her sake—no: or anyone else.' She was aware of the people about them now. 'Call me soon, please.'

'I will; 'bye.' He turned to his car.

Big Max Johnson, towering above the welcoming group, glass in hand, roared: 'Stay and celebrate, Sterning!'

The back wheels of the car screeched as Sterning got away fast.

'He'll never stop running,' Johnson said disgustedly.

Martha supervised the collecting of her baggage and the group went into the little house. They were all there, the officers of the Press Union and the senior members of the working Press. They had all been waiting for the best part of two hours; and while waiting they had consumed vast quantities of liquor so talk was loud and uninhibited. They welcomed her with the noisy demonstrativeness that liquor engenders. Only one colleague, the normally aloof Social Reporter, seemed distressed by Martha's homecoming. The others had steadily fed her rum punch on an empty stomach and now she sat weeping loudly and all by herself in a corner, repeating over and over that nobody loved her. When she saw Martha her weeping took an aggressive turn and she blamed Martha for the fact that nobody loved her. In the end someone took the Social Reporter to the back and fed her. She came back half an hour later, considerably sobered by the food, steady, not weeping, her normal aloof self.

Max Johnson made sure that there was always too much noise and too many people about for Martha to be able to talk to him. And when the eating and drinking were done and it was close on midnight, he hustled everybody out and tried to get away himself. But Martha, anticipating this, was waiting at the gate.

'Is this all there is to it, Max?'

'Yes! Did you want roses and champagne as well!'

'You know what I mean.'

'Well don't be a damn fool. You know the score as well as I do.'

'And all you have to do is supply liquor and food and everything is made right. Even the best of you whites cannot help being arrogant and patronizing with us.'

'That's nastier than I thought even you could be,' Max cut in angrily.

'Fraternize with them a little, say a few nice words, declare your belief in racial equality, marry one of them, and you have a license to walk all over them, to use and manipulate them. I think you'll either have to be humiliated racially, as we have been, or you'll never get over the built-in racial arrogance that has been nurtured in even the best of you for centuries.'

'You're lucky you're a woman!'

'You going to let that stop you?'

There was a long, long silence, then Max sighed heavily.

'Have you done?'

'But for one thing.'

'What?'

'I know it's an impertinence on my part—sir . . .'

'I've had enough of your crap——'

'Have you sold out to Josiah? That why I had to be out of the way?'

'You listen to me——'

'Because if it does I'm not for sale . . .'

'You go to hell!'

He walked away from her.

'I'll see *you* there first!' she yelled after his receding back.

Her anger was like dry ice; her body was under control, not shaking as with hot anger. She stood there till the tail-light of his car disappeared. Then she went into the house.

The maid, Lydia, was collecting glasses and emptying ashtrays. She had opened all doors and windows and a cool freshness was spreading through the house. After a while Lydia came into the sitting-room with Martha's golden Labrador, Sheba. When the dog saw Martha she went silently hysterical.

'She miss you—we both miss you—Miss Martha.'

Martha fondled the dog. 'I missed you too.'

'How was it? Over there.'

'Not like here,' Martha said thoughtfully. How do you tell a person like this of things that are outside the range of her experience? How do you make her know what it feels like to have your self-assurance and sense of humanity undermined in a thousand subtle ways by the whites among whom you were—to such a point that you were ready to deny them their humanity? 'Not at all like here, Lydia. You won't like it. It will upset you.'

'Because of the cold?' Lydia asked. 'My sister over there is always bawling about the cold.'

'That too, yes. But really because it isn't home. You know, for us who are coloured and who are of the western world, who live in the western world, only this chain of islands is home. Once we leave these islands we're outsiders. We're outsiders in continental America, in Europe, in Africa, in Asia. Our ancestors came from these great land masses but they are no longer home to us. And so we're outsiders even among those who look like us but who are not of these islands. I think this is true for even the white-skinned islanders. We are a new breed, a kind of outpost of the future trapped here in the twentieth century. I think we would have a sense of being insiders, of belonging, in the twenty-first or twenty-second centuries. In today's world the people of these islands of ours are, in racial terms, trapped at a point of time that is primitive, barbaric and out of joint. Another way of putting it is that we've outgrown the prevailing racial mores of the times and because we are such an infinitesimal minority this is likely to drive us mad or else to being crucified by the majority. That is why some of us want to invent and create racial problems for the islands . . . Sorry, I'm wasting time and it is late.' Lydia did not understand, but she smiled warmly and said:

'I like it when you speak so, Miss Martha.'

'Time for bed,' Martha said briskly. 'How's your boy-friend?'

'He leave me two months now.' The maid laughed happily.

Martha knew she had wanted an end to the relationship but had been too afraid of the man to break it off.

'So everything is fine.'

'Yes'm! I never thought day would come when man leaving me would make me so happy. Funny, heh?'

'Good night, Lydia.'

' 'Night, Miss Martha.'

Lydia shut all the windows, except those in Martha's bedroom. In that room she drew the blinds against prying eyes. All the windows of the house had 'burglar bars', a feature common in the homes of all except the poorest sections of the island's population.

Because her mistress was back Sheba did not go out to the maid's little back room with Lydia. Instead she led the way into Martha's bedroom and curled herself into a contented ball on the bedside rug, both guardian and companion.

Martha stripped, went into the bathroom, lit the geyser, turned on the shower and allowed it to run hot; then she stepped under it and scrubbed herself vigorously till she felt free of all the sweat and grime that had collected during the long air passage. Some of the ugliness in her mind and spirit seemed to go with the dirt that left her body. She turned off the water; she towelled her boyish body vigorously, making it tingle. Her mind relaxed the tight control it held on her body. Her muscles relaxed, became soft, flabby. Weariness, no longer held in check, took over. She felt faintly lightheaded. It was all she could do to make the short passage between the bathroom and her bed. The sheets made her nerves tingle, raised goose pimples about her shoulders and sent a shiver down her back. She leaned out of bed, unplugged the telephone connection then switched off the light. It took a few minutes for the heat of her body to warm up the bed. When body and bed were the same temperature, she burrowed a little deeper in the bed, curled her body into its most natural, foetus shape, closed her eyes and fell asleep immediately.

She woke late and the mountains were outside her window assuring her that she was really home. Lying in her bed in the sunfilled room, with the mountains just out of reach, and the whole world a place of living green, yesterday and yesterday and yesterday all seemed unreal: New York with its acres of concrete and steel reaching up even unto the heavens and all but blotting out the sky; London with its filthy stifling industrial air where the few parks and the sickly-looking trees and grass only intensified her nostalgia for the vibrant green of the island; the pinched faces of pinched people for whom life was permanently grim and embattled.

And when Lydia brought for breakfast a tall tumbler of freshly squeezed orange juice, a huge golden yellow mango, an egg laid half an hour earlier and supplied by the next-door neighbours as a welcome-home gesture, and a pot of rich aromatic coffee made from freshly ground mountain beans, the unreality of the way of the world outside was intensified. Except that it was as real as this. And not much less ugly, she told herself, recalling last night's encounter with Max Johnson and knowing there would be another soon.

When she arrived at the paper it was close on noon and the telephonist said:

'Welcome home, Miss Lee! Editor waiting for you. Looks like stormy weather.'

The storm warnings were all over the editorial room. People called greetings to her, but quietly, in case they offended the editor.

She tapped on his door and waited.

'Come!'

She went in, closed the door, leaned against it, waited. He spent a full fifty seconds on what he was doing, then he looked up at the clock above her head, noting the time so that she knew he was noting it, and then he said, brusquely: ' 'Morning.'

' 'Morning, sir.'

'Not much of it left.'

She ignored that. 'I was told you wanted me.'

'Yes. Sit down.' She hesitated so he exploded. 'I said sit down! Dammit!'

She moved forward, slipped into the only chair in the room and waited.

After a while Max Johnson looked up, examined her face searchingly, pursed his lips.

'Last night,' he said carefully, coldly, 'you foisted your colour complexes on me.'

'This is our place of work, sir,' she cut in, equally coldly. 'And it was your rule that what happens outside this place is not to be brought in here.'

'It is the business of this place when you accuse me of selling myself; I can only sell myself as editor of this paper.'

'I didn't accuse, sir; I asked.'

'Bloody clever; but I've forgotten more about the trick

use of words than you'll ever know. "I didn't accuse, sir I asked", hah! Like the prosecutor asks when he's satisfied beyond all doubt that the person he asks is guilty. I suppose it'll be part of my white superiority complex if I tell you you're just not clever enough.'

'You could have answered my question,' Martha snapped. 'You could have told me I'm wrong.'

'I see. So I'm accountable to the great almighty Miss Martha-bloody-Lee! Pray tell me why! Because I was unfortunate enough not to be born in your sunny paradise? Because I'm a poor bloody pale-skinned bastard who must forever bend over backwards to prove that I'm without prejudice? Go on! Tell me why I'm accountable to you?'

'I didn't say you're accountable but I'll accept your clever wording—so much more clever than mine. I think we're all accountable to friendship, to shared ideals; if there is a mutual commitment to values then we are entitled to measure each other's conduct against those values.'

'Now you're getting airy-fairy and a little arsy: save that for Sterning. Our commitment, yours and mine, is professional: we're a couple of journalists. That is the one thing that is between us. Our business is to get the news and to present the news and when we go beyond the getting and presenting of the news then our so-called commitment goes to hell. When you start interpreting and analysing and slanting, when you start crusading because your tail is moved by the patriotic itch, then I become the boss and I decide what you do and where you do it and when you do it and I don't owe you or anybody else any damned explanation. As long as I sit here that is how it is going to be and no crap about friendship or ideals will make any difference to that. Journalists are not politicians, are not supposed to play God. We have great authority and no responsibility. Don't ever forget that. So we have to build in the responsibility ourselves, within ourselves. If you, or anyone else, try to use this paper in a manner that goes outside the scope of the getting and presenting of the news I shall stop it in any way I see fit, all your charges of racial arrogance notwithstanding. If you don't like it you are free to get out—or to use the influence of your friends to get me fired.' He paused to light a cigarette, then he continued but with less of a hint of passionate anger. 'Disraeli, who was the first Jewish gentleman to become Prime Minister of Great Britain—because he was a better Englishman than he was a Jew—wrote in one of his books that the world is a wheel and it will all come round right. Unless the journalist who is supposed to be the chronicler of the events of his day understands this he or she will end up no damn good as a journalist.' He shrugged as though suddenly grown bored. 'Anyway, you do your job and I'll do mine and forget about friendship and shared ideals and commitments.'

'Right, sir,' Martha murmured impersonally.

It's gone that deep, he thought, pursing his lips and watching her carefully.

Martha Lee noted the cool detachment with which Max Johnson examined her and realized how wrong she had been to assume his involvement. For all his years here, for all his great love of a woman of the island, this one had never made, will never make that commitment to the land which is a thing of the heart and of the mind and of the soul—a wayward thing of dreaming and feeling that sought to establish a link with time and the earth and which would make more of a man's existence than just the brief moment of consciousness we call life.

Max Johnson wished there were more to say, or that what had been said could be unsaid. There had been friendship of a kind.

She said: 'I apologize if I seem to have presumed. I misunderstood.'

It gets lonelier and lonelier, he told himself.

'I think it's a good idea for you to spend the next week or so going about the island. It'll refresh you and it's important to assess the new climate in the country. Something of our bad press outside is filtering through.'

'Right, sir.' She got up and went quickly out of the door.

Max sat very still for a long time, feeling lonelier than he remembered being for years.

The telephone rang and they told him that Mr. Andrew Simpson, the Acting Presidential Secretary, was on the line. He took the call.

'Mr. Johnson? Simpson from the Palace. How are you?'

'What is it, Mr. Simpson?'

'We understand Miss Lee's back.'

'Yes.'

'The President has a suggestion for a series of articles and with your approval he thought Miss Lee might be the ideal person to do this. I think he would like to speak with Miss Lee himself but we thought it best to clear with you first.'

'I'm sorry, it won't be possible.'

'I beg your pardon?'

'It won't be possible for Miss Lee to entertain the idea.'

'That what she says?'

'She has nothing to do with it. At their last meeting the Directors gave me special instructions to ensure that the editorial staff is guarded against any undue outside influences and pressures. I have therefore decided to restrict personal contact between my staff and the Palace, as well as personal contact between my staff and all the major mining, agricultural and business firms on the island. They face harsh disciplinary action if they ignore these instructions and they are under orders to report any attempt——'

'I'm speaking for the President, Mr. Johnson.'

'I know that.'

'And that is what you want me to tell him?'

'Those are the facts. Tell him what you like.'

Andrew Simpson hung up abruptly.

In her own cubbyhole Martha Lee went carefully through the new directive from the editor that she found waiting on her desk.

At his desk in the Palace Josiah listened with an expressionless face while Andrew Simpson told him of his telephone conversation with Max Johnson.

'All right, Andy,' Josiah murmured at the end of it all, nodding slowly, thoughtfully, as a man coming to a hard decision.

Martha Lee walked into Max Johnson's cubbyhole, placed the directive on his desk and said:

'I can't do my job under these restrictions.'

'All right,' Max said, without looking up. He picked up his internal telephone, snapped: 'Chief Accountant!' waited then said: 'Johnny: Max: make a note of this. Martha Lee is suspended until further notice. At half pay. Yes!' He pressed his finger on the rest, breaking the connection, then he removed his finger and said: 'News Editor.' He waited, then said: 'Joe, Miss Lee is suspended till further notice.' He replaced the receiver and looked up at Martha Lee.

'That all, sir?' Martha asked.

'Yes. I'll let you know when I want you back. I still want you to make that tour; in fact I want you to start it immediately. That's an order!'

She nodded austerely, seeming more aloofly Chinese than Negro now, and left him.

Max Johnson thought of the possibility of the Palace reaching her by telephone. If they did it would be hard for her to refuse to go and see the head of state at his own invitation. He thought of calling the head of the telephone service to try and arrange for her number to be rendered unobtainable, then changed his mind; there was some point of law involved and he did not want to get anyone else into trouble. Then he thought of the paper's own technician who was responsible for things like electrical maintenance in the plant. He called in the business manager and told him what was on his mind. The business manager was firmly against the idea. 'He's a staunch union man and all for Josiah.'

In the end, unable to do anything else, Max went into Martha's cubbyhole and caught her on the point of leaving, files of personal papers under one arm and her portable typewriter in the other hand. He told himself: You can't just order this woman not to answer her telephone;

that's beyond the scope of your authority and responsibility. Aloud, he said: 'The Palace has been on to me: your young friend Simpson. It seems the President has some ideas for a series of articles he wants you to write. I told them about the directive. I want you to know in case they reach you before you leave town.'

She said: 'Thank you,' coldly. Then she pushed past him and walked down the long room, between the desks and the rattle of typewriters and the ring of telephones and the buzz of human voices.

Word of her suspension had spread through the newsroom and the men and women at work watched her departure surreptitiously, aware that at times like these the wrath of the editor could be as indiscriminate as falling rain, with only those who are sheltered escaping.

Within an hour of Martha Lee's leaving, and after someone had phoned to say that after loading her little car with provisions and then having it serviced she had taken the road north, the storm-warnings were hoisted down in the newsroom of *The Voice of the Island.*

Andrew Simpson went into the President's office and reported:

'The maid says Miss Lee's gone, sir; on a tour of the island. My information from the newspaper is that she's been suspended from work. A copy of the directive to the paper's writing staff is on the way here. It won't be difficult to get hold of Miss Lee. I have her car number and I am sure our road patrol police can get hold of her within the hour.'

'We don't need her now,' Josiah said. 'Let her go.' Then tangentially: 'Know what a newspaper like that is, Andy?'

Knowing the man, Andrew Simpson waited for the President to answer his own question.

Josiah did. 'It is the most potent weapon in the society, more powerful in its impact on the minds of men than anything else in the country. And this paper, in our society today, is the single most powerful instrument of the neo-colonialism which is the bitterest enemy of the emancipation of our people. That is our problem, and the question is: How to deal with it?'

Simpson waited but Josiah had done speaking and

Simpson realized that he had slipped away into that mental world where he worked out the problems and possibilities of using power with a delicately realistic precision.

Simpson withdrew.

An hour later the President summoned the Acting Presidential Secretary and ordered him to arrange a Cabinet meeting for the next morning. Before he had finished, fat K. E. Powers, now Prime Minister and Minister of Financial Affairs, came in to report that his three-pronged attempt to raise new money had failed. The former occupying power had turned down the island's request for aid in the form of a money grant for development purposes. It had offered instead to examine sympathetically any development projects the island's leaders cared to put forward with the idea of possibly providing technical skills and raw materials and, perhaps, very cheap loan money.

'We will not submit our development programme for their approval,' Josiah snapped.

Second, the International Bank had made it plain that money was available but not cheap money, and in any event, since the island was behind with its dues a loan could not be considered until it had paid off its membership arrears.

'They will only *consider* it after we've paid,' Josiah commented. 'Not good enough. We're a poor country. We can't afford these fancy club memberships unless the gains are worthwhile.'

'I tried to get a commitment out of them,' Powers said. 'They won't say anything till we're paid up.'

'And our great neighbour?'

'The same. Cancel the "Ownership of Foreign Companies" Law, the "Ownership of Property" Law, amend the "Control of Profits and Wages" Law, and then come and talk.'

'So they won't lend until we break our promises to the people and go back to being a lucrative investment field for foreign capital.'

'That's about it.'

'And the state of the treasury?'

'Not too bad, and not too good. Some of our loan

repayments are going to be difficult. And a number of businesses are pulling out.'

'Flight of capital?'

'The banks are not forthcoming with the information.'

'So check on Exchange Control regulations, Andy. Tell our people to draft something, if it is needed, that would stop the flight of money. That's all for now, gentlemen.'

Very late that night a nondescript, poorly dressed black man appeared at the Palace gates. The guard on duty grew forbidding as the man approached; but before he could send the man about his business the man fished a piece of square cardboad from his breast pocket, held it out as far in front of him as his arm would stretch and advanced behind it as though behind a shield.

'What you want?' the duty guard snapped.

'Josiah pass,' the man said, pushing the bit of cardboard close to the guard's face.

The guard had been informed of these things called 'Josiah passes' and he wanted to have nothing to do with them so he turned his head away, snapped: 'Come!' and led the way to the guardhouse.

The old sergeant who had been on duty on the night Moses Joshua died was again the officer-in-charge.

The duty guard saluted.

'This man got one of those pass things, Sarge.'

'All right. Back to your post.'

The sergeant took the card from the man and examined it, waiting till the guard was gone before speaking.

'What you want?'

'I have word for the President.'

'It is late.' The sergeant looked up at the guardhouse clock which said it was a little after ten.

'He will see me,' the man said.

'What name?'

'Tell him the number on the card.'

The sergeant grew angry. 'I can't call the Palace except you give me your name.'

'You better, Sarge,' the man said softly, 'or else you catch a whole heap of trouble.'

The sergeant knew all about these special passes and the type of people who had them. Odd people, he had been told they were, not the kind you would expect to turn up at the Palace; and he had been warned that the new President set great store by these people. He picked up the telephone that connected him with the Palace and dialled the number of the Presidential Secretary's apartment. The number rang and kept ringing. Fleetingly, he thought of John Stanhope, wondering where in the world he was at this moment, aware of the rumour that the new President was quietly driving him out of his job. All this was part of the change that had come over the Palace and over the country and that was symbolized by this man standing in front of him and demanding access to the President without giving his name. The sergeant looked up.

'Nobody answering.'

'Who you calling?' the man asked.

'Mr. Simpson, Acting Presidential Secretary.'

'Call the President.'

'I can't just do that, man.'

'You better, Sarge. He will want you to.'

The sergeant examined the card once more, waving it slightly from side to side, hoping, it seemed, to gently shake from it the secret of its power.

'This thing important?' the sergeant murmured and it was half question, half statement.

'It is important,' the man said, a hint of anger creeping into his voice.

The sergeant noticed the man's growing anger and it shook him. The impossible had come to pass: a man whose whole upbringing, whose history and tradition had conditioned him to be humble and ingratiating in the presence of ordinary policemen, let alone sergeants, was getting angry with him.

'These are new days,' the man said, checking his anger. 'We run the law now. Call the President, Sarge.'

'Brand new world,' the sergeant murmured to himself.

The man heard and nodded. 'Yes, Sarge.'

The sergeant dialled the number of the President's

office, silently praying that the great man had gone to bed.
He was wrong: the President himself answered instantly.

'Yes?'

'Duty sergeant at guardhouse, sir.'

'Yes, sergeant?'

'Man here, sir. Don't want to give his name, sir. Man
with a card, sir.'

'My card? A blue one with a number?'

'Yes, sir. I tell him . . .'

'Send him up immediately!'

The sergeant said: 'Yessir' but the phone had already
gone dead.

The sergeant raised his eyes to the face of the man. He
knew this type from long experience. This man came from
that half-world inhabited by the 'operators': people who
had not passed the school examinations that would get
them admitted into the island's vast, cumbersome and
overstaffed public service, but who were sufficiently educated to impress the mass of their fellow-men who were
either totally illiterate or semi-literate and who put great
store by the ability to read and write and speak in the
pseudo-accents of the island's great northern neighbour.
Since the change these had become the people on the
fringes of political power—hanging on to the coat-tails of
the successful politicians, arranging their meetings, driving
their cars, selecting their bodyguards or the strong-arm
squads that are so important in keeping marches and demonstrations peaceful. The more successful of these people
also operated as contact men introducing businessmen,
especially foreign or out-of-town business people, to the
right persons in the right ministries. A small number of
these 'operators' had grown rich and powerful and respectable. The majority scrambled desperately not to sink
back into the vast faceless mass out of which they had to
claw and fight their way. These people were not criminals,
but they knew the criminals and used them when the need
arose. They battened on ignorance, on fear, on hope, on
ambition, on greed, on human vanity. And the society,
composed mainly of those who used them and despised
them, a minority, and those who envied and looked up to

them, a majority, had been ambivalent about them until
Albert Josiah appeared on the political scene and described them as symbols of the wasted manhood of a
nation. The police force in general and this sergeant in
particular had never had much time for these symbols of
the wasted manhood of a nation. And this man had told
him that they were running the law now, and the man who
sat in the President's office seemed to agree.

'Well, Sarge,' the man said. 'Was that the President?'

'Yes. I'm to send you up.' He pressed a buzzer, summoning a constable in the back room awaiting his turn to
go on guard duty.

'Take this—gentleman—to the Palace. Tell the guard
there he's to be taken straight up to the President's office.
The President's waiting.'

The man held out his hand for the pass, and his mental
attitude and his physical bearing made of the gesture a
demonstration of power. The sergeant reached up and
placed the pass into the outstretched hand, acknowledging
the reality of the power.

The young constable also recognized the man for what
he was but, being younger, his mind adjusted to the new
importance of the operator more easily so he led the man
off to the Palace showing no feeling, doing nothing to
ruffle the man's sense of self-importance.

The two men on duty at the great doors had escorted
other such men into the presence of the President late at
night, so they too took it in their stride.

The constable handed over his responsibility and
marched briskly back to the guardhouse, determinedly
blanking out of his mind all thought of the unlikely visitor
to the President. While one of the guards led the visitor up
the wide stairs the other hurried into a small office rest-
room down the corridor and woke the security officer on
duty who slept fully clothed on a camp-bed in a corner.
The guard told the officer of the visitor. Instantly the
officer was wide awake and on the alert; while his feet
worked their way into his shoes he grabbed his shoulder
holster from a chair, slipped it over his head and through
one arm, put on his jacket and hurried out and up the
stairs. He burst into the Presidential office in time to see

Josiah rising to meet the stranger. The smile froze on Josiah's face, his outstretched hand seemed petrified for a brief fraction of time, like a film that had been stopped in mid-motion, then he played out the action by dropping his hand and looking at the door.

'It's all right,' he said coldly. 'I was expecting this gentleman.'

'But, sir,' the security man protested, caught between anger, fear and exasperation, 'I'm held responsible for security and you don't inform me of this.'

'There was no danger; no risk,' Josiah snapped. 'You can leave.'

'But, sir.'

'Don't waste my time!'

The security man moved his head so that he could take a quick careful look at the visitor's face, then he withdrew.

The man said: 'They're very mistrustful. That sergeant.'

'It's their job,' Josiah cut in. He sat down abruptly. The security man had interrupted his gesture of cordiality; he could not go through the performance again. 'Well?'

'A friend of mine,' the man began.

'What is this about?'

'A meeting.'

'What meeting?'

'Fairways and others and a plot to overthrow the government.'

Josiah sighed.

'All right; sit down. Want something to eat?'

'A drink, please.'

Josiah depressed the switch on his desk and spoke into his little black box: 'Bring up some rum, coffee and sandwiches, please.' He lifted his finger off the switch, breaking the connection. He examined his visitor's face searchingly. The man became uncomfortable, nervous, a little frightened even, under the steady gaze of Josiah, so much so that he sighed audibly when Josiah looked away, seeking, by looking into space and therefore inwardly, the words with which to make this man understand the gravity of what he said.

'You understand what you are saying?'

'Yes, sir.'

'You know you face serious trouble if this is false?'

'It is not false.'

'Those who informed you could be wrong.'

'No, sir.'

'You and they could go to jail if they are. You understand that?'

'Yes, sir.'

'All right. Who are these people? Your informants.'

'Two work in the house of Fairways. One is my woman; one is her brother. The other is a woman who works in the home of that big rich white man, the one who is in oil and shipping.'

'Bulmer-Whyte,' Josiah murmured.

'That's the one. My other contact is a man in charge of the waiters who serve in the private rooms upstairs at the Imperial. You know him; he's a strong party man.'

'And all these people told you of a meeting where Fairways and others plotted the overthrow of the government?'

'No. There have been many meetings. Some with only two-three people in the Bulmer man's house, some in Fairways's house, some at the Imperial upstairs. Sometimes you have a big party at some place and these selfsame men manage to get together in a private room or in a quiet corner of the garden. And always others join them as though they are taking orders and go and pass on these orders. It is like just before we had the election which made you President, sir. You know how they tried to scheme then. Only thing is it is more serious now. The man at the Imperial once heard them talking about arms; my woman once heard them talking about guns too. And the woman at the Bulmer man's place swears there's a packing-case full of guns locked up in the basement of the house.'

'Your conspiracy becomes real, my friend.'

'The meeting I came to tell you about is tomorrow. I hear it is planned for after the big reception for the visiting trade delegation.'

'You hear?'

'Yes, sir. From the same people and it build up in the same way as the other information I gave you: one person picks up a little here, another picks up a little there and because we're all suspicious we come together and check each little bit of information against all the other bits of information. Believe me, sir, what I'm telling you is true. The people are plotting to go back to the days when the black man was a nothing in his own country.'

'Let me see your card again,' Josiah said; and when the man gave it to him he noted the code number carefully. Later, in his private suite, he would open a small steel trunk jammed with files and look up this man, and the contents of the file would guide him in assessing the weight of this man's information.

Josiah rose and extended his hand. 'Thank you; you've done a big job for your country. I must now get the experts to sift what you've told me. You know where to report to. Tell them I say to give you fifty.'

The man rose and took the President's smallish brown hand in his big black one.

'I'm not doing this just for money, you understand.'

'I understand,' Josiah said, 'but a man must live.' He pressed a button summoning one of the guards to come and escort the man out.

'It's for our people—the black people.'

'Yes,' Josiah said, 'yes; I understand.'

He came round the great desk and walked with the man to the door. When they reached it there was a light tap and it opened, but instead of one of the guards the security officer had himself come up to escort the stranger out.

Josiah mocked the security officer with his eyes and said: 'As you see, nothing's happened. You wouldn't have been so anxious if my visitor had been your Mr. Bulmer-Whyte and yet I'm safer with this man than with him.' He paused and looked at his visitor and a smile, rare and humourless, flashed across his face and was gone. 'This,' he said dispassionately, 'is the disease known as the "White Bias".'

The tall, handsome, strongly-built brown-skinned security officer relaxed his body and blanked out all thought so that there was nothing for the President's probing eyes to see.

Abruptly, Josiah said 'Good night', eased the stranger out, turned back into his room and shut the door.

'This way,' the security man said and led the way to the great stairway.

At the foot of the stairway the stranger paused and looked back up the stairs. 'That is *our* President,' he said. 'It's the first time in our history that the President belongs to the black people.'

'He belongs to the whole country,' the security man said. 'Just as President Moses Joshua did.'

'No, sir!' the stranger said. 'That one didn't belong to us. He used us and the white people used him. This is the only one since the slavery day leaders who belongs to us.'

'And what of the other people of the country?'

'You worrying about them? Then go on worrying. We won't. They had their innings, good and long innings, and they didn't worry about us. We're not going to be as rough as they were; we're not going to put them in chains and make slaves of them; we're not even going to have colour bars to keep them out. We're not going to rob them or lynch them. But we're not going to worry about them any more, and we're not going to serve them any more, and we're not going to put their interests above our own any more, and the sooner they and people like you, Mister Security Man, learn that, the better because then maybe we won't have to bust their asses and yours to show them and to show you that it is our turn now and we've taken over. I don't suppose you and your friends, Mister Security Man, heard or read about a speech which said "Massa Day Done". Well, all the poor black people in all these islands heard it or read it or were told about it and believe it and we're making it come true here and Josiah, the President, is our man. What d'you think of that, Mr. Security Man?'

'An operator's smooth line of talk,' the security man said.

The stranger looked into the brown eyes and read no fear and no concern, read only indifference which was a refusal to recognize the reality of the new power structure.

A flash of blinding anger, a wild uncontrollable gust of passion, swept over the stranger.

'You! You . . . You facety arrogant bitch! You wait! You white sucker you! You just wait!'

One of the guards, attracted by the stranger's voice raised in anger, pushed his head round one of the great doors.

The security officer called out: 'Will you see this gentleman out before he causes a disturbance. See him right out of the gate, please.' Then he nodded curtly to the man and walked away. He checked his time as he went and it was another two hours before his replacement was due to relieve him. In the rest-room he sat down at the little table beside the cot and wrote out a careful, detailed report of all that had transpired, leaving out nothing. Only when this was done, when he was stretched full-length on his back on the cot, did he allow himself to think of what the stranger had said. And as he recalled the stranger's words, turning them this way and that, exploring all possible meaning and implications, and as he connected them with the stranger's access to the President and the President's cryptic remark about Bulmer-Whyte, his mind gave way to the concern, verging on alarm, his training would not allow him to show in the presence of that type of stranger.

The young security man was particularly concerned about the clamour for nationalization and land reform that came from the people like this stranger. He and his wife had, a year earlier, put all their savings plus a substantial amount they had borrowed into two hundred and fifty acres, a small herd of high-grade dairy cattle and some of the most modern dairy equipment. They had planned everything carefully and according to their plan they would both have been able to give up their jobs in five years' time and go full-time into dairy farming, using the hillier parts of their land to build up a food forest. They had spent all their spare time on the farm for this would be the estate they would leave to their two youngsters. That had been the great incentive.

Then the old President had died and Josiah, the man

upstairs, had come in and the sure foundations on which they had laid their plans and hopes for the future had become shaky and uncertain; and the peaceful and happy people of the countryside seemed less so now than they were a year ago. Then, quite recently, on a week-end he would never forget, one of a gang of men working on the roadside near the entrance to their land had yelled, as they drove past:

'Gi' us a piece a' tail! Red bitch!'

He had wanted to stop and go back to the men, to confront them, to shame them into apology. But she, a daughter of the island, a 'crepe sole' blonde who had grown up in the country, had talked him out of it.

After that, because that incident had alerted him to it, he looked for and found a world of latent prejudice among the dark-skinned people against those whose skins were fair, whether they were native to the island or not, whether they were white or just very pale coloureds like his wife.

And he grew alarmed about the safety and security of their investment and their dreams of a modern, efficient, profitable dairy farm; and about the safety of his wife from molestation; and about the future of his children and his dreams for them; and all these led, in the end, to his being desperately disturbed about the growing instability in the land. It had been comfort of a kind to discover that his fears and feeling were increasingly shared by most of the people he knew, that the spirit of concern for the stability of the society was growing apace among all whose forebears had worked so hard to make this island into what it was.

And now this stranger who had spent nearly an hour with the President had spoken the language of race hatred and resentment and jealousy; and the President had said he felt safer with people like that than with men like Bulmer-Whyte.

That investment had looked so good just over a year ago.

From the shadows just beyond the head of the stairway Josiah had watched and listened to the sudden passionate outburst of his visitor and the surprisingly calm response of the security man. He was not sure that he, in the place of the security man, would have shown such restraint. But then, neither he nor his visitor had gone to a fine old public school started by the missionaries a century and more ago and teaching young men that air of judicious detachment which set them apart from the less fortunate who went to the very few, very over-crowded, poorly staffed ordinary government schools.

Now, with the hallway in silence and the watchers and guardians out of sight and sound, Josiah turned and retraced his steps. He hesitated outside the office door then went past to the end of the passage and up the short flight of narrow stairs to the Presidential apartments. There were two suites: a large one that could house a President who was a family man with a wife and three children, and a smaller one designed for accommodating visiting dignitaries but which old Moses Joshua had used as a place of favour where the most popular sycophant of the moment was put, like a court jester of old, till he fell out of favour. Josiah had moved into the smaller of the two suites, and after ordering all the fancy furniture removed he had turned it into rather austere bachelor quarters. He entered his quarters and went straight into what had once been a dressing-room but which he had turned into a study. The small steel trunk stood on a massive chunk of wood near a desk under a window. Josiah unlocked it and took out the file on his recent visitor. He studied it for the best part of half an hour, replaced it and locked the trunk again. He mixed himself a drink which was just a hint of rum with a great deal of ice and water, then he used the unlisted telephone that went directly out, by-passing the Palace switchboard, to dial the home number of the man he had appointed head of the security service within ten days of becoming President. The men heading the Security Service, the Police Force and the Military were appointed by the President in consultation with his Cabinet of Ministers but without reference to the Services Commission. These offices had been held by expatriate officers under President Moses Joshua. Josiah had replaced all three by islanders: each with a long record of distinguished service, each very able, each very dark.

The telephone stopped ringing as someone lifted the receiver at the other end.

Josiah said: 'Joe? Josiah here. Get here as soon as you can. It's something big. The opportunity to make our show of strength; could also fit in with the pressures we're getting from overseas . . . Yes . . . Set things in motion for a round-up but make sure of your men . . . Yes . . .'

Josiah replaced the telephone on its cradle and picked up the other one beside it. The night duty man at the switchboard answered immediately.

'Do you know where Mr. Simpson is?'

'At a concert, sir; he left a number in case of need.'

'Ring and tell him I want him, immediately.'

'Yes, sir!'

The man at the switchboard phoned through to the booking-office of the National Auditorium where Michael Chen, the world-famous pianist from mainland China, was giving a Beethoven recital.

Up in the Presidential box of the great hall, which had cost twice as much to put up as it would have done in America or Europe, Andrew Simpson, representing the President, played host to senior diplomats and their wives. The young lady he escorted was currently the beauty queen of the island, and she was a willowy-waisted, wide-hipped, big-bosomed, taller-than-average and strikingly beautiful black girl who also had the rare gift of intelligence. Mona Wright's father was Mr. Justice Douglas Wright, President of the island's Supreme Court, and Andrew Simpson could not get rid of the suspicion that the fact that she was the daughter of the great judge had something to do with Josiah's quiet encouragement of his interest in the young woman. The President had said, when urging him to take her out as often as possible: 'We need to restore pride to our women, to make them feel their men are proud of their black beauty. That is the only way to put an end to the present attitude which puts an especial value on paleness of skin, the only way to heal the damaged pride of our black women.' Simpson had not told the President that of all the young women he had ever met this one was least in need of the kind of reassurance the

President urged. Now, he stole a quick, sidelong look at the girl. If there were such a thing as a black aristocracy on the island, hers was its leading family. Behind her were generations of land-owning, highly educated, wealthy black Wrights. He was aware that the wife of the British Ambassador, immediately to his right, had intercepted his look and now her knowing woman's smile showed what she had read into it. Then Mona herself turned to him, touched the back of his hand and mocked him silently with sparkling eyes. The others in the party in the Presidential box were intent on the music.

Then someone came into the box, leaned over Simpson and murmured that the Palace was on the phone. He guessed that he might not return so he put his hand on the girl's arm and whispered: 'The Palace on the phone. Please take care of our guests and explain if I have to go.'

She pressed his hand and nodded. He slipped away.

F. F. Freeways was arrested two days after the night the informer had visited the President. He was taken in a pre-dawn swoop led by the newly appointed Chief of Security himself. Others were taken too, eight businessmen—three local and five expatriate—two great landowners who between them controlled close on a quarter of a million acres, and three professional men—an accountant, a barrister and a doctor. A large quantity of arms and ammunition was also taken. But the real shock was the arrest of Freeways who had until so recently been old Moses Joshua's spokesman both at home and abroad.

The Voice of the Island had already come off the press when the news broke, so it carried nothing about the arrests, but the government-controlled radio and television stations had a field day. And the way they presented the news made it clear that a dangerous conspiracy threatening the life of the island republic had just been averted thanks to the prompt, efficient and courageous action of the security forces. The enemies of the people had planned to seize power but their plot had been uncovered and destroyed.

When word reached back to the Palace that there were people, albeit a small minority, who questioned the charge that Freeways had planned treason against the country, the radio station put on a programme headed 'The Anatomy of Treason' which went back into history to show how the Freeways family came to the island, how they acquired their land, became slave-owners, dealt with their slaves, fought against the abolitionist movement, resisted all progressive change through the years and how they acquired their wealth. The programme was repeated three times at peak listening hours. After that there were no more questionings of the charges against Freeways; certainly not in public.

At eight in the morning the American Embassy telephoned the Palace. The Ambassador urgently wanted to see the President at his earliest convenience. Almost immediately after the American phone call there was a similar one from the British Embassy, then from the French and the German embassies. Each time the person at the other end was very senior so Andrew Simpson handled the calls himself; and each time he regretted that he could not disturb the President at the moment but would see him as soon as possible and phone back.

At ten, armoured cars appeared in the streets of the capital, cruising about showing their guns.

At eleven the radio carried a brief Palace announcement that Mr. Richard Young had been relieved of his post as Minister of Youth and Community Affairs and had been taken into custody because the early morning round-up had produced evidence implicating him in the plot.

A reporter from *The Voice of the Island* arrived at the Palace seeking an interview with either the President or the Acting Presidential Secretary to fill out the details of the Young story. He was turned away, politely but firmly. As he left a fellow-journalist, a member of the staff of the radio station, arrived and was ushered up to the Presidential office. The journalist phoned this information through to his editor.

At noon the American Embassy phoned again; still the

President could not speak on the phone or see the Ambassador. At two in the afternoon an Embassy official delivered a note of protest against the detention of two American citizens among those taken in the raid. The official was kept waiting an hour then Andrew Simpson descended the stairs and handed him a single-sentence reply rejecting the protest because 'all people in this island, native and foreigner alike, are subject to the laws of the land and to the same due process should they violate these laws; anything else would be a denial of national sovereignty'.

When the official got back to the Embassy with the reply the Ambassador himself telephoned the Palace; and because it was the Ambassador the President took the call.

'Your Excellency . . .'

'Mr. Ambassador . . .'

'I have been trying to reach you all morning . . .'

'So I hear . . .'

'About our note and your reply, sir . . .'

'Yes, Mr. Ambassador . . .'

'I had hoped, I still hope it is possible for us to talk about this thing face to face. There are ways of sorting out these things, as you know. With President Joshua . . .'

'I know, Mr. Ambassador; but President Joshua is dead and the rule of law, now, is supreme in our land.'

'But sir.'

'He could and did manipulate the law; I cannot and do not want to. Surely you agree with me. This is what your country always preaches to the world.'

'Could we talk face to face about it, sir? Could you spare me just a few minutes? . . .'

'The matter is out of my hands, Mr. Ambassador . . .'

'There are political considerations, sir. Question of your country's relations with a neighbour who has not been ungenerous in coming to your help in the past whenever such help was needed, a neighbour who has, by treaty, guaranteed the very sovereignty and independence mentioned in your reply to our note. I think, sir, you would not want lightly to turn away from the pattern of traditional relations that has existed between our two countries . . .'

'Mr. Ambassador, only last week two of my countrymen were sentenced to long terms of imprisonment for breaking your laws; and these were not exceptional. Scores of my countrymen have been arrested, tried and sentenced to terms of imprisonment or have been fined or have been expelled from your country. In all these cases we have never challenged or questioned the right of your courts to administer your laws in your land. There is no record of any notes of protest from our Ambassador to your State Department; no threats about the consequence of lightly turning away from patterns of traditional relations.'

'No threat was intended, sir.'

'One was discerned, sir!'

'Then you were in error, sir, because no threat was implied.'

'What am I supposed to do? Reverse myself because you say I'm wrong? This brand of arrogance might have worked with old Moses Joshua! And please note very carefully that I do not like being threatened with the withholding of aid. If you want to withhold it, then do so! You're not the only one we can turn to.'

'I apologize for the unfortunate turn this conversation has taken, sir.'

'It has not been of my choosing, sir.'

'Perhaps a personal meeting.'

'No, sir!'

'Then I'm to transmit your reply to my government?'

'What you transmit to your government is your affair!'

'Your Excellency.'

'Mr. Ambassador! I have accorded you the courtesy of interrupting important work to answer your call. Please accord me a similar courtesy.'

'I'm concerned with your interests too, sir. The critics of our aid programme will seize on your reply to press for further cuts in aid and this could hurt your country badly, sir.'

'That is your business, sir.'

'About our detained nationals, sir.'

'I suggest your Embassy approaches the security authorities who are the people rightly concerned with a matter of this kind. Good day, sir.'

'Your Excellency . . .'

The telephone went dead and the Ambassador let out a single explosive expletive which only his Counsellor, listening on an extension line, heard.

A little later Max Johnson telephoned and the President agreed to see him in the late afternoon.

When news of the detention of the two Americans reached Washington what had up to then been treated as a routine Caribbean political incident became front-page lead matter. A Senator just returned from the island told a nation-wide television audience that the background to the false arrest of two respected American businessmen was a communist takeover which had in fact been financed, through aid, by the American government, and he called for the impeachment of the President.

It was late afternoon and a cool breeze, light and gentle, made the dwarf coconuts below Josiah's office window sway rhythmically, as if dancing. He had turned off the air-conditioning and opened the window wide. All day he had worked in shirtsleeves, poring over the reports of reactions to the day's happenings.

Just before the arrival of Max Johnson he had gone up to his quarters to shower and shave and change into a freshly starched white linen suit. Now he sat back in his chair, clean, crisp, unruffled.

Max Johnson made himself comfortable on the other side of the great desk.

Josiah said: 'I take it you are here because I wouldn't see your man earlier today.'

'That is your privilege, Mr. President. My protest is that you and your staff made it so blatantly obvious that this was an act of discrimination against my paper.'

'And that's a crime, I take it?'

'No, sir. I'm here because I think we understand each other. You know what my paper is and what it represents; we know who you are and what you represent.'

'If we're going to be honest with each other then I must question your "we". Who are your "we"?'

Johnson acknowledged the point with a quick smile.

'Not the directors or shareholders, not even the editor and his staff, but the paper as a corporate concept with a life of its own, stretching both ways in time, into the past predating our existence and into a future which will probably post-date you and me, sir.'

'Probably,' Josiah said drily. 'So?'

'Your job is to run the country. My job is to run the paper. I think you know there is no arrogance of any kind in my coming to you to say I want to avoid any possibility of a collision through misunderstanding. For one thing you are the elect of the people and we—the paper—are not here to play the part of the opposition. We have not submitted ourselves to the electorate. For another, news, however it comes, whatever it is, is our business.'

'And in your "business" you will take guidance from no one? Not even from those whom you describe as the elect of the people?'

'We will co-operate as far as possible, sir.'

A faint smile, bereft of humour, flitted across Josiah's face.

'But not take guidance, Mr. Johnson?'

Max hesitated fractionally then said: 'No, sir,' firmly. Then, after a few moments of silence, he went on. 'Mr. President, you have a special responsibility to the society as its head of state. The paper has a responsibility to the society as well, though it is different in kind and quality. To submit to guidance from anyone, even from the shareholders, when it comes to editorial content would be to fail in our responsibility to the society.'

Josiah rose abruptly, pushing back his chair. The action was so sudden, so unexpected that Max involuntarily moved back, as someone withdrawing from the possibility of attack.

Josiah smiled and it was a manifestation of complete amusement that softened the normally bleakly austere face, made it look youthful, attractive, friendly, charming even.

Waywardly, some marginal area of Max's mind noted that Josiah's waist had thickened visibly over the past few months.

'In this job I get very little time to exercise,' Josiah said, 'so I always take a walk in the grounds at this time. We can finish our little talk while we walk.'

Josiah led the way out along the busy corridor and down the stairs. The rattle and clatter of typewriters, the buzz of the voices of people at work, came to them from the administrative section over which Andy Simpson presided in the absence of John Stanhope. Downstairs the Presidential security officer on duty came out of his little office. It had become routine for the security man on duty to keep the President company on his daily walk. Josiah waved him away with a friendly smile, and went briskly out of the door, looking smaller than his five foot six and lighter than his one hundred and twenty pounds because of the towering white giant on his heels.

When they were fifty yards away from the great building Josiah stopped, looked back and pointed to a small window at the top of the building. 'A man with a high-powered rifle goes up there whenever I go for a walk . . .' Then he pointed at a couple of athletic-looking young men who had emerged from the Palace and were now splitting up, one going left and the other right. 'They're supposed to be my bodyguards and I'm sure they would willingly risk their lives to protect mine. If you'd been black and poorly dressed and not the great editor of the great paper I'm sure they would have searched you before letting you near me. But because you're you they weren't even suspicious of that bulge under your breast pocket. And yet my greatest danger comes from people like you. Come.'

For ten minutes they walked in silence through the great green park with its vast well-kept lawns and its magnificent trees that had been brought from all the tropical corners of the earth and planted here to create the most exotic garden of trees in the Caribbean. Old Moses Joshua had allowed the Scouts and the Guides and other youth organizations to use the far northern end of the great park as a camping site. The land there was farthest away from the city and was the beginning of the climb up into the mountains. Also, out of a high rockface from which ferns grew lushly, and from a small circular hole in what seemed one mass of solid live rock, a clear steady stream of sweet water bubbled forth. It had done so for centuries and in time it had made for itself a path that became a dancing rivulet that had, again many centuries ago, found a hollow non-porous piece of land and worked on it till a miniature lake had been created. And the task of the clear sweet water was to feed the tiny lake. A long, long time ago, but not so long compared with the age of the rivulet and the miniature lake, a flock of wild ducks had come accidentally upon the little lake. They had liked it, staked claim, and settled on it to produce many generations of what became known as Sweetwater ducks. And because an early colonial governor had proclaimed these birds protected and the miniature lake at the far northern end of the park their natural home, the islanders, who were not really interested in animals, feathered or otherwise, except as food or beasts of burden, developed an oddly self-conscious pride in the Sweetwater ducks, so much so that when independence came the Sweetwater ducks and their home became part of the island's coat-of-arms. And for twenty years, until his death, a member of the old parliament before the coming in of one-party government, had regularly during each Budget debate asked searching questions about the health and upkeep of the ducks and the beautification of their environment.

Josiah turned in the direction of the miniature lake, and Max Johnson wondered whether he intended walking all the way there. Max looked at his watch in a way that ensured Josiah seeing him do it. The trees, here, created such an air of peace and tranquillity as to make the setting seem unreal, not of this world.

Josiah said: 'I hope you understand there is nothing personal in what I'm about to say.'

Max looked quickly at Josiah's face and grunted non-committally.

'What you said back there about your paper's responsibility to the society interested me because in a way—and I accept completely that no arrogance was intended—you were saying that I have a responsibility to the society as head of state and you have a responsibility to the society as editor of the paper. And this assumes that the thing common to both of us is our responsibility to the society, no matter how different our capacities or the manner of our discharging this responsibility. Is that a reasonably fair statement of our positions as you see them?'

'I wouldn't have put it in those terms.'

'Then this is not what you wanted to convey to me in the office?'

'Not in those terms. I was not putting myself up as sharing an equal or even corresponding responsibility. I thought I made that very plain.'

'I'm not trying to trap you into anything, Mr. Johnson.'

Max kicked at a tuft of grass, letting go of the hard knot of irritation building up inside him.

'I'm not concerned about being trapped, Mr. President; my concern is to state a position clearly.'

'So is mine, Mr. Johnson; so is mine: so let us try again. Would you accept it if I said that in your statement in my office when you said that my job is to run the country and your job is to run the paper the implication was—and indeed you said it obliquely later—that in your job, in your sphere of activity, no matter how small compared to mine, your primary responsibility, like mine, like that of any good citizen, is to the society?'

The trap, Max thought, calmly curious now to discover the point of it. Up to this moment he had thought it was irritation, or even seeking revenge, over the articles he would not allow Josiah to inspire Martha Lee to write. Now he knew it was something much, much bigger. And in spite of himself he felt calm and at peace, aware of the deep pools of tranquillity the trees made of the shadows they cast.

'Yes,' Max said remotely, almost carelessly. 'And you are saying I do not have the same sense of responsibility to the society that you or any other good citizen have.'

'I go further: I say it's impossible. Let me illustrate it at a very elementary level. In my conflict of interests between this country and the land of your birth who would claim your first loyalty?'

'Is the question real or rhetorical?'

'Real.'

'It will depend.'

'There you are. It is as simple as that.'

'What do you expect?'

'It doesn't depend for me, or for those like me.'

'If I were in Britain editing a British paper and a British head of state asked me the same question I'd make the same answer.'

'No doubt. And you would be one of a dozen or so and for the vast majority there will be no "it depends". I think you see what I'm driving at. In any case, if it depends now when the question is purely academic it means that I can never be sure of the backing of the most powerful opinion-moulding organ in the country in any conflict of interests with one of the two major countries with whom we deal.'

'And you must be sure of that backing?'

'For what we have to do, Mr. Johnson, it is imperative. We cannot as yet afford the kind of press you hold up as a virtue. For us, for our needs, the press must be involved in the struggle to bring into being a completely new pattern of social and economic and political relations in the society. It must be an instrument of change serving the political will, much as I am an instrument of change serving the political will. When you say to me "it will depend" . . .' Suddenly Josiah stopped walking. He tilted his head to look up at Max Johnson, then he spread his arms out, palms upward, in a gesture at once both helpless and deprecating. 'I'm not sure I can make you understand because the state of mind and what it stems from is totally alien to anything you or your people have experienced for centuries.' He let his arms drop to his sides and shrugged slightly. 'You know, I cannot say "it depends" in the way you do and mean what you mean. It does not "depend" for me in the same way it does for you. You are primarily concerned with the salvation of your individual soul. I am not that free. Between me and your kind of freedom stands a terrible wall which I and those like me cannot climb until we have achieved the salvation of our racial soul. Till then your concern about your individual soul is a rare and enviable luxury which I recognize longingly and then put behind me. Till then we cannot be individuals in the sense that you are and until we are all relations between white and coloured must be counterfeit by definition.'

They walked on to a little rising of land. Here the wind seemed to have found a way through a passage in the mountains so the cool breeze blew more strongly through this spot, stirring the leaves, making even the grass bend with its force. Josiah paused once more.

Max lit a cigarette and waited, certain now of what was coming, curious only to see how Josiah presented it. Instead, Josiah moved off again, briskly, so that Max had to stretch his long legs to keep up.

'So according to you, sir, we are to rule out the possibility of any decency in motive or action on the part of any person unfortunate enough to be born white?'

'You're angry,' Josiah said calmly; 'but not even anger is justification for distortion.'

'Only being Josiah,' Max snapped.

Josiah came to an abrupt halt, consumed by a sudden towering rage that hit Max Johnson with an impact that was physical in its force and violence.

'I am the President! Understand! The President! To insult the President is to insult the land, the nation! Everything!'

Startled, Max Johnson said: 'I'm sorry, sir . . . I . . .'

'Would you have done this to your Prime Minister? Your King?'

'I'm sorry, sir. I thought we were talking man to man.'

Josiah's anger left him as suddenly as it had come.

'You don't talk man to man to the President. It is not an eight-to-four job. I cannot, like you, go on the town as a private citizen after hours. But you know all that. It is just that you cannot take our institutions as seriously as you take your own. You remember, no matter how unconsciously, that your forebears were the lords and masters here, so there can be no real humility in your dealings with us and our institutions, no real awe before our sym-

bols of power and authority. Which is one of the reasons
why we have to assert our authority and to insist on your
showing respect.'

'Respecting is not the same as crawling, sir.'

'I agree with you. And yet our people have been taught
that it is. We have been made to crawl. This is something
they understand; it is something they've experienced. They
will only know that they are truly in power, that the
dominance of the white skin has been removed when they
see the whites doing some crawling too. An ugly thought,
isn't it? I'm paying you the compliment of being honest. It
is ugly. I don't like it. But it is real. Without a sense of
pride in themselves, without the confidence of being the
masters, the people of this island will never begin to move,
will never build a future that is meaningful for themselves
and their children. Possibly the biggest block to getting
them moving is the sense of racial inferiority. They must
be shown they amount to as much as a white man and
more, that their institutions are respected and even feared
by the whites, that every job in their land is open to them.
You know and understand all this.'

'Yes. And you want a black or brown editor in my
place.'

'Preferably black. I think you know that's why I agreed
to see you.'

'I know now.'

'There's nothing personal about this, you understand.'

'Please, Mr. President! You use your office to inhibit
any real rejoinder; you tell a man to give up a lifetime's
work and then you say it isn't personal! What am I supposed to do, sir? Fall on your neck? Tell you what a
wonderfully patriotic man you are? No sir! It is very personal to me!'

'I know it is,' Josiah said mildly. 'But it really isn't for
me. Before you came I wondered whether I would be able
to make you understand.'

'Does it matter?'

'You sound bitter now, like a Negro. It does, because I
like you and I don't like doing this.'

'But you do it.'

'I have to. And because you're the most honest and able man the owners of the paper ever imported.'

'A good man fallen among rogues you'll be saying next.'

Josiah laughed, and it was harsh and humourless. 'If you were a Negro, Mr. Johnson, they would call you a ranting extremist for being so bitterly angry. Being white, it is just righteous indignation. Perhaps not a good man fallen among thieves; rather, a good man trapped in the wrong passage in time. In this position a hundred or even fifty years ago you would have made your paper serve this society a great deal better than it did. Twenty years hence the fact of what you look like and where you were born is likely to be irrelevant, once you have the ability and are committed to the country. Today the times are out of joint, as someone said, and we with them. Today, the best service you can do us is to let us do things for ourselves, even if we make a mess of them. There is no other way to attain self-respect and pride in what we are. I don't think I have to tell you that the racial insult hurled at some white on our streets, the aggressive race talk, are all symptoms of our sick need for self-respect.'

'And how you attain it doesn't matter!'

'The angry extremist again. It does matter, but because there is no nice and decent and easy way of attaining it that meets with the approval of what you would call "the free world"—which includes places like South Africa and Portugal and Spain—does not mean we must do nothing.'

Max Johnson stopped under an ancient and massive cotton tree. Josiah went on a few paces then stopped and turned back.

'Want to go back?'

'No point in going on,' Max said. 'They were afraid of you. I see now they had reason to be.'

'You knew it all along,' Josiah said casually. 'You and Martha Lee. The big difference is, in her own way she is as committed as I am.'

'I didn't see the implications as clearly,' Max said thoughtfully.

'Didn't want to, would perhaps be more accurate,' Josiah suggested, then he added musingly: 'I wonder, would you have given me the kind of support you did had you seen the implications as clearly?'

'I don't know,' Max said. 'You're right about Martha. She did see the implications.'

'And made a choice,' Josiah said, 'even though she kept on denying it to herself. The other people who saw the implications as clearly and made their choice as deliberately are the Isaacs crowd. The rest of the merchant crowd sensed, instinctively, that ultimately this man Josiah was a threat to their interests, just as the mass of the people knew, without being able to explain how or why, that Josiah represented hope for their interests.'

Briefly, they had achieved the harmony of men exploring an idea. Now, Josiah felt Max Johnson grow cold and withdrawn once more.

Josiah said: 'If you or anyone else could show me some way of doing what has to be done without upsetting the merchants or the foreign investors or those who believe in your brand of free press and free speech or the free enterprisers or even, ultimately, my own people who have been corrupted into wanting to have their cake and eat it without paying for it, I shall be glad to follow that way. The trouble is there is no easy way.' He made a wide arc with both arms, taking in the hills behind them. 'All this can feed us and provide what we need to make a decent living but it will require total effort, directed and guided to one end and you know our society will not do this of its own free will. That is why I am needed.'

'Why tell me?' Max snapped. 'I'm not needed.'

He began to walk back in the direction of the Palace, too angry to show the traditional deference due to the Presidential office. Josiah followed slowly, a little surprised at himself for not being angry at this insult to his office and what it represented, feeling, instead, more depressed than he wanted to admit over doing what he knew had to be done. He wondered whether Max Johnson had really understood the mood and feeling he had tried to convey, the things that words can only hint at, suggestively, shadow-like.

He found Johnson waiting for him under a tree just out of sight of the men on duty outside the great doors of the Palace.

Johnson said, coldly, making it plain that it was more than a gesture of politeness: 'I'm sorry, sir.'

Josiah shrugged slightly. 'When will you leave?'

'I haven't said I'm leaving.'

'You will. The only thing that kept you here was the job. The grave was just self-deception. Wait! I don't want another display of bad manners. I might do something about it! I'm not saying you didn't care for your wife, that you don't mourn her. I'm saying she's been dead many years and the only thing that's kept you here is your job and you'll prove it by going. You're not a fool clutching at shadows and your commitment was not to us, it was to the job.'

'Then I may not leave the job.'

'You will and you know it, Mr. Johnson. I *am* the President, the elect of the people, as you put it. Please note I've paid you the compliment of not inviting you to stay on my terms.'

'May I go now?'

'You may but you'll have to walk with me to the door otherwise the security people might be concerned and I don't want it to seem that we are parting in anger. They might turn on you if someone else were to do away with me after we'd been seen to part in anger.' Josiah led the way, deliberately strolling slowly. 'When you come to write that inevitable authoritative book of yours on how a dictatorship came to a Caribbean island I hope you will remember the essence of what we talked about this day.'

The policemen on duty saluted smartly. Josiah paused at the great doors and turned to Max.

'When do you leave?'

Max stared stonily at him. Josiah nodded slightly.

'I know how you feel and I apologize. I have felt like that many times in my life and each time the hurt was fresh and new. I am sorry you should feel it.'

Josiah pushed out a slender brown hand. A mulish expression showed briefly in Max Johnson's eyes then he took the President's hand, bent over it in a slight gesture of formal respect and let go of it.

'Good-bye, Mr. Johnson,' Josiah said.

Max Johnson said: 'Mr. President,' nodded again, swung on his heels and walked briskly away, controlled anger in each step.

Josiah watched Max Johnson until he got into his car and drove off, then he climbed the stairs to his office. Young Andrew Simpson was waiting with a large pile of state papers.

'Know something, Andy?' the President said. 'I just sent away a man who could be very useful to us, and I sent him away experiencing probably for the first time in his life the kind of emotions that we grew up with. It's not pretty.'

Simpson nodded knowingly and said nothing.

For an hour and a half the President and the Presidential Secretary worked steadily at the state papers. While they worked people came and went; experts clarifying points of constitutional law, Ministers of government and senior civil servants summoned to supply essential pieces of information. The last to come were the Director of Public Prosecutions, the head of the military and the head of the security forces. With these three the President worked out a pattern for dealing with the fourteen men under detention.

It was decided that those who were natives of the island would be put on trial first, beginning with old Freeways. The strongest case of all was to be built up against him. The Public Prosecutor was to demand the death penalty for conspiracy to overthrow the government. The head of security reported that two of the local businessmen had indicated their willingness to turn on their fellow-conspirators and give evidence for the State. It was decided that these would be used to help build up the case against Freeways. Only when the case against Freeways was over and done with would the others be put on trial; first the natives, as a group; then the Europeans; and finally the two Americans.

'Never forget for a moment,' Josiah concluded, 'that primarily this is a political trial with very clearly defined aims. First, it will assert our authority in the land unmistakably for all our enemies to see, those at home and those abroad, and there will be no more plots and conspiracies. Second, it will make plain to all investors, foreign and local, that this is a break with our neo-colonialist past and that capital, foreign or local, will no longer be permitted to manipulate power in this land. The great powers will get our message too, and it will be up to them to decide what they will do about it. Third, and most important of all, this trial must make clear to the people in the hills and in the villages and in the fields and in the little shacks that this is their government exercising power on their behalf. They must see this trial as the assertion of their interests, the interests of the downtrodden and the dispossessed and the black, against the interests of the rich and the powerful and the fair. If the trial achieves these aims it will be justified; it will represent a twenty-year leap forward in the struggle to implant the *idea* of real independence. We will then be able to put most of our energies into the struggle to create economic independence. Fail in these aims and the trial becomes the pointless act of cruelty our critics are going to make it seem in any case. That is all I have to say, gentlemen. Much will depend on your handling of it. And in legal terms it must be above criticism.'

It was then, under the inspiration of Josiah's clear vision of the aims of the trial, that the chief of security conceived the idea of a carefully selected armed people's militia.

Josiah liked the idea and sent the three men away to work out the details.

At last the President and the Acting Presidential Secretary were alone. The day was over, night had fallen and the administrative offices were dark and deserted. Only a skeleton night staff was on duty: four young cadets, two drinking coffee and playing cards in the staff canteen while the other two slept for four hours. Then it would be the turn of the card players to go to sleep and the sleepers to drink coffee and play cards. Sometimes the cadets had to deal with a surprising volume of telephone calls from consular and embassy and government offices in other coun-

tries where it was not night. Mostly these were routine
matters that they handled by themselves; occasionally a
call from some faraway place was sufficiently important to
warrant the waking of the Presidential Secretary; more
rarely, once or twice, a call had been so important that the
Presidential Secretary had awakened the President. But
mainly, the young men spent the long hours of the night
playing cards and drinking coffee. Periodically they were
joined by the security officer on duty. Sometimes they
went out of the great doors for fresh air and a smoke
under the stars and casual conversation with the two policemen always on guard duty outside the Palace doors.

Except for the kitchen night man, who was on call at all
hours, the domestic staff lived in a cluster of outbuildings
behind the Palace and, like all the workers in the land,
were unionized and worked a forty-four-hour week. Those
who worked late when the President entertained received
time off to ensure that they did not exceed the statutory
length of the work week.

Now, with the day ended, the pattern of the nightly
routine came into play. In the days of old Moses Joshua
two dinner parties a week had been common; there had
been a grand ball once every three months on an average;
and there had been innumerable cocktail parties, recep-
tions and stag parties where the old President and his
cronies and favourites of the moment often drank prodigiously. With Josiah all that had ended. There had been
his inaugural reception and a ball and nothing formal and
official since. Periodically small groups of key party people
from the country areas came to the Palace to dine quietly
with the President. The President used these small informal dinners to keep himself informed of the mood and
problems of the country as seen through the eyes of dedicated party workers on the spot. He also used them to
send back to the party, and the country, explanations of
policies and ideas for future action. At these parties the
President asked questions, posed problems, and spoke
more frankly about the things that were on his mind than
he ever did to the nation at large. Neither parliament, the
Press nor the mercantile community had ever been able to

get any information of precisely what was discussed at any of these dinners. All they knew was that Josiah and the mass of the people of the country seemed linked by a channel of communication and understanding, strong and sustaining as that between mother and child at the moment after birth before the cord is cut.

Josiah and young Simpson finished their work. Josiah looked at the desk clock. It showed that the guests to his small dinner party tonight would arrive in two hours' time. For this particular party he did not want anyone connected with the government present. There were matters he would not discuss in the presence of the most loyally committed of the Presidential staff—and he had made sure that only people committed to him personally were now on the Presidential staff.

He said, casually, without looking at young Simpson: 'Tonight's little gathering is very special. What have you got on?'

'I'd arranged to dine with the Wrights but . . .'

'I want you to go,' Josiah cut in. 'It's important. And let the President of the Supreme Court know what's on my mind and the aims of the trial.'

'He's a very difficult man, sir, when it comes to pending cases.'

'I know, but you tell him all the same.' Josiah rose, stretched and walked to the open window.

Just about ten years between us, Simpson thought with a touch of wonder. Aloud, he said: 'I think it'll come much better from you.'

'Your job is to open the door, Andy. I want him to have time to think before I talk to him.' To himself, Josiah said: He doesn't usually hesitate like this about doing my bidding. 'You think I'm wrong?' Josiah turned to look at the younger man's face.

Andy's wide, open smile disarmed him completely.

'Truth is I'm a little scared of the old man, sir.'

A flash of humour showed on Josiah's face, making it soft and attractive. 'I know. He'll have to be prepared though.'

'I will do it.'

'I mean really prepared to do things our way; but that's my job and I expect him to be difficult.'

'How much do I tell him?'

'Everything we discussed about the trial. D'you have time for a drink?'

Simpson nodded and the President led the way out of the office and to his private suite. For the President Simpson prepared the usual very weak rum and water; for himself he mixed a stiff scotch and soda. Drink in hand, Josiah prowled silently, aimlessly about the austere room, touching a piece of furniture here, a book there, all unseeingly. Simpson crossed the room to the window and looked out on the night, then back at the President.

'Things are going to happen very fast now, Andy.'

Simpson knew, from other times, that Josiah was really speaking for his own benefit, to externalize and so visualize his own thoughts more clearly, so Simpson held his peace. 'If we control these happenings now, manage them now, ride them in our direction now, we will make a great forward leap in the history of our country. The thing to understand, Andy, is that our people have been historically conditioned to submit almost blindly to "duly constituted" authority provided that authority shows clearly and simply and unmistakably that it is strong and will not hesitate to use its strength. In our context a show of strength is a very good thing and you can never overdo a good thing. The people have seen me use it to get the Presidency; they've seen me use it against my political enemies inside the party; against the merchants, where the Isaacs crowd were most useful to me for reasons of their own; in my dealings with the civil service, and especially in the collision with Stanhope. Now, in order to make them work for the good of the nation, in order for them to accept directions of labour, compulsory shifting of populations, controls and taxes on wages, there must be a series of more striking and impressive shows of strength.'

'Not against the people, though,' Simpson said quietly.

'Not unless we have to,' Josiah said.

'Does Freeways *have* to die?' Simpson asked.

'I don't know,' Josiah said, 'I hope not. It will depend on how things unfold.'

'But why call for his life, sir? He's not that important.'

'Symbolically he is, Andy.' Josiah stopped close to Simpson and looked searchingly into his face. 'Symbolically it would also be important for me, the black President of a black country, to decide, as an act of mercy, to spare the life of a descendant of a slave-owner.' Suddenly his face softened. He reached up and rested his small brown hand on Simpson's shoulder. 'Andy, don't you buy the fiction of Josiah as a bloodthirsty black dictator in the making.'

'Of course not!' Simspon said quickly, fiercely.

'There are no easy ways, Andy; no simple, painless solutions to our problems. I don't like sending Maxwell Johnson away or putting old Freeways on trial, or driving certain types of investors away. But you know why I'm doing it, Andy. You were in it when we began our secret movement inside old Moses Joshua's party. We knew then there were no easy ways. Now we are in power; and we have to act out the not-so-easy ways.'

'I know, sir!' Simpson said.

'But it's hard, heh?'

'At times, yes.'

'At those times, Andy, just ask yourself what it's like for me.'

He turned and walked away then. And to Simpson, so much taller and broader, he looked very small suddenly, weighed down by the burdens of state he carried so ably that he seemed to do it without strain or effort. We sometimes forget he is as human, as subject to hurt and depression as we are, Simpson told himself.

'I'm sorry, sir,' Simpson murmured.

Josiah smiled warmly at him across the room. 'Time for you to go.'

CHAPTER TWO

For them this night will never end, the woman told
herself. They will weave a legend out of the happenings of
this night, and with the legend they will bind and imprison
their minds and make it easy for someone else to come
and gain ascendency over them, as that dead old man in
the Palace had done. She wanted to feel angry with them,
but she could not. This is how they are, and to be angry
with them is to be angry with man, and with God, and
with life.

She pushed her way through the thick mass of people,
raising her voice now and then to insist that some big
brute of a man make room for her to pass. They stared
briefly at her, and they let her pass. Here and there she
heard murmurs of resentment, but these bothered her no
whit, and she went on her way, weaving in and out of the
large crowds, observing, listening, periodically imprinting
a face or a voice or an expression on her memory with
precise care. Thus she made a complete circle of the
Palace and its vast throng of mourners. The journey took
her the best part of ninety minutes and she was dog-tired
when she got back to the Palace gates. The guards knew
her, so there was no need to produce her Press pass, but
all of them were under strain so she showed it all the
same. They let her through and she went into the little

which she necked and petted and the casual assurance with which she had joined in any discussion of sex when it arose.

Afterwards they had gone into the warm sea then they had lain on the beach for a long time, her left hand in his right, and he had found himself bereft of speech, like a man struck dumb.

She said, softly, breaking the long silence: 'I'm sorry it was so messy.'

'Oh God!' he exploded, a mute bursting into sound for the first time. 'I didn't know! I didn't know!'

'Would it have made any difference?'

'Yes! No! I don't know! Yes! I would have married you first!'

'I hoped you'd say that.'

'Why didn't you tell me?'

'It might have frightened you away.'

'But I love you.'

'You never said it, Andy. I thought I was just another of your dates.'

'And still you let me?'

She laughed: a caressing maternal sound.

'Virginity isn't as important to women as it is to men. We're not as fascinated by firsts as you are.'

'But you are—were—'

'I wasn't saving myself for you or anybody else, Andy dear. I just never wanted to make love to anybody before. Tonight I did.'

He turned on his side and propped himself up on one elbow and tried to look into her eyes.

'So it is just my luck that I am with you tonight. It could have been someone else . . .'

She laughed again, at him this time, with a gentle hint of mockery.

'No, my dear, I wanted you, Andy Simpson, personally. No one else would have done. Now preen yourself.'

He gathered her to him then, in a flood of tender feeling that soon transmuted itself into a wave of passion. Then they made love once more. And for the woman, this time the glowing purity of the passion wiped out the memory of the earlier pain and made their loving a thing of gloriously bubbling joy.

Afterwards they lay as they had done before, on their backs, hand in hand.

He said, voice charged with compulsive passion: 'I love you, Monal'

She turned only her head so that she lay looking at him instead of the starlit sky. She quoted dreamily: 'Lo I am black but comely O ye daughters of Jerusalem, as the tents of Kedar, as the curtains of Solomon.'

He said, trying to sound businesslike: 'Will you marry me?'

'Pray ask my daddy, sir.'

'Be serious. Will you?'

'Now I know why the President calls you "Young Andy". All idealism and high-mindedness.'

'Nonsense! You're rich, you're beautiful, marriage to you raises my social status immeasurably.' He hesitated, trying to control the note of rising passion. 'You make love as no other woman I've known . . .'

'And you've known many,' she mocked, but tenderly.

'A few,' he said. 'Will you?'

'Marriage is for ever, dear Andy; a thing that must outlast the passion of sex. It must still be there when my waist is as wide as my hips and my breasts are sagging bags from feeding many babes. In my family we grow big and fat and shapeless as we age; you've seen it in my mother and my aunts and my other relatives. And I adore my neat and trim father for still being able to penetrate Mama's folds of fat and flesh and still see the real woman. For him she is still the same trim young woman he possessed those many years ago. That is how I want it to be when I'm old and ugly.'

'You'll never be.'

'I will.'

'For the last time: will you marry me?'

'Dear, dear Andy; young Andy. Tell you what: when you are ready to face the fact of my growing old and shapeless, and you still want to marry me, I'll be ready and willing.'

'I'm ready now! Don't you understand? I know what's happened to me tonight. It's all very well to "young Andy" me but I've had experiences with other women; I've slept with other women, I've had affairs, I've even thought myself in love before and I *know* that this is for good. I didn't want to make love with you. Don't *you* understand what's happened to me?'

'You've fallen in love,' she said gently, calmly, as a mother to an only child or a teacher to a favourite pupil. 'You made love to me—mainly because I wanted you to. You discovered that I was what you would call "untouched", that no one else had known me. Perhaps it was the first time this had happened to you———'

'It wasn't,' he insisted.

'All right. Still, this discovery touched that strong streak of idealism in you, that impulse to nobility of thought and action. And so you're in love, cleanly, purely, idealistically. But marriage is not all moonlight and singing surf and white sand beaches and it would be unwise to make commitments that must last a lifetime on just this.'

'If telling you I love you is not enough, what must I do? Enter into a legal contract swearing that I will do so for the rest of my life?'

'You're getting angry now, Andy, and that doesn't help. Marriage is precisely such a legal contract. All I'm saying is let us not enter into such a contract on the basis of one sexual experience, no matter how wonderful. You might come to regret it and being you—high-minded and all that—you might spend a lifetime doing your duty and silently regretting it.' She paused for a long time then, as casually as she knew how, she added: 'And that would break my heart, my dear.'

Suddenly, in spite of and because of his newly born special feeling for Mona Wright, Andrew Simpson saw and understood the mood and feeling and intent behind her words. Something of the undercurrent of tranquillity that was a part of her mood crept into him.

He said quietly: 'I'll wait till you are ready.'

'It's really till I'm sure you're ready.'

'Every night before I go to sleep I'll imagine you as old

and as ugly as possible, and awfully fat. How will you know when I'm ready?'

'I will know.'

'And you'll marry me then?'

'If you ask me.'

'You know I really do love you. I must have done for a long time. It isn't just sex, though making love to you brought it out.'

She raised herself and leaned over him, and now he could just see the sparkle of her eyes. She kissed him on the forehead.

'I love you too,' she said lightly, 'very much and very much and very much.' Then she jumped up, wrapped a large towel about her body and walked away from the beach to the little family cottage nestling among the dwarf coconuts on sloping land a hundred yards back.

Simpson stayed on the beach until he thought she had had enough time to shower and change and put on her make-up, then he wrapped his towel about his naked body and made his way to the cottage. She was on the little veranda, dressed, combing her hair. He went in, showered, dressed, mixed a couple of drinks, turned down the oil-lamps, and carried the drinks out.

She was humming softly to herself, radiating a mood of quiet contentment that made him feel very good. He gave her one drink and touched her glass with his.

She said: 'I want to remember each detail of this night so that I can tell my daughter on the night she comes of age. And I will say he was one of the most striking young men of the day in spite of his humble origins; tall and handsome and clever and with a driving impulse towards noble deeds.'

He said: 'And you will add that he loved you—loves you.'

'I will.'

There was a long stretch of silence. And in it they watched a shooting star streak across the heaven and being young, made wishes; and listened to the distant, unending song of the surf.

At last, reluctantly, he broke the silence.

'Something I should have said to your father at dinner this evening.'

'I felt there was something on your mind. Important?'

'About the coming trials. Something the President wants him to know.'

'You can still do it. Daddy rarely goes to bed before midnight. All this passion's got me into a drugged and desperately hungry state so I'd be glad to get back, have a snack and go to bed.' She hesitated a while then went on: 'Daddy's not happy about these arrests so I hope you don't have to do anything that will make him more unhappy.'

'It is something the President wants him to know.'

And having grown up in a home where the head of the family was privy to state secrets and often had to make grave decisions that affected life and death, Mona Wright questioned Andrew Simpson no further.

They finished their drink, locked up the cottage, pushed the key under the door of the shack of the sleeping old watchman, got into Simpson's car, and took the coast road back to Mosesville.

The road was free of traffic, and the bright moon, high in the sky now, made it almost clear as day. Mona Wright nestled against Andrew Simpson as they sped through the beautiful night.

Mr. Justice Wright was a smallish man, five foot seven, with a trim and delicate air about him. His hands, feet, face, nose, eyes, ears, mouth, were all small and so his body always looked larger than it really was. His face, almost jet-black, showed none of the strength his adversaries knew he had. He was sixty-six, smooth of face, with a thick, well-groomed mop of kinky grey hair. In repose there was an air of sadness about him and only the wintry wetness of his eyes hinted at the boredom of age with the business of living.

The Judge looked up as Mona knocked and opened the door. Then he saw the young man with her and rose smiling politely. She crossed the book-lined room and leaned down a little to embrace and kiss her father. He held her off and looked at her face, aware of some subtle change in his daughter.

'You're home early.' His voice was surprisingly deep.

'We went to the cottage,' she said, 'and had a swim.'

'I asked her to marry me,' Andy said, still near the door.

'I see,' the Judge murmured.

And it seemed to the two young people that he knew what had transpired at the beach and they grew self-conscious.

'We're engaged, but secretly, Daddy dear. I don't want it known yet.'

'Why?'

She hesitated for a few seconds, seemingly unwilling to say, then she burst out: 'I want him to have a chance to be absolutely sure.'

'I am,' the young man cut in. 'I am absolutely sure.'

'He idealizes, Daddy.'

'I see.' He patted his daughter's cheek then he turned his eyes on the young man and smiled benignly. 'This calls for a drink.' He went to a small liquor-cabinet in a corner of the room, poured three touches of brandy into three tiny snifters and handed two to the young people. The third he raised in a silent toast.

'You'll tell your mother, of course,' he murmured.

'Of course. Daddy, there's something else. Andy has a message for you; something private, so I'll go and find myself a snack. Anybody else interested?' She moved towards the door while speaking: now she slipped out and shut the door behind her.

With Mona's going the atmosphere of the room became cold and impersonal as a judge's chambers. The Judge returned to his desk and motioned Simpson into a chair near it. He leaned back, elbows on the armrest of his chair, thumb against thumb with the rest of his fingers intertwined making a canopy of his hands. He waited, head slightly cocked, eyes searching, alert.

Andrew Simpson told him of Josiah's summoning of the heads of the military, the police and the security force and of what had transpired and of Josiah's explanation of the aims of the trial. When it was over, the Judge sat thinking for a very long time, withdrawn into himself and not seeing the young man watching him. Simpson waited; he understood this type of withdrawal; this was how it was when Josiah had to work out some difficult problem.

At last the Judge's thinking was over. He looked curiously at Simpson.

'The President must be very sure of himself.'

'He works out things very carefully, sir.'

'And letting me know what's on his mind is part of this working out?'

'Yes, sir.'

'Did he tell you when he will speak to me himself?'

'No, sir. But I think it will be soon. He's anxious to get this over with.'

'And what of you, young man? I hear he trusts you completely.'

'I don't understand you, sir.'

'Don't these things bother you? The manipulation of the police and the civil service? The attempt to manipulate the law? Do you really think the law should enter into this conspiracy against Freeways for daring to oppose Josiah?'

'He's the President, sir.'

'You don't need to teach me that, young man. The question is: don't these things bother you?'

'Of course they do!' Simpson paused to bring his rising passion under control. 'Of course they do, sir. As much as the hunger and homelessness and miserable poverty that is the lot of most of our people. I am bothered by the fact that something like ninety per cent of our population is black and after half a century of independence the wealth of the nation is still concentrated in the hands of the ten per cent who are not. I know the poor in all nations come from the majorities in those nations so the faces of the poor will be the same colour as the faces of the majority; but the faces of the rich would be that same colour, and so would be the faces of the powerful and the influential. It is not so here, sir. And I am bothered by that too, sir.'

'Must I now match your declaration to show I too am concerned?'

'No, sir.'

'For that at least, thank you.'

'I know the President is bothered, too, sir. He expressed it to me today.'

'All right, young man, so we're all concerned. How does this justify what the President proposes?'

'He will tell you, sir: much better than I can.'

'I would still like to hear what you say.'

The young man was alert and intent now, an advocate pleading his case before the great judge; he chose his words with care and used all his body—hands, eyes, head, motion—to dramatize his presentation. Watching him, Mr. Justice Wright thought: He would have done well at the Bar.

'This is an unjust society, sir: harsh and cruel to the majority of its people. You talk about manipulating the police and the civil service and the law and you imply it is something new. But these forces have been manipulated first to run the slave state, then to run the colonial state, then to run the independent state which was handed over not to the mass of the people but to the descendants of the slave-owners and the heirs of the colonial state. Is it such a crime then for us now to manipulate the police and the civil service and the law in the interest of the majority of the people?'

'I take your point, young man: the past has been unjust and cruel and evil. Does this now justify a counter cruelty and injustice?'

'That is not our purpose, sir. All we want to do is break out of this situation. It was the resistance of the mercantile community that compelled the President's strong economic measures. It was in order to prevent a flight of capital that he was forced to freeze assets; it is the massive land-hunger that forced our nationalization measures. It was——'

'Yes, young man, I'll concede you can make an overwhelming case for the evils of the past, for the greed and selfishness of the wealthy and for the massive inequalities of our society. What I'm asking is whether you personally are prepared to manipulate the police and the civil service and the law to change this situation. You've asked me just now whether it would be a crime to do this in the interest of the people. Would you answer that question yourself?' The Judge leaned back and waited.

'Yes, sir, I'll answer: I don't think it is a crime at all.'

'Let's go a stage further, young man. Let us assume that all the things the President proposes and you endorse are carried through and it still does not end up as serving the interests of the majority of the people . . . please! It isn't such a unique proposition. It's happened before and since you are playing with life and death you should at least be prepared to think out the consequences . . . So I ask you again: what happens if, after you've carried out your programme you still find that the interests of the majority have not been served?'

'I can't answer a question based on the supposition of failure. I don't think we'll fail. He's not that kind of man.'

'We all are "that kind of man", young man. For each one of us one final failure is certain; most of us experience many before we get to that final one. Let me tell you one thing. I'm not as hostile to your changes as you seem to think. What I fear, and I fear it for the land and for the people, is the way in which the President destroys the way back to where he started from each time he takes a step forward. We need to be able to retrace our steps if we get lost or suffer defeat. And we talk about the interests of the majority. How do we know what those interests are? How are they expressed after he has destroyed all opposition and criticism? And how do the people remove him if the day ever comes when they want to get rid of him? These are the things that worry me, young man. And it worries me that you, the people around the President, accept him as infallible.'

'I don't think that's fair, sir. No man is as committed to the people as is President Josiah.'

A wave of impatience swept over Mr. Justice Wright. 'And no man is as committed to the President as you are! But unlike you I'm not interested only in the person and position of the President, young man. I'll accept his and your sincerity but I'll defend and uphold the law against anyone because I believe that in the long run the law, independent and defending the letter and the spirit of the Constitution, is a greater guarantor of the real interests of the majority of the people than any one man, no matter how benevolent, wise, all-seeing or committed he might be. I had hoped you might understand that, young man.'

The Judge rose, and it was an act of dismissal that reminded Andrew Simpson of that other time when John Stanhope had dismissed him in similar mood.

'I hope you can find your way out,' the Judge said curtly. 'It seems my daughter's gone to bed.'

'Yes, sir, good night.'

'Good night.'

But Mona was on the veranda, sleepy but waiting to see him off. She sensed that he was upset and murmured: 'Rough?'

'He doesn't seem to understand; and yet one feels that he does. I don't know.'

'Is he as upset?'

'Think so. Dismissed me coldly.'

She said soberly: 'I don't say this because he's my father and I don't know what it's about, but just remember Daddy's not a fool, Andy. And he is a very good man, which is why he's honoured all over the world as a great judge.'

'And I am young and idealistic,' Andrew Simpson said with a touch of bitterness.

'Which is why I love you,' Mona Wright said.

'Then tell him——'

She put her hand over his mouth and stopped him.

'You tell him whatever you want to, Andy. In my family we don't influence each other's ideas except in the course of normal conversation. Please remember that always.' She removed her hand from his mouth, kissed him quickly, murmured 'Good night', and slipped into the house.

Andrew Simpson stalked angrily to his car and drove off, cursing the island's black aristocracy for refusing to face the realities of the problems of power.

Inside the house the Judge met his daughter at the foot of the stairs leading up to the bedrooms.

'Thought you'd gone to bed.'

'I waited to see Andy off.'

'Yes.' He waited awkwardly, not knowing what to say.

'Don't judge him, Daddy.'

'All right, I won't.'

She took his hand and they went up the stairs together.

It was early morning, three days later, when the summons from the Palace came. Mr. Justice Wright was in his Chambers high up in the Supreme Court building going over the evidence of a complicated rural murder case that had aroused unusual national interest because it was a crime of passion in which the accused, a man widely known for his generosity and gentle nature, was said to have come upon his woman, mother of three of his children, and his best friend, in sexual embrace. The Judge was reading the conflicting expert evidence about the man's state of mind when he clubbed the two to death with a tree branch. The telephone rang.

He answered it absently, not registering young Simpson's voice until the boy said it was the Palace and the President wanted to speak. Then he was alert at once.

The President's voice said: ''Morning to you, Judge. Josiah here.'

''Morning, Mr. President.'

'Young Simpson told you I wanted to have a word with you?'

'Yes, Mr. President.'

'When's convenient?'

'Any time that suits you.'

'This morning? Now?'

'Yes.'

'All right then, sir. Come over now, please. I'll have a cup of coffee waiting for you.'

Mr. Justice Wright replaced the receiver and sat thoughtfully still for two minutes. Then he pressed the buzzer summoning his clerk; after that he phoned downstairs ordering his car. When the old clerk, the Judge's senior by a year or two and not as well preserved, entered, Mr. Justice Wright rose.

'I'm going to the Palace, Edwards.'

'He called you?'

'Yes.'

'About the Freeways case?'

'What else? He's a practical young man, is our President.'

'He wouldn't dare try to bully you.' But the old clerk sounded doubtful and a little frightened.

'We'll see.'

'I still think you should have summoned all the other judges and told them what you told me.'

'Listen, old friend. There is no trade union of judges to arrive at a collective decision in order to engage in collective bargaining. Each judge is appointed individually and his business is to uphold, to interpret and to instruct in the execution of the law. My trade union is here.' He made an arc with his arm indicating the four walls of the room, all lined with legal books. 'You know how greatly we can differ in our interpretations of a point of law; and that is a good thing. What I hope is that there will not be one of us who will be prepared, for any reason, to surrender the independence of the judiciary to political expedience. But this, in any case, is a private decision for each man who sits on the bench. Now! I must not keep the President waiting.'

Together the Judge and his old clerk entered the lift and were carried down. People stood aside respectfully to let the great judge out; and along the corridor leading to the street they acknowledged his passage and honoured him with bows and the look in their eyes.

Outside on the street people pointed him out to each other as, in other countries, they would point out a well-known film star.

'That's him, the great judge. Judge Wright. Them say he's one of the biggest in the world and when there are big big cases they sometimes call him to sit with the other great judges in the World Court.'

'That's something, heh! And him black too!'

'Black man day coming!'

'And him not much to look at!'

'It's the head that count! Not the prettiness.'

'Right name for him, too, Wright!'

'Yeah. Judge Wright never wrong!'

The chauffeur held the door open for the Judge. The bolder among the spectators waved. The Judge bent his head in acknowledgement. The car moved off and gathered speed. At every intersection the policeman on point duty held up other traffic to let the Judge's car through.

Ten minutes later the President himself welcomed Mr. Justice Wright outside the doors of the Palace and escorted him in.

'It was good of you to come, sir.'

'My duty, Mr. President.'

'I hope it isn't only that, sir.'

Upstairs, Josiah led the Judge into a large, cool, cheery sun-filled morning-room. A steward wheeled in a coffee-trolley. Josiah gestured for the Judge to sit and set about pouring coffee.

'We're both very busy men, sir, so I'll come immediately to the point. I understand young Simpson told you why this trial is so important to me—to us, to the country.'

'As I understand it you want to make a political demonstration of strength.'

'Precisely.'

'That would have nothing to do with me, sir, or, I expect, with any other member of the Bench. We must judge the case strictly on its merits in law. That is the law and we are all bound by it. I know I don't have to refer you to the Constitution, Mr. President.'

Josiah handed the Judge his coffee, poured a cup for himself and sat down.

'You understand, sir, that I am faced with a political problem?'

'Yes.'

'Do you understand what I am trying to do?'

'I think so.'

'Are you hostile to what I am trying to do?'

'No.'

'Then why can't you, whom I know to be a patriot, help me, sir? What is the problem?'

'You know your country's history, Mr. President, so you will remember how your predecessors came to power. I was a very green young barrister when I defended, in my very first big case, an agitator called Moses Joshua who was accused of plotting the overthrow of the duly constituted government of the day.'

'It was a colonial government; the people had not voted it into being. It's not the same thing.'

'My point, Mr. President, is that the judge who presided at that trial judged the case on its merit in law solely. He was not an islander, not one of us by birth or colour. It would have been easy and understandable for him to have seen the political interests of his own country, the colonial power, and to have judged accordingly. And if you had been in that court you would have seen how the prosecution tried to make him see the case in a political light. But he refused to and I won my case.'

'I take your point, sir,' Josiah said. 'That is the ideal situation. That is how I would like it to be, but my position is not strong enough for that; if it were I wouldn't have you here . . .'

'I doubt that,' the Judge murmured.

'What!' Josiah's eyes popped with a sudden flash of anger. He began to get to his feet.

'Please!' the Judge said coldly. 'Don't tell me I'm acusing the President of my country of being a liar. I'm sure you mean what you say, you believe what you say, but I question the validity of what you say. The rule of law must never depend on the strength or weakness of the position of any ruler. It must be a constant, above person and position.'

Josiah said, suddenly grave and thoughtful and quiet: 'What are you saying, Judge? That you put the judiciary up against the will of the people? Is that what you are saying?'

'No, sir. If you will pass a law making the courts subordinate to the political will, subject to direction by it, then, Mr. President, it would be my duty to do what you ask.'

Josiah exploded. 'You know I can't do that in under three years! The Constitution is riddled with so many damned safeguards on this point!'

'I know, Mr. President. I helped draft it.'

Josiah jumped up and walked away, and now there was no doubt about his blazing anger and the herculean effort it required to keep it in check. He stormed across the large room from window to door, then he swung back and criss-crossed it from wall to wall. He kept up this brisk walking till he grew calm. He went back to where Mr. Justice Wright sat.

'Do you really understand how important this trial is to me, Judge? Did young Simpson really make my position clear to you?'

'So clear, Mr. President, I think I understand it better than he does.'

'What's that supposed to mean?'

'Simply that you've got him to believe in the idea of liberation by personality rather than by principle and the habit of good rules. Which is probably why my daughter wants some of his idealism shaken up a little before she marries him.'

'Please let's get back to the case, Judge.'

'It must go to court like any other case, Mr. President. It's already had all the preference possible by upsetting the entire calendar.'

'I can't afford not to win.'

'If it's a good case, properly presented and conclusive, you'll win.'

'I must be absolutely certain of a conviction, Judge! Look! If I promise you to exercise mercy and spare Free-ways's life, and if I promise you that I will never ask anything like this of you again, will you give me this case? For the sake of the country, will you?'

Josiah rose abruptly. He stood waiting till Judge Wright got to his feet. He stared coldly into the Judge's eyes.

'I am the President,' he said harshly; 'elected by the people; and you who have not submitted yourself to the people have chosen to defy me.'

'No, sir,' the Judge said stiffly. 'I am not defying you. I am simply stating my sworn responsibility to uphold the law and the rule of the law according to our Constitution.'

'Good day, sir!' Josiah said coldly and swung on his heels.

'Mr. President,' the great judge said and inclined his head slightly at the President's back. Then he walked slowly from the sun-filled room, down the long corridor, down the wide, carpeted stairway and out of the great Palace.

The early afternoon news bulletin on the government-controlled radio station opened with the announcement that the President, exercising the powers vested in him under the Constitution and in consultation with the Cabinet, had relieved Mr. Justice Douglas Wright of his position as President of the Supreme Court.

The news of the dismissal of the great judge brought Martha Lee hurrying back to the capital.

And that evening when Andrew Simpson phoned to let Mona Wright know that he would be coming round later, she put him off. He wanted to explain about what happened between her father and the President. Still she would not see him. The thing that distressed him was that she was not angry and she did not blame him; she just sounded tired and listless, like someone drugged.

Later the President tried to comfort him. 'I didn't want to do it, Andy; but you know how important the trial is.'

And that night, too, John Stanhope came home after a long time away.

Martha Lee finally tracked down Max Johnson in the early hours of the following morning. He was maudlin drunk. He told her he was leaving because he wasn't wanted. The next day Joel Sterning, bitter with disgust of himself and the Isaacs family, brought her up to date on all that had happened in her absence.

A week later, early one September morning, just under a year since old Moses Joshua died and Albert Josiah took over the Palace, Maxwell Johnson left the island for good. He had come as a young man, more than thirty years earlier. For the best part of twenty years he had edited its only daily paper. His roots had gone deeper here than in the land of his birth. He knew he would never again be able to give of himself as he had done here, to the job and to those he had come to love and to the land; he would never again experience the quality of hurt he had known when he lost those he loved, and that he was experiencing now as the moment of departure approached.

He had been shocked and embittered by the ease with which his directors had accepted Josiah's will. They had been sorry but if that was how the President really felt . . . Well, he was the elect of the people. And so they had taken over his house and beach cottage at a reasonable price and given him a severance settlement in lieu of notice and his accumulated pension right that ensured his financial security for the rest of his life. He had, in short, been generously paid off. And immediately after that Board meeting the chairman had sought an interview with the President. This had been followed by the dropping of two of the old Board members and the election of Solomon Isaacs and Joel Sterning to membership of the Board. An able, veteran black journalist, news editor of the state-controlled radio station, and hitherto regarded as too radical, had been selected to succeed Max Johnson.

It was a bleak morning, cloudy and overcast, with periodic drizzles, and the airport was a miserable place. He had come in by this same airport a long time ago, young and full of high hopes and the spirit of adventure, planning to spend a year or two. No more. Same airport but not these massive new buildings and miles of runway; not this streamlined place where the great giants of the air left with clock-like regularity every so many minutes. It had had a pioneering air then; the pioneering airport of a pioneering colonial town, hustling and bustling and on the make, and fun to arrive at for a young man in search of adventure.

. . . But I overstayed my time because the warmth of their welcome deceived me. I assumed they would look into my heart and see what I really am, how I feel and what I was willing to give. And yet he's right. Everything he said is true. Then why did you expect your directors to tell you not to leave and that they would stand behind you in any showdown? It is they who are dishonest, not he; and you were prepared to play along with them. He is the man of principle: they the opportunists. How aptly he described them! The margin-gatherers. So what does that make you? What have you to be bitter about? You know you wouldn't have done as well if you'd stayed home. You're hurt because this happened to you. Had it been someone else you would understand and be on *his* side. You've had a better time than you would have at home, and you're going back well heeled. So what do you feel so bitter and upset about . . .

He saw his baggage through the weighing, paid the excess and headed for the departure lounge where the bar would be open even this early in the morning.

. . . I arrived alone, with no one to welcome me: I leave alone, with no one to say God-speed. And it took nearly forty years to make this circle. Ageing is growing lonely. That is why it is sad . . .

But he was wrong. With a full five minutes to departure time still left Martha Lee came striding into the lounge. For a terrible blinding moment the great, hulking Englishman thought he would break down and weep. Then he regained control.

. . . Not quite the same circle; not alone. There is one to say God-speed. Not much of an upward spiral in a forty-year circle—just one hundred per cent. Ageing is also a deepening of perception, which is what gives its brand of sadness that tinge of distilled purity. We see and understand a little more clearly but we are too tired to invest it with the conquering hope of youth . . .

Martha climbed on the high stool beside him. He stared steadily into his glass and said: 'I'm glad you came. I was feeling bloody sorry for myself.' Then he turned his head and looked at her.

'Black coffee,' she said to the barman, then to Johnson: 'You could have decided to stay.'

'And do what?'

'Of course,' she said evenly. 'With the job gone there is nothing to stay for.'

'Except to be a spectator of the unfolding of a not pretty picture. He paid me the compliment of not offering to buy me. I was too angry to appreciate it at the time.'

'What will you do?'

'Probably blossom into the latest expert on the Caribbean.' He looked away from her and said, thoughtfully: 'You know of course that I hate to go.'

'I know.'

'I'm going among strangers; to what's become an alien place. It's like going into exile.'

A voice over the loudspeaker announced the departure of his flight. They got off the bar stools.

'The real reason why I'm going,' Max Johnson said, 'is because I feel guilty. Josiah made me see it. I am part of that white crowd that was in control for so long that it could have made the necessary changes gradually. Think what we could have done with this island over the past fifty years. Then think what we did do. And if my Board had said stay and defy him, I think I would have; they didn't and for the most disreputable reasons.'

'Some may envy you your "exile",' she said coldly. 'We cannot all pack up and go.'

. . . She has a right to judge harshly, cruelly; the right of those in battle who are there because of our failures . . .

'Yes,' he said lightly. 'The compensations will be great. There'll be theatres and concerts and books. And one always makes new friends. And the leisure to write that book.'

The loudspeaker called Max by name.

'And cold winters,' she said, allowing him now to look into her eyes and see that she, too, was sad.

'Yes, and cold winters,' he said softly.

'And later others will come and judge us for our failures as we now judge you.'

'But at least you are making more of an effort than we did.'

'I'm still not with him, Max.'

'And not against him. You won't run and you won't sabotage.'

'I love my land and my people.'

'It may not be enough.'

'Good-bye, Max.' She was remote now.

He shrugged slightly, a small gesture of irritation.

'Good-bye; and thanks.'

He walked briskly through the door and to the plane.

. . . Only the native sons and daughters bear the full brunt . . .

As the plane rose the sun broke through and the island was warm as usual.

From the viewing-gallery Martha Lee watched as the plane climbed into the blue sky, grew smaller, silvery, tiny, then merged into the mistiness of space.

She had wanted the parting to be on a warmer note for she knew that Max had just gone into a lonely exile for which nothing would compensate. She knew that at bed-rock, when stripped of all the jingoistic rubbish of race and class and colour and nationality, all humans were plain people; made richer and more beautiful by their variety, but still only people; the same under the skin. And yet the history of the skin thing and what lay behind it had made for an invisible wall that had made impossible a parting on a warmer, more personal, more human note. He had, she knew now, always been the stranger within the gate for her and many others like her: and it was not a thing of her wanting or his wanting. It was so because of what had happened long before they were born. And so what you would give your heart and mind to, what you would do as an act of will, what you would do as a man using the blessed gift of conscious intelligence, is denied you because of a past over which you had no control, for which you have no responsibility.

Awareness of this was no new experience for Martha Lee; but it was personal now, and sharp and clearcut. It brought the anguish and the despair known only to the creature that knew it was trapped in a hopeless situation. Perhaps for others, coming later, a point in time would be reached when there are no strangers within the gate any-where on this earth of ours.

She left the airport and made for the paper and her first conference with the new editor.

The trial of Freeways was postponed for a week because of the sacking of Mr. Justice Wright. During the week the President summoned three judges of the Supreme Court, individually and in order of seniority. The conference with each started cordially and ended foully. For the first one, the most senior judge after Mr. Douglas Wright, the President had a small intimate but formal dinner party. Then he and the judge retired to his private quarters. They remained there for two hours while the guests—old Nathan Isaacs escorting his daughter Clara Sterning, the judge's wife, K. E. Powers's wife acting as hostess for the President, Andrew Simpson and the dark beauty he had called in to substitute for Mona Wright as his dinner partner—ran out of topics to discuss and grew restive. Then the judge emerged alone from the President's quarters, shaking and in the grip of such strong emotion that he was unable to speak. His wife of forty years had looked into his face then left her seat, taken his arm and led him out of the drawing-room and the Palace.

The President had returned to the remainder of his guests ten minutes later, calm but distant and preoccupied. Andrew Simpson had quietly taken over and another ten minutes later all the guests had gone.

For his meeting with the second judge the President arranged a simple informal dinner for two. This, too, ended prematurely and disastrously.

The next day the President ordered that all the files and submissions and memoranda that had been used in the drafting of the Constitution be brought to him. He also ordered that the opening date for the trial be put off for yet another week. He telephoned the new editor of *The Voice of the Island* and said he did not want any mention made of these postponements or anything connected with the judges, other than what the Palace itself put out officially. The new editor was a man committed to the ideas and principles Josiah was working to translate into practice: there was real understanding and respect between them. He assured the President of the paper's co-operation as long as he occupied the editor's chair.

Josiah summoned the third judge to lunch. Again the meeting was very brief and explosive.

After that a day passed, then, late in the afternoon of the following day, the car of the chief of the security forces stopped outside the house of Mr. Justice Douglas Wright and the security chief and two of his men went into the house.

Still later that evening the President appeared personally on radio and television and explained to the nation that the former President of the Supreme Court had been taken into custody because he had tried to use his high office to give comfort and protection to the political enemies of the nation. Josiah ended with tears in his eyes: 'We are not against him; we do not even say he has committed unconscious treason: we do not want to take any of his great honours from him and we do not want to smirch his high reputation; he is one of us and his great honour is ours; so we do not love him any less. It is only that we love the nation and its children more. We cannot allow even this great and honourable man to stand in the way of the nation. And so, with great heartache I have used the special powers reserved to the President to detain Mr. Justice Douglas Wright. I hope it will be a short detention and that it will be possible for him to return to his great work after.'

The next day a Palace announcement gave the date when the trials would begin and the name of the presiding judge. He turned out to be the second of the three judges the President had interviewed.

A week later this particular judge was appointed to act as President of the island's Supreme Court.

The new editor of *The Voice of the Island* took his time to finish reading Martha Lee's piece on the detention of Mr. Justice Wright. He had read it twice before, each time with a glow of admiration for the first-rate piece it was; this was the kind of writing the island had been so short of when it was most needed, when the nation had to be agitated to demand its independence. It was brilliant but it was the wrong time.

At last he shuffled the sheets together and looked up to meet Martha Lee's impersonal gaze.

'The only reason for my killing your story,' he said softly, almost tenderly, 'is that it is inappropriate at this time. We're at war, Miss Lee, the war of the underprivileged and the hungry and the homeless against those who have and who will not give up what they have without a fight.'

'A journalist's first duty is to present the truth, no matter how inappropriate the time,' Martha Lee said evenly, suppressing all hint of feeling. She pointed at the manuscript on the desk. 'And that is the truth.'

'Not *the* truth, Miss Lee: a version of the truth. The President gave a version too. We sometimes forget that even Christ held his peace when Pilate asked him "What is truth?" '

'And so . . .'

'It is my responsibility to decide which version is in the public interest, and this piece, now, is not. I know you don't agree but I'm the editor and the decision is mine.'

The face and the voice are different, she told herself, but the words could have been spoken by Max. In spite of herself, of her anger, she felt respect for this new man who sat in what had been for so long Max's chair. How Max lingered! But then, the paper, an indispensable part of the life and thought of the island, had also been the reflection of Max: sober, balanced, slightly aloof in its detachment; above the battle and making a virtue of seeing as many sides of a question as possible. Now, with this new man, the paper, she knew, was going to become involved, engaged, partisan, an instrument of the changes Josiah desired. And that is why the memory of Max's régime was so lingering: she knew it was dead.

What now? she asked herself.

Her editor said, a world of understanding in his voice: 'I know what this means to someone like you so don't make any snap decision. Think it over before you decide whether you want to carry on or whether you want to quit. I don't want you to quit. You are much too valuable. But I also want you to understand frankly that as long as I sit here this paper is committed to the President and his policies. I don't have to tell you what is involved. If you decide to stay, which I hope you will, I cannot promise not to kill another of your stories. What I can promise is that my decisions will be based solely on what I regard as the public interest.'

'And truth is relative . . .' she said softly, musingly.

'Yes,' he said. 'Relative and with a point of departure.'

She left her new editor then, without another word; attempting to resist admitting the knowledge that she would stay on because there was nothing else to do, no other paper to go to, and, unlike Max, no other place to go to. Exile for her would not be to the land where she was born. This was the land where she was born; this was the only job she could do; these were her people; and they had chosen Josiah, freely, to change their society.

The thought of the cost frightened her; and she knew, as she had known from the very first time Josiah made his bid, that the people would have to pay the price of his dreams if he succeeded. He had succeeded; he was doing the things he said he would do, changing the power structure of the society. And a few people had started paying the price already.

. . . And I can't turn against him. I'm not for him but I can't be against him either for he is the elect of the people . . .

She phoned John Stanhope, ex-Presidential Secretary, who late in life was for the first time setting up a law practice. He had been trained for the law as a young man but the government service had claimed him until the emergence of Josiah. His first case was to be the defence of F. F. Freeways.

She said: 'John, my story on Douglas Wright has been killed.'

'What did you expect?' The bitterness in Stanhope's voice distressed her. 'Come over for dinner.'

Over the telephone she recognized one of the voices in the background behind John. The reactionaries, those Josiah called the margin-gatherers, those who had used old Freeways and pompous little Richard Young, were now pushing John Stanhope into the posture of opposition. She had tried to warn him but he had come home blind with anger over the arrest of Freeways. And they had used his anger.

She said: 'No, thank you, John,' unhappily and hung up quickly.

Martha Lee decided to spend the evening alone, and at home. Sterning had telephoned her at the office shortly after she had spoken to Stanhope. He had sounded disturbed, unhappy, and she had been aware of his need for comfort. All she had to do was ask him to pick her up and he would have jumped at it and they would have driven up into the quiet hills to watch the sun set or else to some secluded beach to swim and then to lie and be at peace and talk a little. She had not asked him; and his pride had forbade him to beg. So he had told her—and she was aware of his disappointed withdrawal—that he had an important business dinner that evening.

She had relented a little, in spite of herself.

'You can come by afterwards, if you like.'

'It might be late,' he said. 'We are negotiating with an Eastern Trade Delegation on behalf of the government; and you know how these things can go.'

'I'll be up.'

'All right. Martha——'

'Yes?'

A pause, then: 'Nothing.'

She said, making her voice cold and impersonal: "My story on Mr. Justice Wright has been killed because truth is relative and with a point of departure. So my new editor says.'

'I see.' His voice now had grown cold too.

'And your friend, John Stanhope, will soon be in the same position as Mr. Justice Wright. I may not even bother to write about it when the time comes.'

Sterning had remained silent at the other end of the line so Martha had said, harshly: 'Later then, unless you change your mind,' and hung up on him.

262 THIS ISLAND, NOW

Lydia, the maid, was off for the evening, gone to the pictures with the latest boyfriend; but with the great Labrador bitch, Sheba, for companion, Martha Lee was neither afraid nor alone.

When darkness fell she flooded the little house with lights, turned off the music she had been listening to, and switched on the television to catch the early evening news. It was all very carefully selected and edited, and the presence of the Eastern Trade Delegation took up about half the film footage shown. Then there was a new list of things put on specific license, things that could not be imported without the permission of the trade ministry. This one was longer than all the previous ones had been; it included all brands of spirits, cigarettes, chocolates, perfumes; shoes above a certain price, and a long list of fresh, tinned, and frozen food and vegetables.

'It's getting drabber,' Martha murmured.

For answer Sheba bounded up and, barking, dashed to the door: then there was knocking. The woman switched off the television, lit a cigarette, and went after the dog.

'Who is it?' she called, not opening the door.

'Simpson, Miss Lee: Andrew Simpson.'

'What do you want?'

'May I come in?'

'No. I don't want to see you; I don't want to see anybody.'

'Please.'

'I'm not opening. Tell me what you want and go away.'

Reassured, though not entirely disarmed, Sheba retreated six feet from the door, but in line with it, and went down on her belly in the position heraldry describes as couchant.

Martha remained silent, waiting, for the space of half a minute; then she said: 'Well?'

'It's all right, Miss Lee,' Simpson said from the other side of the door. 'Sorry to bother you.'

She heard him turn away; and without knowing why she opened the door. Then she herself turned from the door and walked back to her sitting-room. Sheba remained quietly on guard, watching the man.

'Shut the door behind you,' Martha called from the liquor cabinet.

Simpson came slowly into the well-lit room, escorted by Sheba, who only considered her job done when Martha murmured: 'All right, girl,' permitting her to relax completely and curl up on her favourite rug.

'I can only offer you rum,' Martha said without turning, then added with a sting; 'unless you've brought your own whisky. I hear that's the fashion under your new dispensation.'

'A little rum, please,' Simpson murmured.

She poured two drinks, then turned to him. He seemed unchanged, not invested with the cockiness of victorious youth she had expected to see in his face, his eyes, his bearing. If anything, he seemed a little sobered by the responsibilities of power.

'Well? What do the great Josiah and his faithful Presidential Secretary want of me this time?'

'May I sit down?'

'Of course.' She waved an arm to embrace the house, the land, and everything on it. 'Of course. You may sit or stand or take or reject or imprison or release by simple Presidential decree. You are the new gods of power, so why ask! You want to sit? So you sit. It's all a matter of power, isn't it? D'you think I want you in my house? But you represent power so I open the door and you walk in. So cut the social crap. What do you want?'

'I came to see you; personally, privately, socially, as a man, as a friend.'

For a moment Martha Lee stared at him in speechless bewilderment, then she threw back her head and let out an ugly, derisive snort. 'You what!'

'I came to see you.'

'Privately? Socially? Not to tell me the great Josiah wants this or that? Not to try out your latest idea? Or parade your latest victory?'

'No. Personally, privately; nothing else.'

'Well, well,' said Martha Lee. 'This *is* something and I'm flattered. And now that you've seen me personally and privately and for nothing, will you kindly get the hell out of here. I don't want to see you!'

'I love Mona Wright,' Andrew Simpson said quietly. 'I love her desperately.'

A stillness, as physical as a cool breeze, swept over Martha Lee, dispelling the harsh and strident anger within her. And now, freed of the blindness of her anger, she saw and felt the new sombreness about the young man.

'You'd better sit down,' she said.

'It changes nothing,' he said. 'Josiah had to do what he did.'

'And you love the Judge's daughter.'

'Yes.'

'Sit down,' she said again, taking his glass and going to the liquor cabinet for a refill. She asked: 'Have you seen Mona? I mean since——'

'No; she won't see me and I can't force myself on her.'

She turned and carried his drink to him. He sat relaxed and calm; a man reconciled to a cruel necessity, suffering its cruelty but not fighting it.

No longer Young Andy, Martha Lee told herself: never again Young Andy.

'What do you want me to do?'

He mustered a smile, but not with the dashing charm of old. He raised his shoulder slightly, gestured deprecatingly with his right hand; a very Jewish movement that brought the image of Joel Sterning to Martha's mind.

'Nothing,' he said lightly.

Only comfort, she told herself. And that is what I do not have for you.

'Have you eaten?' She forced herself to be brisk and business-like.

'I'm not hungry.'

'Well, I am! Give me a hand and let's make a quick curry, Indian style. Come!'

She led the way into the little kitchen. By the time he got there, she had taken a piece of steak out of the refrigerator and was now down on her knees in a corner picking out onions from a vegetable-box. 'Better take off your jacket. There's an apron behind the door. You'll have to do the onions; they always make a mess of my eyes.' She looked up briefly and noted the slight wry smile that tugged at one corner of his mouth. It tugged at her heart. It would have been easier if he had wept, for it was a time to weep. 'Please fetch me my drink and help yourself to another.'

When he returned with the drinks she was sitting at the kitchen table cutting the meat into neat little cubes. She took a long swig at the glass he handed her, then waved him to the sink where a small mound of onions was ready for peeling. 'It's less devastating if you do it under running water.'

'All of them?' he asked.

'All of them.'

For the space of ten minutes they worked in silence. When the woman had done dicing the meat she went into the sitting-room, piled a stack of records on her player, and switched it on. She reduced the volume so that the folk songs of the island, sung by native singers, swept softly through the little house. Then she gathered up her bottle of rum and container of ice and carried them into the kitchen.

Simpson had nearly finished preparing the onions, with only the faintest hint of wetness about his eyes.

'My eyes would have been running like taps by now,' she said, refilling their glasses.

'A racial weakness,' he laughed. 'Not enough black in you.'

'Liar,' she retorted. 'My black Lydia is even worse.'

'That's because she doesn't *feel* black,' he teased. 'I think I'll do a scholarly tome on race and reduce everything to a matter of feeling. And you know something, if science goes on as it is now doing with people able to reshape their features and lighten or darken their complexion at will, race will, in a relatively short time, be largely a matter of feeling.'

'And of loyalties,' she said, thinking of Max Johnson, wondering how he was making out in the land of his birth to which he had returned as a stranger.

She made a quick, abrupt gesture of face, eyes, body, hands, mind, turned away from Simpson, scooped up the

plate of diced onions, and poured it into the saucepan of
hot coconut oil. There was the sudden hiss of the explosive
meeting of boiling oil and water. A wave of hot steam
replaced the almost invisible bluish haze the boiling oil
had given off. And the smell of onions browning perme-
ated the kitchen and spread through the little house.

'Yes, of course; and of loyalties,' Andrew Simpson said,
caught up in Martha Lee's new mood; thinking of Mona
Wright and her father, the great judge now in detention.
Then, a hard unhappy edge to his voice, he added: 'The
question is: Loyalties to what, Miss Lee?' And without
waiting for an answer he took his drink and went quickly
into the other room.

She stood over the onions, stirring them so that they
browned evenly, making a little ritual of it, which helped
to blunt the edge of thought and feeling. When the onions
were done she squared her shoulders as though for some
hard effort, then, without turning, and making her voice
louder than all the other noises of the house, she called:
'The onions are brown.'

And when she sensed his presence back in the kitchen,
she said: 'The red tin on the top shelf. It says pure Madras
curry.' Then: 'You know I didn't mean to get at you.'

'I know,' he said. He gave her the curry and she put two
heaped spoonsful on the brown onions and kept up her
stirring.

'Now the meat,' she said; and when he handed it to her
she put it in, cube by cube, ensuring that each piece was
completely covered with curried onion goo before putting
in the next; and all the while keeping up the stirring.
When meat, curry, onions, oil were all integrated into a
beautiful golden-yellow goo, popping and bubbling like a
miniature appetite-stirring volcano, she turned the flame of
the fire very low, covered the pan, and left it to simmer.
She scrubbed her hands vigorously, but there was no getting away from the clinging smell of the curry-onion-meat
combination. She set her kitchen timer to go off in half an
hour, then she gathered up her liquor and made for the
sitting-room.

Simpson sat staring into space, his refreshed drink untouched; no longer dashing and godlike, a very mortal young man now whose sharp and strong and clear vision had been weakened and blurred and diffused by hurt and uncertainty. Martha Lee fought down the impulse to speak words of comfort.

'How did you think it would be?'

'Like this,' he murmured.

'Then why the self-pity? Why the running to me?'

He winced as though struck. She thought: He's going to get up and walk out.

'I suppose I deserve that,' he said calmly after a while, surprising her, making her feel awful. 'It isn't really self-pity,' he went on thoughtfully, a hint of the old detachment of the pre-Josiah days in his voice. 'I think it is surprise, or bewilderment, or both, that I had shut my mind so firmly to this aspect of things; this personal human aspect.'

'So you lied when you said just now that you'd expected things to be as they are?'

'I suppose you have to be aggressive. We did push you around. But I didn't lie. I remember warning John Stanhope about his friendship with Joel Sterning and the Isaacs crowd. And it wasn't simply because Josiah told me to do so. I believed in it and I believe now that public officials cannot have personal relations with people whose interests are opposed to public policy.'

'The Isaacs crowd are agents of public policy, on your side, so you were wrong.'

'Not at the time. At that time they had to be frightened into becoming agents of public policy. But that's not what I'm getting at. The point is that it was very simple for me then. I saw things clearly and simply.' He emptied his glass in a single long draught, got up in one uncharacteristic jerky movement, and went to the little liquor cabinet for a refill. There was the faintest hint of a sway in his movement.

'So you're bawling because you can't see things as simply and clearly any more.'

'Yes!' he said harshly. 'Yes!'

'And you are angry with God and with man. And upset

and unhappy because you can't have your woman and be a hero of the revolution too! Well, it would seem that's how it is, Mr. Presidential Secretary! Perhaps you now understand how John Stanhope and Max Johnson felt.'

'But what we did was right, had to be done, if we were to get things moving. You know that!'

She turned her back on him and walked across the room to the open window. Outside, the night was black and moonless; but the sky was clear of cloud and the stars hung bright and low over the earth.

From inside the room Simpson spoke again, insistently: 'You don't dispute that we had to do what we did?'

'I dispute nothing,' she retorted without turning. 'You've ensured that no dissenting view is heard. You've muffled me, so it is silly to come here and ask what I think of any view you or your master put forward. In the silence you've created there are no voices, except your own, to listen to. Is that what you find so hard to live with?'

'No! We can live with that because it is an unhappy necessity. What is hard is that the necessity should have arisen; what is hard is that selfishness and vested interest made such drastic measures necessary.'

'Then you ought to be happy, Andy.' She swung about and looked across the room at him. 'You should find comfort in being right and having the strength to strike down those who are selfish.'

'I come to you for comfort and you mock me,' he said, but calmly, almost lightly. He remembered how it had been on that night that seemed a lifetime away now when he had taken her to Josiah and there had been that flash of intimacy between them.

The timer went off in the kitchen.

She said: 'The food is ready,' pointed to a drawer and added: 'You lay the table and I'll get it.' Then she went briskly to the kitchen.

Simpson opened the drawer and found the tablecloth and the knives. It was the memory of the intimacy of that night that had brought him here now. There was the irrational hope that that long-remembered moment might be recaptured, and with it some of the assurance and inner tranquillity that had been part of his make-up in those days.

They ate in silence, washing down the hot rich curry with a chilled light lager produced in the island. Martha used her fingers to break the bread and dip it in the curry goo, and after a while Simpson abandoned his knife and fork and followed suit. The measure of his enjoyment of the food surprised him: the last time he had experienced this kind of sensual pleasure was the night Mona had made him make love to her. The remembrance of it was an arrow of sweet-bitter grief.

When they had eaten Martha rose and cleared the table. And it was while she passed close to him that Simpson reached out and got hold of her, one hand on her thin bony arm, the other on her waist. She pulled away. He held on, lightly but firmly. She became very still, very calm, very relaxed, very remote. She cocked her head to the right and looked into his face with expressionless Chinese eyes.

Whatever Simpson's original impulse, holding on to the woman, feeling the warmth of her flesh, evoked a sharp undercurrent of sexual desire. The look in his eyes became a plea.

For a wild moment the woman was possessed of a strong urge to comfort this unhappy young man with her body. She had done as much for other men at other times, and not all of them as worthwhile as this one. Then the moment passed. Not this one. The expressionless eyes came to life, looked at him with a hint of mockery. She let out a coarse gurgling laugh, tinged with teasing vulgarity.

'So that's it: belly full, now a piece of tail! Sorry, me love, that's not part of *my* plan. Loyalty or whatever else you want to call it ends here. I'm no substitute for your Mona and no comforter of lonely young men, not even if they are Presidential Secretaries! No piece of tail from me, ducky! Not now! Not ever!' Then she let out her cruel deliberate laugh again.

All expression went from Andrew Simpson's handsome face. The normally vibrant black-brown skin became

tinged with a ghastly hint of green. His eyes seemed lifeless and suddenly sunk far back in his skull. He let go his
hold on Martha Lee as though burnt by the touch of her.
Then, without a word, he pushed back his chair as he rose
from the table and walked out of the little house.

Martha Lee closed her eyes and held on to herself and
let him go.

Outside, at the gate, Andrew Simpson all but collided
with Joel Sterning, coming in to call on Martha Lee.

As soon as Sterning looked into her face he knew that
she was all knotted up, and because he was tired and the
dinner for the Eastern Trade Delegation had bored him to
the point of irritation, it angered him that Andrew Simpson's presence could have so affected her that she did not
respond to his need.

'And what did he want?' His irritation broke through.

'Comfort,' she said coldly. 'And being a man it meant
one thing.'

'Not giving it to him seems to have upset you.'

She choked down the quick retort that sprang to mind.
He's tired and fed up and I'm not helping, she told herself.

'It wouldn't have really comforted him,' she said mildly.

He poured a drink for himself and moved restlessly
about the room. She thought: I should have done that for
him; any such gesture would help ease his bloody-minded-
ness.

'And that's the only reason why you didn't give it to
him?'

'Please, Joel,' she murmured.

He turned and stared at her with head cocked to one
side. Spoiling for a fight, she thought, registering the chal-
lenging posture. I should have been more demanding
earlier; I should have made him come to me; it was wrong
not to.

'What's happened to the proverbial Lee honesty? Come,
tell me: would you have bedded him had you been certain
of the comfort part? After all, he's one of your people,
entitled to the special compassion you reserve for those
born here.'

'Drop it, Joel, please.'

'Is it that hard to answer?'

She sighed. 'All right, Joel; since you are determined to have it: I might have.'

'Is "might" the best you can do?'

'All right! I would have!'

'That's better! That's how the public knows the great Miss Martha Lee: straight and honest and upright!'

Looking into his eyes, very sensitive now to his mood, she realised he was enjoying himself, that this verbal violence on her was a pleasurable release, as needed as is cursing to the inarticulate. Had he been a different man, a man of the island perhaps or one from a different cultural background, he might have sought this release by knocking her down.

'I think you better go, Joel.'

He threw back his head and laughed; it was a mirthless, mocking sound.

'Just like that! When she wants she says come, when it ceases to please she says go. Just like that!'

She lowered her head so that she should not see his face.

'Forgive me,' she murmured: she hesitated, then added: 'I thought you'd done, and not being a Semite myself I do not have the Semitic capacity to appear nobler for being kicked.' She felt the change of mood in the room; it was as if a current of electricity had been turned off. There was no need to look up to see the changed expression on his face. In place of the bright hint of human cruelty of a moment ago the eyes, now, will be guarded and calm, and with a touch of the sombre desolation which is part and parcel of the knowledge of just how alone each one of us really is on this earth; knowing or not knowing this is the real gap between innocence and experience. And the racial thing is still the easiest weapon with which to force each other back into our particular aloneness.

He said: 'I'm sorry. Perhaps I had better go.'

She looked up then and Sterning saw the hint of tears in her eyes; but he knew she would not allow them to take over. She chewed at her upper lip.

'It's my fault,' she said. 'This wouldn't have happened if I'd asked you to come here to eat. Instead you had your Eastern traders and I had Andy Simpson.'

'Whom you would have bedded had you been sure it would work.' But he could not, now, revive his anger at the thought.

She nodded. 'Yes.'

He turned to the liquor cabinet then, but she moved more quickly, got there first and fixed a drink for him.

'I should have taken a chance,' he said musingly, recalling that far-off day nearly five years ago when he had suggested in this very room that they live together openly and so force Clara to divorce him.

Martha Lee made the connection immediately.

'I had something to say too, remember.'

He shrugged slightly. She gave him the drink; they looked into each other's eyes and there was the intimacy of knowledge shared. And he knew that she also remembered the quickness with which he had welcomed her rejection of the suggestion. The gesture had really been a bit of mental strutting, a showy piece of shadow-boxing for her benefit, not to be taken seriously. And she had done the expected thing. She was again doing the right thing now. The difference was the mutual awareness this time that it was part of the show.

'But I didn't have the guts.' He turned from her and walked to the open window. 'We both know I didn't intend to do anything, even if you'd agreed. I would have found some way of wriggling out.'

'We must stop this, Joel.' She went to the table where she and Andrew Simpson had eaten and sat down, overwhelmed by a sudden weariness of body and mind. "This is what husbands and wives do to each other and still live together because they have to. Friends and lovers cannot go in for this type of spiritual striptease without ceasing to be friends and lovers. You know, my dear, I never thought very much of the cult of showing guts and I never thought of you in terms of having or not having guts. So there's no need to lacerate yourself or to savage me.'

'I can't take it any more, Martha,' he said. Then, explosively: 'I've decided to go! To leave.'

Martha's body jerked upright, all weariness forgotten. She stared at Joel's stiff back, knowing as a passing thing that he was holding on with all his might. She waited till she felt calm, till the tension left her body, then she spoke, making her voice flat, impersonal: 'When?'

His body relaxed visibly.

'I don't know; haven't decided yet.'

'I meant when did you make the decision?'

'I don't know; I thought of it just now but I probably made it a long time ago.'

'Alone?'

'It was you who warned against this kind of stripping.'

'Too late. Is she going with you?'

'I expect so.'

'Do you want her to?'

'Yes. I think so.' He turned then and looked across the room at her. 'Would you come?'

She smiled and a rare tenderness showed in her face.

'No.'

He nodded at this bit of knowledge confirmed. Now they were as close as they had ever been.

'What would you have done if I'd said yes?'

'Gone into a blue funk, I think; and then, blue funk and all, I would have taken you with me.'

'And your Clara and your children?'

'Why speculate? The question doesn't arise.'

'It could have very easily, a moment ago.'

He shook his head, making it a gentle motion of denial. A terrible sadness was mingled with the love he felt for this woman who had not tried to bind him to her. In some odd way that he himself could not understand she had helped him make this decision.

'And you,' he said, caught in the mood of the moment, 'what will you do?' How would she fare under the new dispensation? Would she end up one of the victims? Something he wanted to promise her, some commitment that would show the nature of his love.

Again the soft smile flitted across her face.

'What I did before you came, dear Joel. Live and work and survive. And perhaps, with luck, there will occasionally be a man with whom I can have moments of intimacy and companionship.'

'That all?'

'That is all.'

'What can I do?'

She was deliberately obtuse. 'Do what you decided. Take your Clara and go.'

'I mean for you.'

She swallowed hard.

'I want you but you'd be a fool to stay; they'll break you so badly that in the end I may stop wanting you.'

'You know I didn't come here——'

'I know,' she cut in quickly, and he felt the weariness in her voice.

He came towards her, uncertain and self-conscious suddenly despite the years of intimacy. She rose and put a hand on his arm.

'Don't blow it up in your mind, Joel. It wasn't a thing of high passion. I'll miss the quietness between us—and the talking—much more than the bedding. Think of me sometimes, and if you can do it without messing up things between yourself and your Clara write me.'

In a sudden, wild, impulsive gesture, Joel Sterning flung his arms about Martha Lee and held her tight.

'Come with me!' he urged over and over again.

Martha Lee willed her body into total relaxation and waited calmly for the moment of passion to pass.

At last Sterning stopped pleading; the tightness of his grip relaxed, then he let her go.

'I wish——' he began; then he turned away from her and walked stiffly to the door.

Martha followed him out to the veranda. He turned to her, awkwardly. She tilted her face up for him to kiss her. He did so, tenderly, lingeringly.

She said: 'Go now, Joel. Good-bye.'

He left her quickly. He looked back when he reached her gate. She waved to him; then he turned and went to his car.

Martha Lee went back into the house, locked up, and then poured herself a nightcap. It startled her a little that she should feel so calm, so composed, so self-possessed. But she knew herself, knew that reaction would set in later, slowly, when loneliness and need for a man came on her and fastidiousness made finding the right man difficult. That, she knew, was when she would really miss Joel Sterning and the rare kind of man-child he is. She tossed down the drink, called the dog Sheba, and went into her bedroom, utterly weary but knowing sleep would be a long time coming. For the present her mind shut out all thought of Joel Sterning or the affairs of the island. She thought, instead, of the black father of her deaf-mute child. He had been the first, and in a sense the only one, who had aroused her physcial passions fully. He had also taught her the reality of loneliness. Those others who came later had only reached a small part of her, the fringes of her being: all of them, except this last one now gone. With him there had been a strange kind of understanding to which sex was a small physical overtone. And because this had been something new, a thing of the mind, its end carried the promise of a greater loneliness than she had known before it . . . But that other one, the first one, the man who had made a woman of her, where was he now? Alone? Unhappy? At the end of one situation, as she now was? Or gay and happy and taking everything some other woman had to give?

She stripped; got into bed, lit a cigarette, turned out the light, and lay on her back, relaxing body and mind and allowing a confused and jumbled pattern of thought and feeling to course through her mind. After many hours and many cigarettes and just as the first signs of light appeared in the eastern sky, she slipped into an uneasy, restless sleep that made her toss and turn all the time. And the uneasiness of the mistress passed to the dog, and it too spent a restless night.

Clara Sterning woke in the small hours and was instantly aware that Joel was not in bed. Since the Old Man's death she had slipped back into the habit of crawling into Joel's bed whenever he was out late at night. This had made of the physical thing between them a strong bridge on the way back to where they had started from.

She turned her head and the luminous dial of the bed-side clock told her it was eleven minutes after four. She remained still for a minute or two longer, then she flung the blankets back and swung out of bed. What remained of the night was a world of discernible shadows so there was no need for light. She left the bedroom and padded, barefooted, across the thick carpet to the living-room.

It was as she had hoped. He was home; deep in his favourite chair by the picture window. She thought he was asleep and had forgotten to turn off the little side light. Then she saw the liquor on the side-table and her heart sank a little.

'Clara—?'

'Yes, Joel. I thought you were asleep.'

'Or drunk?'

'No,' she lied. 'Not that.'

'I didn't want to disturb you, and I needed to think. Come; let me give you a drink. I have something to tell you.'

Something about his voice made her feel peaceful. She remained at the door.

'Not that stuff. Let me hot up some chocolate for both of us.'

She left without waiting for him to agree; and when she returned with the hot chocolate he was as she had left him. She looked out of the picture window, and Mosesville was a city of twinkling stars on the face of the earth.

He said: 'I'm going, Clara; I'm leaving the island.'

She braced herself and forced her eyes to focus on the twinkling stars down below.

He went on: 'I want you to come with me. I would very much like you to come with me, but I think you should also know that I'm going in any case.'

She relaxed, and now she could not see the stars on the earth, and there was a weakness in the pit of her stomach, like that nightmare weakness after the big black girl had hit her, but without the accompanying terror.

'I will go with you if you want me, you know that, Joel. When do we go?'

'The sooner, the better.'

Now the stars on the earth were in focus once more.

'Where will we go?'

'To Europe, of course. London, Paris, Rome. Not Germany: not Germany for a very long time; perhaps never. I'll have to find something to do. We must go where we'll both be happiest. I rather suspect we'll end up in London. But we'll see.'

'And the children?'

'I was thinking about them. I know your family would prefer them to finish their education in the States . . .' He paused for so long that she turned from the window and came to him and knelt beside his chair.

'It is what you want, Joel. They are our children, yours and mine.'

He slipped his hand behind her neck and massaged it gently.

He said: 'All you have to do is look at me to see all the weaknesses in a European education.'

'But that is what you want for them.'

'Yes, especially for the boy.'

'Then that is how it will be. They will come with us.'

'It won't be easy, Clara. You'll miss many things.'

'We'll set things in motion tomorrow—I mean today. You know the family's going to be very upset.'

'Especially your father.'

'But he'll understand too.'

Under the influence of his gentle massaging a drowsiness began to spread through Clara's body. She removed his hand.

'If you go on I'll fall asleep at your feet.' She rose, reached down to his hands and pulled him up. 'We have much to do, so let us rest while we can.'

Side by side, hand in hand, they looked down at the twinkling lights of the city.

He said: 'I saw Martha Lee last night. It's over. I told her we were leaving.'

So many things we are going to miss, Clara told herself.

'Come,' she said, and led the way to their bedrooms.

CHAPTER THREE

ALBERT JOSIAH could not sleep. He got out of bed, groped his way across the darkened room, and pulled back the heavy curtains. Instantly the room was lit up with soft, subdued moonlight. He opened the window wide and brought his favourite armchair to the window.

There was the thud of running feet on soft earth then a voice called up, anxiously: 'Mr. President, sir! You all right, sir?'

'Yes, guard. I'm all right.'

'Right, sir.'

The light footfalls went away. Josiah settled down in the chair. The hills were the darker shadows on the light land. He wished he had developed the distracting habits other man had: smoking, drinking, women, deep personal attachments. Trouble is these things diffuse your energies and you end up trapped. Changing things is no part-time job. The real truth is that he'd never needed or desired any of these things. He'd tried a couple of times with women and it had left him cold. The only really important thing was the commitment to free the land and its people. He couldn't pin down quite when it had begun, or how. Looking back now, trying to think it out, it seemed always to have been there, born with him, but lying dormant until that moment.

A small moment, nothing ugly or dramatic. Some un-named, unknown, unimportant, white person had called out kindly: 'Hey! you! Boy! Black Boy! You've dropped a book.' There had been kindness and no malice and the quiet, subtle understanding of difference. A thing of the mind and of feeling. And the great restlessness, which was the commitment, had sprung alive instantly and forever.

But where had it gone wrong?

Not with the trial.

That had been the master political spectacle he had planned. The nation had been behind him. The ardent advocacy of Stanhope had added to the whole thing. No; not the trial. That had been a smashing national suc-cess.

And there had been the great psychological thing when he had commuted old Freeways's sentence and ordered the expulsion of the expatriates and the people's armed militia had first appeared on the streets. In those days his rule had shown all the hallmarks of a people's government and you could sense the pride and the confidence and the new-found self-assurance of the nation.

It was on this high note of a people who were masters in their own home that the next phase had been launched. And the nasty press the island had received from the out-side world had had its useful aspect too in making honest fence-sitters like that Martha Lee move closer to the gov-ernment.

And then the next phase, the assault on the economic problems, had begun. As expected, they had run into trou-ble here. A history of corruption is not undone overnight, and it was almost impossible to persuade the working peo-ple to give some of their labour to the nation, for the good of the nation, without being paid. And so an element of force had to be introduced to get the unemployed into the labour battalions for the great national terracing and irri-gation drives. There had been that unhappy week of riot-ing and over two hundred people had to be killed before the situation was brought under control. There had been no more trouble after that. Perhaps that had been the beginning of it all. Only thing is that was over two years ago, and these people are not known for nursing long angers. One of their main faults has always been that they hate too lightly, forgive too easily.

And still there had grown up this sense of things gone sour between him and them.

. . . And I have done more for them in five years than old Moses Joshua did in twenty-five. Today all the children go to school from the age of five onwards. And the labour battalions have wiped out unemployment. We have eliminated most of the margin-gatherers and those who remain work for us. We have started on the road to economic self-sufficiency and if food is short it is the fault of the farmers who withhold their crop. The other things, the luxury items, the foreign clothes and cars and wines and spirits we will keep out until we can afford them . . .

All this had been made plain to them so they know it; they know why they make the sacrifices, and they know what the rewards will be. And each one from the President down, makes the same sacrifices. No one is exempt.

Perhaps they had been promised for too long that there were easy ways out of situations like this. There is no way out except through hard work.

. . . No way except through hard work, I had told them. If I had permitted elections after my four-year term expired they would have been fooled by those who promised easy ways out and I would have lost the election . . .

So, at the beginning of the fourth and final year of Josiah's first term of office there had been a referendum and the people had voted—under pressure of a massive and vigorous party campaign—to suspend all further elections until the economic revolution was completed.

By then Josiah was already aware that things had soured between himself and the people; by then they had long ceased calling him names like 'The Liberator', 'The Dark Crusader', 'The Guardian of the People'. And he had increasingly come to depend on the military, the police and the security forces as well as the very much smaller but also very much more dedicated 'people's militia' to see that his will was carried out. The controlled Press and radio were also useful.

But this was not how he had wanted it. To use force in order to crush the enemies of the people, yes. That he had done without compunction. To use force against the people themselves because they do not know their own interests, that hurts in a way nobody understands. It was not the sort of thing others could be made to understand. Not even young Simpson, for all his sensibility and commitment, could understand that. So there had been a souring of things between them too. Nothing had been said, nothing done; he had just felt the souring process, as with the people. Only once, fleetingly, had he felt that someone understood his hurt. It was at the big political rally after the riots and the shooting. In the midst of trying to make the silent mass of people understand what it was all about he had turned his head and there was the Lee woman. She had looked at him as his mother had looked at him, seeing and understanding the hurt and suffering he dared not admit to himself. It had made him yearn for comfort as he could not remember ever yearning before, with a heavy ache at his heart. But after the rally, when he tried to talk to her, to make contact with that flash of understanding and sympathy, she had withdrawn with the frightened touchiness of a whole person in the presence of a leper. He had dismissed her, and the experience, then, as an illusion. Her air of understanding sadness, that look in her eyes, did not stem from seeing and understanding his hurt but from the fact that her lover, that fellow Sterning, had taken his wife and gone to Europe, leaving her behind. The look was simply that of a woman acquainted with grief.

Or was it?

One of the problems about controlling Press and radio is that it is difficult to know what people think. Yet, with a free press he would not have been able to do a fraction of what he had done.

And the more he did, the more withdrawn his people became, the higher the invisible wall of coldness between them and him. As though he were the enemy.

. . . I was prepared for everything except this . . .

Sitting by the open window in his unlit bedroom Josiah

took careful stock of the situation. He had conquered all his enemies, all those who stood in the way of the great revolution, and then his people had turned sour on him. How? Why? He had explained to them what the revolution meant, he had written it down for them, the party had conducted political classes throughout the country. But still the sourness was there. And he knew it would not be long before this sourness would express itself as opposition. And so, he knew, it was inevitable, only a matter of time, before he would have to be as harsh with the people as he had been with their enemies. For the job of creating a proud and independent island people, standing on their own feet, had only begun. The great battle was still ahead. It would have been glorious fighting it with his people solidly behind him. It would be hard and it would hurt to have to use the party and the police and the military and the security to drive them.

... It will be hard. It will be done ...

And for a moment, there in the moonlight, feeling as lonely as he had ever felt, doubt came to Albert Josiah. And fear touched him. And the thought that this way might be wrong; that this was not the road to freedom for his people.

But if this was not the way then there was no way. The lion does not lie down peacefully with the lamb. The exploiters do not suffer a change of heart and cease to exploit. The great powers do not suddenly discover a morality that tells them it is wrong to manipulate small countries and use their lands as bases and battlefields and their people as living targets in the power game of showing muscle. If this way is wrong then there is no way out for the peoples of the so-called underdeveloped world. The people of that other world were lucky; they had had centuries in which to work out their institutions and to grow rich and strong and stable; and of course they had the resources of the underdeveloped world, human and material, at their ready disposal. And in spite of their lip service today they are still bent on exploitation: subtler and more sophisticated it is true, but no less real for that.

And thinking along these lines, the moment of doubt passed and Albert Josiah knew that this was the way it had to be. Many things he would not have chosen to do this way. Freeways spending the rest of his life in jail he did not mind: keeping proud and stubborn old Douglas Wright in detention hurt deeply. The old man could have been a rallying point for popular support; and his detention meant the frustration of young Simpson's love for his daughter, and this had gone deeper than he thought it would. If it had been up to him this would not have happened.

And the two hundred killed in the riots. But he doubted if there could ever have been any way of avoiding that without giving in.

Now there were the hard decisions that lay ahead, the harsh actions that would have to be taken when the wall of coldness from them to him became thought-out, active opposition.

Not things he would have chosen to do; things forced on him if he was to carry through the great work of his life, the liberating of the land and its people.

He sighed and got up. He took his light dressing-gown from the foot of the bed, pushed his feet into his slippers, and walked quickly out of his quarters, down the long and silent corridor to young Simpson's private quarters. The boy had gone off to the other end of the island on a two-day job. He'd been expected back this evening but he hadn't reported. Perhaps he had come in late and did not want to disturb Josiah till morning.

The Presidential Secretary's quarters were deserted. He had not come back. On an impulse Josiah picked up the telephone by Simpson's bed. The sleepy switchboard operator was startled by the President's voice at this hour of the morning.

'Any word from Mr. Simpson?' Josiah snapped.

'No, sir! I mean yes, sir.'

'Which is it, man?'

'Mr. Simpson called earlier, sir, Your Excellency.'

'Well?'

'Said to tell the secretary to tell you he won't be back till tomorrow evening, sir.'

'Then why wasn't I told?'

'It was late—after midnight—when he phoned, sir.'

'That all he said? Nothing else?'

'No, sir. Just that everything was under control and he would be back tomorrow evening.'

'All right. Thank you.'

Josiah replaced the receiver on its cradle, looked about the room then left it, carefully turning out the lights he had put on when entering.

Pity young Simpson would not be back on time. He hated travelling alone.

And the trip up to the hills tomorrow evening was important. The man in charge of the champion labour battalion had thought it a good idea for his people to stage a massive country feed. Having the President taking part in such an affair might just spark off a revival of the type of emotional interest that had been there when he first took over. He did not really think it would happen, but there was always the off-chance and he dared not let it pass. So he would go up into the hills tomorrow because of the faint, desperate hope for a miracle that would make it possible for him to do what had to be done without having to drive his people as savagely as he had been forced to drive their enemies. But deep inside him he knew the gesture would be futile. There are no easy ways, no shortcuts, no way of doing what had to be done without drinking deeply of this bitter cup of loneliness and harshness.

He left Simpson's rooms and returned to his own, sure now of what had been done and of all that was involved. In the years that lay ahead, long and bleak and lonely years possibly, this moment of doubt, of weakness, would not return again.

... Once you start on this road there is no way back ...

Back in his bedroom he drew the curtains to shut out the light, got into bed and fell asleep almost immediately.

The man on night duty returned to his partner and said:

'President restless tonight, but him gone to sleep now.'

'Perhaps he had a dream,' the partner suggested.

'Yes; perhaps he had a dream.'

Tʜᴇ ʟɪᴍᴏᴜsɪɴᴇ came easily round the bend in the road and through the sights he could see how worried and preoccupied Josiah was.

Now! Pull the trigger! Now!

"There are no interest-free shortcuts. If you skip a stage in one way, you pay for it in another.' Martha Lee had said that to him a long, long time ago and he had been angry with her.

'So if things ever change, don't let the change change you and what you are and what you believe and hold dear.'

Now or he'll disappear!

'You are fine the way you are, and what you're after is right both for yourself and our people.'

You are losing him! Pull now!

Thou shalt not kill.

Now!

And though I have the gift of prophecy . . .

Josiah's limousine passed out of sight along the winding road. The man lowered his head over the beautiful precision instrument with which he could have ended so much.

He burst out crying; he wept with the desperate abandon of a lost child for whom there was no comfort.